Baking and Babies

(Chocoholics #3)

by Tara Sivec

Annette —
Babies are
delicious.

Tara
xo

Other books by Tara Sivec

Romantic Comedy

The Chocolate Lovers Series:

Seduction and Snacks (Chocolate Lovers #1)

Futures and Frosting (Chocolate Lovers #2)

Troubles and Treats (Chocolate Lovers #3)

The Chocoholics Series:

Love and Lists (Chocoholics #1)

Passion and Ponies (Chocoholics #2)

Tattoos and TaTas (Chocoholics #2.5)

Romantic Suspense

The Playing With Fire Series:

A Beautiful Lie (Playing With Fire #1)

Because of You (Playing With Fire #2)

Worn Me Down (Playing With Fire #3)

Closer to the Edge (Playing With Fire #4)

Romantic Suspense/Erotica

The Ignite Trilogy:

Burned (Ignite Trilogy Volume 1)

Branded (Ignite Trilogy Volume 2)

Scorched (Ignite Trilogy Volume 3)

New Adult Drama

Watch Over Me

For Buffy –

You were right; I had nothing to lose. I love you, asshole.

Table of Contents

Prologue

Molly

THERE IS A phrase in the English language that I believe should be banned for all of time. Two little words that will fuck up life as you know it and make everyone around you certifiably insane.

"I'm pregnant."

You just shuddered a little didn't you? A small chill wound its way up your spine, your eyes got wide, and you looked over your shoulder like a monster might be standing there waiting to rip your head off. Maybe you even put your hand to your stomach and said, "Awe, shit." It could be out of sympathy for the words you just read or maybe it's real. You could be knocked up right now and not even know it. If you are currently with child…my condolences are yours for the taking. I mean, sure, once the baby gets here you'll probably be happy, but you have nine months—give or take—of people riding full speed ahead on the crazy train and dragging you with them.

I had a good life. No, I had a GREAT life before I uttered those stupid words. Twenty years old, almost finished with my two-year accelerated program in culinary school, and perfectly content staying hidden in the background around my nut-job family. I learned at an early age to keep my mouth shut so I'd have a good chance at never being publicly humiliated by them. It worked great until a couple of months ago when I just HAD to open my mouth and make my presence known.

My older sister, Charlotte, seems to think all of this is a great "learning experience" for me. Of course she would say that considering everything that happened is HER fault, but I guess she sort of has a point. I definitely came out of my shell in the last eight weeks. For the past two years I'd done nothing but eat, sleep, and breathe culinary school. When I finished and finally had some free time, I got a life. It was a fake life for the most part, but hey, at least it was a life.

Unfortunately at this point, I'd much rather still be the girl who spent two years secretly daydreaming about her pastry chef instructor and what he would do if she walked up to him and swiped the flour off of his cheek that always seemed to be there.

Luckily, I got to find out what would happen when I did that. I also got to find out a lot of things about my instructor and what he would do, like lie right to my face about something extremely important—and after I let him make me a non-partial virgin, too! But at least we had a few good weeks. That poor guy put up with a lot—a black eye, everyone knowing how he masturbates, me puking on his brand new chef coat, learning things about afterbirth he probably never, ever wanted to know, eating an actual bag of dicks…oh yeah, and telling everyone he was the father of my baby that wasn't really my baby without even knowing that the baby wasn't my baby because he's just a damn good guy. You know, if he wasn't such a liar-face liar pants.

So, this is the story all about how my life got flipped-turned upside down…no, seriously, it is. Stop singing, you heartless bastards.

I'm pregnant.

Those words can just fuck right off.

Chapter 1

– Can I Get A Woohoo?! –

Molly

"I F YOU WHIP and fold in the egg whites last, you'll get the best volume in your finished soufflé."

Listening to the deep timber of my pastry instructor's voice as he wanders around the test kitchen, I pause with my whisk in my hand and imagine Marco Desoto naked for probably the thousandth time. Today.

"Very nice, Molly," he speaks softly right behind me.

He continues watching over my shoulder, and I don't even care that I'm the only one in the class who already had the foresight to add my egg whites in last. Everyone else is scrambling around to start their soufflés over while I'm just standing here with a kitchen utensil in my hand thinking about slathering his body with the egg whites and licking them off. Shaking away my lust-filled thoughts and the idea of consuming raw eggs and the possibility of Salmonella, I go back to manically whipping my whisk through the fluffy white mixture in my bowl until I have perfect, soft peaks.

"You have beautiful peaks, Molly," he adds quietly.

Usually, nothing breaks my concentration in the kitchen, and even though I know I have perfect egg white peaks in the bowl in front of me, hearing my instructor say the words right by my ear turns me into an idiot.

"Do you think so? They're a nice, full B-cup, but I've never thought of them as beautiful before," I ramble.

"Did you say something, Molly?" he asks.

I notice he moved a few feet away and didn't hear me talk out of my ass like...someone in my family. Quickly shaking my head, I concentrate on the peaks in my bowl instead of the ones on my chest.

For two years I've had to try and be stealthy about my obsession with our student-teacher, Marco Desoto, and I can tell I'm losing my edge. He's caught me staring at him more than once, and the few times (okay, more than a few) I've quietly walked up behind him just to smell him while he was busy at the stove, he knew I was there and called me out on it. I can't help it. He smells like the best damn cookie in the world. Like vanilla and almond dipped in brown sugar and butter. Girls buy *lotions* to smell like that crap and this guy oozes it from his pores.

I was once the queen of stealth. I walked through our house completely naked because I realized we were out of towels right when I was getting into the shower and I had to grab one from the dryer. Our living room was filled with all the adults in our family, and no one even noticed me strolling bare ass across the carpet to the laundry room off the kitchen. That was the day I found out my Aunt Claire smoked pot and licked the walls at Seduction and Snacks.

Another time, I stood over my sister, Ava's, shoulder and spent fifteen minutes watching her text her boyfriend, Tyler. I learned about "accidental anal" and a bunch of other shit I can never scrub from my mind, but hey, I got some more dirt to add to my ever-growing laundry list of things about my family I've titled "Things I need to know in case anyone ever tries to fuck with me". It's not that I don't love my family, I just like to cover all my bases. I like being the only quiet person everyone forgets about until I speak up, and then they all look at me like they're trying to remember who I am and what I'm doing there. It's not their fault. I've spent the last two years living and breathing culinary school studying to be a French Pastry Chef.

"I thought I heard you say something about cups, my mistake," Marco says with a smile.

"Nope! No cups here. Just beautiful, firm peaks that will not drop no matter how old and wrinkly they get!"

Marco Desoto is turning me into the princess of bumbling idiots and my family will never let me live it down if I don't get my shit together. Uncle Drew was disappointed when I told him I was going to culinary school and had to inform him that there was no such thing as "ninja school". He truly thought he would get to tell all of his friends that he had a niece who was a real-life ninja. I'm pretty sure that was the first day I ever saw him cry.

Monday through Thursday, every day including summers for twenty-four months, I've been up at school from six in the morning until eleven at night. I'm lucky my family even remembers my name at this point. Even before that though, I usually kept to myself. My family is plenty loud and annoying enough to make up for my lack of enthusiasm.

It makes this unhealthy obsession with Marco all the more annoying. Even though I remembered the whole egg white thing today, I've been flakey and off my game the last few weeks. Being a pastry chef is my dream and I'm on the verge of making it a reality. Tomorrow is my last final exam and I will finally be done with school. I need to stop thinking about Marco covered in eggs and concentrate on what I'm supposed to be doing. I have to finish writing an essay about the history of soufflé's, and then all day Monday, I have to do my final presentation, which includes making eight different desserts and showcase them in an exhibit. I've already spent over twelve hours researching my paper and getting most of it typed up, but I still have a few more things to add as well as doing a few practice baking runs when I get home so that everything is perfect. It *has* to be perfect. Nothing can distract me, especially Mr. Sugar Cookie, who I can't stop staring at as I fold my egg whites into my other mixing bowl.

Why did he have to show up in one of my classes two years ago? WHY? Ever since then I've made sure that I sign up for whatever courses he's teaching that corresponds with my schedule like some kind of creepy stalker. I stare at him instead of concentrating on my food, and for God's sake, I started talking to him about my BOOBS a minute ago.

As everyone finishes up what they are doing and Marco reminds us what time we all need to be here in the morning to start our final, I am determined to do absolutely nothing for the rest of my night but think about Monday and my dreams finally coming true. In just a few more days, I will be a classically-trained French Pastry Chef with a bachelor's degree in Baking and Pastry Arts. I will be able to bring some classiness to Seduction and Snacks and maybe get a life. I really, really need to get a life.

THE SCREAM FROM the bathroom across the hall is deafening and so loud that I can hear it through my earbuds as I blast Mozart's Piano Concerto No. 21 while flipping through *The Baking Bible*. Charlotte stopped by to do a load of laundry since hers and Gavin's washing machine is on the fritz, and I'm assuming she found a red sock mixed in with her whites. Oh, the horror.

Turning the volume up, I go back to writing down a few notes to add to my final paper, leaving my sister to the domestic bliss of washing her soon-to-be husband's tighty whities.

Gavin and Charlotte have been up each other's asses ever since they got engaged and started planning their wedding. I'm pretty sure she only asked me to be a bridesmaid out of family obligation. We're not really that close and it's probably my fault. I haven't had time for anyone ever since I started taking college courses my sophomore year of high school and then went right into culinary school after graduation. On top of that, I like to keep to myself. My family is crazy, loud, and so inappropriate that most of the things they say and do border on being illegal. I've wondered many times if I was adopted, but I'm just too chicken shit to ask anyone. I've never felt like I belong in this family.

Sure, I have a sense of humor, but it's more sarcastic and dry instead of in-your-face like everyone else. Charlotte and Ava have much more in common with each other than with me. They care about love and guys and fashion...all that shit you read about in women's magazines. But me? I just care about baking. Cookies, cakes and pastries never let you down. People think it's all about recipes, but it's so much more. It's the science and chemistry of using exact measurements and the right temperatures, and when you follow the rules everything comes out perfectly. I like knowing exactly how something will turn out. I know if I do what I'm supposed to, it will be exactly how I want it. Even if you plan it all out and follow everything to a T, life will fuck you right up the ass. Without lube.

Just as the genius idea pops in my head for making an apple-chutney-stuffed soufflé to add to my presentation tomorrow, another scream breaks through my concentration. With a huff, I yank my earbuds out and quietly make my way across the hall to the bathroom, gently turning the handle and slowly peeking my head inside. Sure, I probably could've stomped across the hall and angrily flung the door open so that it banged against the opposite wall, but that's not my style. Remember, queen of stealth. It's much more productive to sneak up on someone. There isn't all that wasted time of asking things like, "Are you okay?" or "What's wrong?" Standing silently behind them for a few seconds usually gives you all of the information you need. Like right now, for instance. Charlotte is standing in front of the sink staring in horror at a pregnancy test in her hand.

"Look at you, with a bun in the oven," I tell her, pushing the door open wider and leaning my shoulder against the doorframe.

She jumps and turns to face me, then lets out another God-awful scream. I wince and shake my head at her. "I think the screaming part comes at the end when you're trying to push that thing out of you."

Charlotte starts shaking her head back and forth and begins muttering to herself. "This can't be happening. I'm getting married in four weeks. Oh, my God, what am I going to do?"

"Well, clearly we're going to have to take you into town for a back alley abortion since only trollops and floozies get in the family way before marriage," I deadpan as I step further into the bathroom.

She opens her mouth to scream again and I quickly smack my hand over her lips. "It's not 1912. Who cares if you're pregnant? Your fiancé was the product of a one-night stand at a frat party. Do you really think anyone in this family is going to judge you?"

Charlotte grabs onto my wrist and pulls my hand down. "I don't care about that shit! It's Gavin! He doesn't want kids. We've talked about this and we both decided it wasn't something we wanted. He's not going to want to marry me now. I'm going to be pregnant and alone and no one will ever want me! I smell bread. Were you baking bread? Does my stomach look fat to you?"

The speed with which she changes subjects makes my head spin, and all I can do is stare at her as she pulls up her shirt and touches her perfectly flat stomach.

"Yes, you look like a heifer and you'll never fit your fat ass into that wedding dress. You should just call it off."

She nods her head in agreement. "I have to call it off. This whole wedding is a sham now."

"Oh, for fuck's sake, stop being so dramatic. How about you just act like an adult and tell Gavin. Clearly it was an accident, and I do believe it was his dick that did this to you," I remind her.

"I'm going to wind up on *MTV's Real Life: I'm a Crack Whore in Love With a Brony*," she mutters to herself.

"Um, what?"

She looks up at me and pulls her shirt back down. "Well, you know, I'll be alone and I'll be so depressed without Gavin that I'll turn to crack to take the pain away. At that point I'm sure Tyler will start looking pretty good to me so I'll most likely steal him away from Ava and then she'll kill me. I'll wind up a crack whore dead in an alley. It's what I deserve!"

This, right here, is why Charlotte and I have never been close. She's certifiably insane.

"HON! ARE YOU UPSTAIRS?"

Gavin's shout from downstairs immediately throws Charlotte into more of a panic than she's already in. Her eyes grow so wide I'm surprised they don't pop right out of her head. I hear stomping up the stairs and I know it's only seconds before Gavin walks in here and sees Charlotte holding the positive pregnancy test in her hands.

"Oh, my God, oh, my God, oh, my God!" Charlotte whispers frantically. "I'm not ready! I can't do this! OH, MY GOD!"

Gavin is at the top of the stairs now and the thump of his shoes echo on the hardwood floors.

"Char? You in the bathroom?" he calls.

Her eyes immediately fill with tears, and I sort of feel bad for her until she thrusts the pregnancy stick towards me.

"Take it!" she insists in a hushed voice.

I throw my hands up in the air and take a step back. "Eeeew, you peed on that!"

"TAKE IT!" she snarls through clenched teeth as she presses the purple and white stick up against my stomach.

"Get your pee stick away from me!" I whisper back in horror.

Her bottom lip starts to quiver and her eyes fill with tears as she looks over my shoulder.

"Hey! What are you guys doing in here?" Gavin asks from behind me.

Without giving it a second thought, I grab the test from her and quickly twist around to face him, hiding the thing behind my back and trying not to think about the fact that my sister's pee is most likely touching my hand.

"Oh, you know. Just girl stuff," I reply with a nonchalant shrug.

Gavin looks back and forth between us and then cranes his neck to try and look around me. "What's behind your back?"

"Nothing. It's nothing," Charlotte tells him in the guiltiest voice imaginable.

I silently curse her and her inability to lie in a believable fashion. Every time she lies, her voice goes up at least twenty octaves until she sounds like a mouse being stepped on by someone wearing stilettos.

Gavin laughs. "Nice try. Seriously, what's going on?"

He keeps trying to get a look behind my back and I keep turning my body in the opposite direction. Too late, I realize we're standing in front of a fucking mirror. Gavin looks up into it and his jaw drops open.

"Is that what I think it is?"

"I don't know. Do you think it's a hot new shade of lipstick that Charlotte was just about to put on me?" I ask innocently.

"No, no I don't. That's a fucking pregnancy test," he replies in a low, slightly angry voice.

In that moment, I see now why Charlotte was freaking out. Gavin does NOT look happy about the possibility that she could be pregnant. I love this guy like a brother. I've known him since birth and in four weeks he WILL be my brother through marriage, and I've never wanted to punch him straight in the mouth more than I do right now.

I always think before I speak. Always. I carefully process every word to make sure I get the desired outcome.

Until now.

"I'm pregnant!" I blurt out.

Charlotte starts to cry loudly and Gavin's eyebrows rise up into his hairline.

"Yep, I'm knocked up. With child. In the maternal condition. Pregers. Can I get a woohoo?!"

I raise my arms in the air and shake them around, wondering what the hell is wrong with me. Who the hell says *woohoo?*

"Why is Charlotte crying? Hon, why are you crying?" Gavin asks gently.

She sniffles and wraps her arms around my waist from behind. "I just love Molly so much."

I lower my arms and shrug, trying not to roll my eyes.

"Charlotte is just overcome with excitement about the love child in my womb."

I pat my stomach for added emphasis, figuring I might as well make this a stellar performance for Charlotte's sake. She is seriously going to owe me for this shit. Like, name her damn kid after me or something.

Gavin sighs and runs his hand through his hair. "I don't know what to say. I mean, are you happy about this? I didn't even know you were dating anyone. Shit, ARE you dating someone? Who is he? I'll kick his fucking ass."

Gavin goes back to being pissed and now I don't know what the hell to do. I didn't exactly think this whole thing through when I blurted out I was pregnant to save Charlotte. Everyone is going to see right through this charade. Shit. Everyone is going to KNOW. There's no way Gavin is going to keep his mouth shut. Oh, my God, my parents are going to kill me.

"It's horrible, Gavin! He's a horrible man! He got her pregnant and now he doesn't want anything to do with her!" Charlotte wails dramatically.

I look over my shoulder at her and give her the most evil eye I can muster.

"Seriously?" I whisper in irritation.

I turn back around to see Gavin looking at us in confusion.

"I mean, SERIOUSLY. She's serious. It's horrible. I'm so distraught."

With a sniffle, I rub my eyes and curse Charlotte to hell.

Gavin reaches out and pats my shoulder. "Don't worry. You're not going to go through this alone. We all love you, and we're going to find this guy and make him pay."

Awwwww, shit. What the hell have I done? Why didn't I just stay in my room and ignore the blood curdling scream from down the hall like any sane person would have done? When I said I needed to get a life, this isn't really what I had in mind.

Chapter 2

- *Satisfaction and Sugar* -

Marco

"**H**EY, MA! WHAT was that secret ingredient you use in your Zeppole filling again?" I shout from the living room, trying to finish up a few last minute questions on my laptop to add to the final exam for the students tomorrow.

I should know the answer to this question considering I've been helping my mom make her favorite Italian dessert since I was five, but just like everything in my brain lately, it's turned into a pile of mush thanks to one beautiful, shy student I haven't been able to stop thinking about for the last two years. Stupid fraternization rules.

My mom pokes her head out from the kitchen doorway and points her wooden spoon covered in red sauce at me. "Get off that gadget and help your sisters set the table before I whoop you with this spoon."

She disappears back into the kitchen and I shake my head, closing the lid to my laptop and pushing myself up from the couch. I'm twenty-four years old and I still tuck my tail between my legs and run when my mother scolds me. It's not like I'm sitting in her living room writing porn on the Lord's Day. Well, not really. I guess it could be considered food porn to some people.

Walking into the dining room, my ears are immediately assaulted by the sounds of my two older sisters arguing.

"You're just jealous because I can date whoever I want and you're an old married hag at twenty-six!"

"And by date, you mean screw anyone with a penis. Give me a fucking break," Tessa groans, placing a fork next one of the plates.

"Contessa Maria Desoto! Watch your mouth!" mom scolds, setting a huge bowl of pasta in the middle of the table. "We are going to have Sunday dinner like normal, civilized people for once. No swearing, no fighting, and no throwing food."

She looks directly at me as she says the last part. You throw one dinner roll six months ago when your sister calls you a *tool* and you never live it down. It's not my fault it ricocheted off her shoulder and up into the ceiling fan before one of the blades sent it flying into our mother's face.

Rosa looks across the table at me and sticks out her tongue. I slyly flip her off without our mom seeing as we all take our seats. Even though it might not look like it, we really do love each other. We're your typical loud, eating, breeding Italian family, although our mother likes to remind us on a daily basis that we aren't doing our part in the breeding department. She met our father (God rest his soul) when they were sixteen years old, got married at eighteen, and popped out my oldest sister Contessa nine months later. Rosa followed a year after that, and I came screaming into the world a year after her.

"Alfanso, honey, say grace."

My mother folds her hands in front of her and closes her eyes, thankfully before she can see the scowl on my face and the laughter my sisters are just barely holding in.

"Ma, how many times do I have to tell you not to call me that?" I complain, trying not to whine like a little girl.

I spent my entire childhood saddled with that name and constantly being teased—mostly from my sisters, and when I left middle school behind and started high school, I refused to let anyone call me by anything other than my middle name of Marco. Sadly, my mother continues to ignore my request.

"Alfanso is a strong, Italian name and you should be proud you share—"

"The same name as my mother's father's uncle's brother from Sicily," my sisters and I cut her off and finish in unison.

"And by Sicily, we mean the planet Melmac, Alf," Tessa snorts, earning a one-eyed glare from my mother who still has her head bowed, eyes closed, and hands together in prayer.

I bow my head and close my eyes, refusing to take my sister's bait when she uses the same, tired joke comparing my name to some furry creature on a TV show long before any of us were born.

"Rub-a-dub-dub, thanks for the grub. Yay God!"

Mom's hand smacks me upside the head as soon as I finish and Tessa kicks my shin under the table. One of these days I should try not being an asshole, but it's just too much fun.

We all start digging into our food and the only sounds that fill the room for a few minutes are forks scraping plates and ice cubes clinking in glasses. It reminds me of every single Sunday dinner we've ever had, even if it is surprisingly quiet for the time being. Regardless of my sisters and I being adults with our own lives and our own homes, it's an unwritten rule that no matter where we are or what we're doing, that we always come home for Sunday dinner.

"So, Alfanso, when are you going to bring a nice woman home to meet the family?" mom asks casually as she slathers butter on a slice of homemade bread.

"He doesn't know any nice women; he only knows skanks." Rosa laughs.

"Skanks with the I.Q. of a banana," Tess adds.

I glare at both of them with my fork halfway to my mouth. "Hello? I'm sitting right here. They aren't skanks and they aren't stupid. I prefer to call them 'scantily-clad ladies with limited vocabulary.'"

Mom sighs. "All of my friends have photos of grandchildren on their bookshelves. Do you want to know what I have on my bookshelves? I have porn."

In a moment of insanity and a little bit of depression after my father passed away, I got the genius idea to write a cookbook, filled with my family's favorite Italian dessert recipes. When the publishing house I sent it to told me it was too boring, instead of getting drunk and crying about it, I got drunk and added a bunch of tips for men on how they could get any woman they wanted just by making those recipes. It included the best recipe for Italian buttercream that wouldn't leave grease stains on their sheets after they smeared it on their girl, as well as how to give a woman an orgasm using only cannoli filling and a spatula.

"Hey," I bristle at her porn comment. "That's a signed copy of *Satisfaction and Sugar*. If you announce on Facebook you have that, women will start clawing each other's eyes out for it."

I don't mean to sound conceited, but it's true. I get emails from a ton of women on a weekly basis, thanking me for spicing up their sex life while teaching their significant other how to bake and asking if I give in-home demonstrations. It's really great for the ego and it's made my popularity grow so much in the book world that the publisher has requested another cookbook from me.

Rosa snorts. "Try not to break your arm patting yourself on the back there, little brother."

My family really is proud of my accomplishments, even if they don't sound like it sometimes. They are my biggest supporters and always tell me how impressed they are of everything I've done at such a young age, but to them, I'm just Alfanso Marco Desoto. The son and brother who refuses to settle down, gets a cheap thrill out of teasing his older sisters, and had to grow up real fast when our father died suddenly of a heart attack three months before I was supposed to go to Paris to be the head pastry chef for one of the most popular restaurants in the city. I'll never regret the decision to stick close to home to teach at my alma mater and take care of my family, but I'm not going to lie and say that I don't still dream about Paris, although helping men all over the land get laid with desserts does take the sting out of things.

"What's the deadline for your next cookbook? Do you still want me to edit?" Tessa asks, wiping her mouth with a napkin.

Tessa is a copy editor for our local newspaper. It's nice to have someone in the family with editing skills that I can trust my cookbooks with, who won't dry heave when I confirm that I try out every piece of advice I give before putting it in a book.

"I want to have this thing finished in a few months. If all goes well, and I don't have any distractions for the next four weeks, this puppy could be on shelves in bookstores by early next year," I tell everyone proudly.

"Rosa, put your phone away at the dinner table," Mom chastises.

Rosa ignores her, scrolling through something on her screen and laughing. "It's Marco's phone and I'm just checking the notifications on his cookbook page. You really pissed this chick off."

Rosa has floundered between jobs ever since she graduated college, never quite being able to figure out what she wanted to do with her life. When my cookbook started gaining popularity a couple of years ago, I was spending more time answering emails and dicking around on Facebook, instead of doing lesson plans and preparing finals. So when I offered her a job as my social media assistant, she jumped at it. I might be regretting the decision of giving her my Facebook password right now though.

Tessa leans closer to Rosa and looks over her shoulder. "What did he do?"

"Some guy on the page asked if all of the tips and recipes still gave you the same outcome if you had kids, and Marco told him that his first mistake was *having* kids," Rosa snorts with a chastising shake of her head.

"ALFANSO MARCO DESOTO!" Mom yells, bringing out my full name for extra, angry emphasis.

I hold my hands up in surrender. "Ma, it was a joke. I was just being my usual charming, sarcastic self."

I turn back to Rosa. "Who commented and what did she say?"

Tessa grabs the phone from her hand. "Her name is Molly and she said, 'You're an ass. You probably don't even know how to bake and just copied all these recipes from your mommy. Cut the cord and get a life.'"

Rosa takes the phone back and Tessa smacks her in the arm. "Ooooh, burn! She's got your number, Marco!"

I roll my eyes and help myself to another serving of pasta. "Whatever. She's obviously got a stick up her a..." I glance quickly at my mom and correct myself. "...foot, and doesn't have a sense of humor."

"Her name is Molly Gilmore, and it says she's from Ohio too,"

Rosa continues, completely ignoring me.

The spoon slips out of my hand and drops with a loud *clatter*, splattering red sauce all over the table.

"Ooops, slippery little bugger." I laugh uncomfortably, grabbing a handful of napkins and sopping up the mess, hoping no one notices I lost all bodily functions as soon as I heard that name.

Tessa gasps and points at me with wide eyes. "Oh my Gosh, you know her! You know her and you like her and she thinks you're an ass!"

Seriously, how does she *do* that? People drop spoons all the time; it doesn't mean they like someone. How does she know my hand didn't go numb? Maybe it's early onset Parkinson's or a stroke. I could be dying and she doesn't even care.

"I have no idea what you're talking about," I mutter as I wad up the dirty napkins, getting up from my chair and heading into the kitchen. "Who wants dessert? I brought my special Tiramisu!"

Not even chocolate, mascarpone, and the special thing I do with the Lady Fingers can deter the three women in my family when they smell something fishy.

They bum rush me in the kitchen so fast all three of them get stuck in the doorway pushing, shoving, and arguing until one of them manages to break free and get to me first.

"Is she pretty? Can she cook? When are you bringing her to dinner so I have enough time to bring out the good china and your grandmother's lace tablecloth?" Mom asks in a rush of excitement.

Figuring there's no point in lying to them since I already planned on making my move with Molly as soon as she finished her final tomorrow and will no longer be my student, I grudgingly answer my mother's questions, hoping it will shut her up.

"Yes, yes, and never."

She puts her hands on her hips and my sisters do the same, standing behind her and giving me equal looks of annoyance.

"So, you know who this Molly Gilmore person is, but clearly she has no idea you're the same Alfanso D. whose Facebook page she was on, cookbook author and the guy she just knocked down a few pegs," Tessa states. "What does she look like? How old is she? Where did you meet her?"

I roll my eyes at all the questions that just won't stop. When I first found out my cookbook was going to be published, I spoke with the school I worked for to make sure it wouldn't be a conflict of interest. They suggested using some sort of penname just in case and since I'm only known as Marco Desoto at work, Alfanso D. was born. None of my students know I'm the author of that widely-popular cookbook and only a very small handful of the faculty knows.

"She's got long dark hair and pretty blue eyes, she's twenty, and ooooooooh, she's one of Marco's students! You naughty boy, you." Rosa giggles with her eyes glued to the phone in her hand. "Forget writing cookbooks, you could write one of those *'I Bent the Rules and Bent Her Over My Desk'* taboo student/teacher romances."

Mom turns around and flicks Rosa's ear, causing her to yelp and complain loudly, distracting her enough for me to reach around my mother and snatch my phone from her hand. Glancing down at it, I see that Rosa found Molly's Facebook page and was knee-deep in her investigation, going by the fact that she was in a photo album dated five years ago.

"After tomorrow, she will no longer be my student, so there won't be anything taboo about it," I inform them, clicking out of her Facebook page even though all I want to do now is sit and scroll through her pictures. "If any of you say one more word about this, I will pack up that Tiramisu, go home, and eat the entire thing myself."

I can see each of them struggle to keep their mouths closed, their nosiness at war with their stomachs.

"Did you soak the Lady Fingers in hazelnut coffee?" Tessa asks with wide, hopeful eyes.

I nod.

"Did you put vanilla AND almond extract in the mascarpone?" Rosa questions with a dreamy sigh.

I nod again, crossing my arms in front of me and refusing to budge until they all agree to stay out of my love life. Or what I hope will be a love life and not a complete disaster when Molly finds out I'm the ass she thinks can't bake.

After a few seconds, they concede reluctantly.

"Fine," Tessa mutters. "But if that tiramisu sucks, all bets are off."

I laugh, long and hard, as they trudge back into the dining room and I grab dessert from the fridge, knowing without a doubt I would never make a sucky tiramisu. I'm insulted she would even suggest such a thing.

The rest of the night continues with only a few more minor arguments and no more violence from my mother for my behavior. With a kiss on her cheek and three Tupperware containers filled with leftovers, I leave my childhood home and head across town to my apartment to put together a plan of charming the pants off of Molly Gilmore, and hope my comment about kids on my Facebook page doesn't come back to bite me in the ass.

Chapter 3

— Soup —
Molly

S TARING PROUDLY AT my soufflé display that still sits on the middle of the stainless steal counter in the kitchen at school, I look around the huge room, making sure I'm alone. Confident that the rest of my classmates have long since gone home after receiving their pass or fail grades, I start shaking my ass and dancing around the counter. When I get to the other side, I pause my celebration long enough to grab the sheet of paper next to my display that officially declares me a French Pastry Chef, waving it around above my head as I resume my horrible moves.

"What are you doing?! You can't be dancing like that in your condition!"

I freeze mid hip thrust with my arms in the air and watch Charlotte stalk across the room, snatching my final exam out of my hand and smacking it on the shiny surface.

"Shaking your hips like that could hurt the baby," she continues. "It could also hurt my reputation if anyone else witnessed that horrible display that resembled white girl wasted drunk moves."

With a sigh, I drop my arms and start unbuttoning my pastry coat. "In case you forgot, you're the one with the fertilized egg in your uterus, not me. What are you even doing here at my school?"

She crosses her arms in front of her as I toss the white fabric onto the countertop. "I didn't forget, Molly. It's hard to forget something like that when you're constantly puking. If this is going to work, you have to be one hundred percent dedicated and that means behaving exactly like a pregnant woman would. I wanted to catch you here at school before you got home."

Reaching into the giant purse she has slung over her shoulder, she pulls out a thick book and thrusts it at me.

"Here, I got you this. Skim through it and pay close attention to the things I marked with post-it notes."

Taking the book from her hand, I stare in irritation at the picture of the happy pregnant woman on the cover and the big bold words that say *"What to Expect When You're Expecting"*. My hopes that Charlotte would forget this shit, come to her senses, and tell Gavin the truth was clearly a waste of time. Going by the fact that there are post-it notes in a multitude of colors sticking out of practically every page in the book, she still hasn't grown a brain and has instead boarded the crazy train to La La Land and offered to drive.

"Charlotte, this is insane. I am not going to learn about…" I flip through the book and pause on a random page, realizing *this* thing is probably the cause for her puking. "Growing hair on your nipples and hemorrhoids."

I close the book with a *snap* and shove it back at her. "I did you a favor by taking one for the team yesterday when you panicked. That doesn't mean I'm going to keep up with this charade just because you're too chicken shit to tell Gavin."

Her bottom lip starts to quiver and her eyes fill up with tears.

"Oh, no," I scold, pointing my finger in her face. "Don't even try that shit with me. I know for a fact you can cry on command, and you do it every time Dad tells you no."

The tears immediately disappear and she huffs, moving on to a different tactic.

"Molly, please," she begs. "Just do me this one favor. Just until after the wedding and I have enough time to ease Gavin into the news. I've never asked you for anything in your entire life…"

She trails off and I laugh, shaking my head at her audacity.

"Took the blame for the dent in Mom's car when the mailbox magically jumped out in front of you so you wouldn't get grounded and miss prom. Took responsibility for the vodka you puked all over the bathroom floor the day AFTER prom so you could still go to a pool party. And let's not forget the week I spent in my room after I falsely admitted to dying the cat's hair pink so you wouldn't miss Stephanie Johnson's birthday party," I remind her, ticking the items off on my fingers.

"Oh my GOD, that happened when you were six! Get over it already!" she complains. "See? Look how good you are at making Mom and Dad believe whatever you say. What's one more tiny little favor?"

I roll my eyes at her as I turn away and pull my display to the edge of the counter. It's a three-foot-long thick piece of cardboard covered in foil with my different soufflés resting neatly on top. It's heavy and awkward, but I need to move it to the display case in the lobby with the rest of the pastry student's projects.

"It's hilarious that you can call this a tiny favor, Char," I tell her as I slowly lift the makeshift tray with both hands and turn to face her. "You're asking me to tell our parents I'm pregnant. To lie to our entire family for four weeks, have them spend that whole time being disappointed and upset with me, just because you couldn't remember what a condom looked like."

Tears fill her eyes again and I can tell she's not faking them this time. I hate that I actually feel sorry for her. She's the most selfish person on the planet, and I feel sorry for her stupid ass. She hasn't even asked about finals when she knew what a big day this was for me. Two years of not having a life and working my ass off and she comes in here thinking only about herself.

"You don't understand, Molly," she whimpers. "I love Gavin more than anything else in this world. You have no idea how dead set he is against having kids. I thought I felt the same way until I took that test. I know it will just take him time to get used to the idea. I just need a little while to convince him how good it will be."

I close my eyes and count to ten, trying really hard not to give in.

"Mom made me clean up your vodka puke," I remind her, trying at the same time to remind myself all the reasons why I shouldn't cave. "I had to listen to a forty minute lecture about knowing my limits, and then she made me watch fifteen episodes of *Intervention* with her."

Cleaning up Charlotte's puke wasn't as bad as my mother trying to convince me that vodka was a gateway drug to meth and I should think about how embarrassing it would be if she put me on a reality show where the entire world would see me huffing air dusters and sleeping with eighty-year-old men to pay for crack.

"I know, I'm sorry," Charlotte whispers. "I'll make it up to you this time, I promise."

My arms are starting to get heavy, and if I don't agree to this, she's never going to leave me alone. It's not like I have anything else going on in my life now that I'm finished with school. I start working full-time at the Seduction and Snacks headquarters in a few days, but that's a regular job with regular hours and nothing like the time I had to put in for school. And it's not like I'll be busy having a hot romance since I was too much of a chicken to finally try and have a real conversation with Marco instead of just sniffing him. He didn't say one word to me when he studied my project earlier, made several notes on his notepad, and then walked away. He didn't even look in my direction when we came back into the kitchen a few hours later and he handed out our final scores. Now that I'll be walking out of this school for the last time, I'll probably never see him again, and I completely blew whatever opportunity I had to flirt with him and see if he might be interested. My life sucks. It's only four weeks, I guess I can handle a month of this nonsense to save Charlotte's marriage.

"I want every baking item and pastry utensil you get at your shower. Including the KitchenAid mixer I know Aunt Claire already bought off your registry," I inform her.

Charlotte squeals and claps her hands together happily. "Deal!"

"I also want ten percent of your profits from cards at the actual wedding."

Her smile falls and she glares at me.

"Five," she counters.

"I'm fake carrying your baby for four weeks, and you know Mom is going to want to talk about nipple hair! TEN!" I argue.

She stomps her foot and huffs. "Fine! Ten. But you better be the most convincing fake pregnant woman in the history of the world."

"I'll even dump a can of soup in the toilet when I have fake morning sickness," I reassure her.

Charlotte quickly clamps her hand over her mouth.

"Dnsh shtak ashtok shtup," she muffles against her palm.

The look of confusion on my face makes her pull her hand away, swallowing a few times to keep, what I'm assuming is a little vomit, in her throat.

"I said, don't talk about…soup."

She whispers the word *soup,* and I can actually see her face turn an interesting shade of green.

"You are so weird," I mutter, shifting the display in my hands as my arms start to cramp. "So, what's the plan?"

It's her turn to look confused and she's lucky I'm holding twenty-five pounds of soufflé's or I'd smack that look right off of her face.

"How and when am I supposed to tell Mom and Dad this joyous news?" I growl in annoyance.

"Well, I told Gavin not to say anything until you could talk to them, but he might have already said something to Tyler who probably told Ava. So you should do it really soon. Like, as soon as you get home," she tells me, having the decency to wince delivering the news that our sister and her weird boyfriend might already know about my fake delicate condition.

"So, I'm supposed to just walk into the house and say 'Hey, Mom and Dad, good news! I passed all my exams, I'm finally done with school, graduation is Friday at seven, I made a chocolate cake to celebrate, and oh, by the way, I got knocked up by a guy I never told you about and who you'll never meet because Charlotte already told Gavin he was a horrible man that wants nothing to do with me. What's for dinner?" I ramble, picturing my father's head literally exploding all over the living room wall if I said that.

"Perfect!" Charlotte says with a nod, not hearing the sarcasm in my voice.

I open my mouth to call her a range of creative names, but a male voice coming from the doorway cuts me off.

"That won't work at all. What if I go home with you and pretend to be the father?"

I jump and turn so fast towards the doorway that my display slips right out of my hand and splats to the floor, sending pastry crust and pounds of different flavored fillings all over mine and Charlotte's shoes.

"Eeeeew, it looks like tomato soup," she whines, probably talking about the cherry filling dripping from her shins.

I ignore the gagging sounds coming from her and stare with my mouth wide open at Marco as he lounges against the door jam, not even caring that I just ruined my display that I spent weeks agonizing over and all day today baking and perfecting.

"You're not doing this alone, Molly. Let me help you out," he tells me softly.

I'm too mesmerized by the sound of his voice and how his eyes got all sweet looking when he said my name, that it takes me a couple of seconds to process what he said. He cocks his head and smiles at me, and it finally hits me that he must have overheard the last part of my conversation with Charlotte and he's offering to help me. He thinks I'm pregnant with another guy's child and he just volunteered to walk right into the lion's den of my parent's house and take some of the heat off me.

Butterflies flap around in my stomach and a giddy grin starts to take over my face, realizing I didn't blow my opportunity with him and he clearly likes me a little bit if he's being so sweet and offering to stand in as the baby daddy for me.

OH, MY GOD HE'S OFFERING TO BE MY BABY DADDY BECAUSE HE THINKS I'M PREGNANT WITH ANOTHER GUY'S CHILD!

"Yes. YES!" Charlotte shouts next to me in between gags as she shakes her leg to try and get the cherry filling off. "This is perfect! I don't know who you are, but you are a very nice and generous guy to help Molly out like this."

I'm still unable to form words as she takes over speaking for me, telling Marco about the fake horrible man that fake knocked me up whose name she can't even bare to utter (BECAUSE HE'S FAKE) and how he left me in this condition and it would be just awful if I had to face it alone.

Marco nods in understanding while she prattles on, wrapping her arm around my shoulder and giving it a sympathetic squeeze when she tells him how much she loves me and how she feels so much better now that I won't be going through such a trying time alone.

When she finally finishes her long-winded, TMI explanation to the guy I've had a crush on for what feels like forever, who is now looking at me like he wants to give me a supportive hug instead of ripping my clothes off like I always dreamed, I finally find my voice.

Turning away from Marco's sad smile, I look right into my sister's eyes and whisper the words I know will hurt the most.

"Soup, soup, soup. Cream of mushroom soup, green pea soup, chunky gelatinous globs of soup from a can. Soup."

Our faces are so close I can literally hear the vomit fly up into her mouth. Her cheeks puff out to keep it in, her eyes widen in fear, and without another word—thank God—she turns and runs from the room as fast as she can, bumping into Marco on her way out.

"She has a thing about soup; so weird," I tell him with a shrug as the clack of her shoes running down the hall to the closest bathroom fades away.

"Listen, Marco, you don't have to—"

"Molly, stop," he cuts me off, moving out of the doorway and walking towards me. "I know I don't have to, I want to. I've wanted to get to know more about you for a while now, so I guess this will give me that chance."

He stops when he gets to the counter, resting his palms on top and leaning across it towards me. I can't help myself from leaning towards him as well, the smell of cookie dough filling my nose and making my knees weak.

"Let me do this for you. We can go get some dinner to get our stories straight, and then I'll give you a ride home so that we can talk to your parents together," he suggests.

All I can do is nod in agreement when he gives me another smile. I've waited two years to be alone with this guy and now I'm getting my chance. By making him the father of the baby I'm not really pregnant with.

"How about I clean up this mess on the floor and you check on...?"

"My asshole sister," I mutter as he comes around the counter to grab some towels from near the sink.

Marco laughs as he bends down and begins cleaning up the floor.

"She's probably still got the soup pukes, she'll be fine," I tell him.

He smiles up at me as he stands and drops the dirty towels into the sink. When he finishes washing his hands, he walks to my side and threads his fingers through mine, pulling me gently to the door of the kitchen.

We walk through the school and out into the parking lot, and all I can think about is that Marco Desoto is holding my hand. Marco Desoto is taking me on a date.

I mean, a date where we'll talk about hairy nipples, hemorrhoids and afterbirth, and how my father's brain matter will stain his blue dress shirt when his head explodes, but still.

If being the pretend father of my pretend child is the only way I can get him to spend time with me, so be it. I'll just ask Charlotte if I can catch a ride on that crazy train of hers when this is all over.

Chapter 4

- *Toxic Spooge* -

Marco

I STARE AT Molly across the table as she picks at her food, wondering if she's going to puke. Do pregnant chicks puke at night too or just in the morning? Should I go sit next to her and hold her hair back just in case? What if she doesn't have pregnancy sickness but Marco sickness? Maybe I disgust her. I kind of disgust *myself* right now that I opened my mouth without really thinking about what I was doing.

The girl I've been fantasizing about for two years is having some other guy's baby, and instead of doing what any normal guy would do, I offered to pretend to be the father. I've lost my goddamn mind. I can't be a fake dad to someone else's kid, even if I AM hot for the woman carrying said kid. My dreams of Molly included seeing her naked and asking her to help me test out a few new ideas for my next cookbook, not watching her hot body turn into an alien WITH SOMEONE ELSE'S KID.

She didn't say much on the drive over to the diner aside from letting me know the girl with the long, dark brown hair who has a strange aversion to soup was her older sister, Charlotte. She pretty much gave me one-word answers to every question I asked, or flat out refused to answer them. Dinner isn't going much better, no matter how hard I try to get her to talk. As much as I *don't* want to know about the other guy she was seeing, I still think she'll feel better if she talks about it, and it will give me a way to ease into telling her I made a big mistake.

"I can't do this," Molly suddenly mutters, dropping her fork onto her plate.

Oh, thank God. Thank the good sweet lord I don't have to go back on my word and tell her I changed my mind.

"You're the sweetest guy in the world for doing this, but…I can't," she whispers with a shake of her head.

Good, because I still want to put my penis in her, but I don't think I can stomach it knowing some other dude's baby would be looking at it, judging it and saying something like, "My dad's was bigger than yours, asshole." She still looks like she might throw up. I need to say something nice and comforting.

"Okay. Want to order dessert?"

Yeah, real smooth, buddy.

Molly sighs and I wonder if she's mad I gave in so easily or because the diner's dessert selection sucks. What self-respecting diner doesn't serve apple pie?

"Stupid, selfish, irritating moron…" she mumbles, resting her elbows on the table and dropping her head into her hands.

So, I guess it's me, then.

"Look, I'm sorry, Molly. I really like you. Like, *really* like you. You're smart, beautiful, and the most amazing pastry chef I've seen come through that school. I like you too much to be able to just sit back and be okay with you….you know."

I wave my hand and move my eyes down in the general direction of her stomach.

"I think my services would be better served if I…I don't know, beat the shit out of the guy who did this to you," I continue, talking faster so she doesn't hate me too much for going back on my word to help her. "Give me his name, and I'll make sure he steps up to the plate for you. I can roundhouse punch his face and give him a nice left hook kick to the kneecaps."

She slowly lifts her head from her hands and stares at me.

"Have you ever been in a fight?" she asks skeptically.

"Uh, hello? Have you seen these guns?" I ask, flexing my bicep and giving it a nice little pat for emphasis. "I'm a fighting machine."

She doesn't need to know the one and only fight I participated in happened in the fourth grade with Tommy Knittle when he called me a sissy for bringing in a plate of cookies I'd made to share with the class. I showed him, though. He said he'd give me two black eyes if I didn't eat all three dozen cookies myself in front of everyone on the playground. It only took *one* black eye, thank you very much.

"That's sweet, but it's roundhouse *kick* and a left hook *punch*," she informs me, trying to hide a smile.

"I'm Italian. We do things a little more hardcore where I come from."

"Aren't you from Ohio?" she asks skeptically.

"I meant my mother's house. If you can dodge a wooden spoon, you can dodge a fist," I inform her, trying to maintain as much coolness as I can. "Enough talk about me, let's talk about the scum bag who put you in this situation."

So what if I haven't been in a fight since elementary school? I can beat the shit out of bread dough and I'm sure it's the same thing as some guy's face.

"Did you mean it when you said you liked me?" she whispers.

I can't believe that hasn't been obvious over the last few years, especially from the number of times I leaned over her shoulder to compliment whatever she was making just so I could smell her hair. She always smells like cinnamon and apples and it drives me crazy. Now she's going to smell like cinnamon, apples and someone else's sperm. I don't know who this loser is, but I'm sure his spunk smells like toxic waste. I shouldn't have waited so long to make my move. She stuck with toxic waste spooge when she could have had pineapple spooge. (Page 35, Section 2 of *Seduction and Sugar: Pineapple Dump Cake and Making Your Jizz Taste like a Tropical Island Getaway*)

"Yes, of course I meant it," I tell her, saying good-bye to my fantasy of Molly telling me I taste like a Piña Colada while I take a big sip of ice-cold water to cool my libido.

"Why do you have to be such a nice guy? Why can't you be a jerk like that cookbook author, Alfanso D., who hates kids?" she complains.

"I bet the D. stands for dickhead."

The water immediately goes down the wrong pipe, and I start choking and coughing, slamming the glass onto the table to smack my fist against my chest. Molly jumps up from her seat and races around to me, sliding into my side of the booth to pat me on the back through my coughing fit.

Even hacking up a lung of ice water, I can't avoid the scent of cinnamon apples as she leans in close to me and asks if I'm okay. Dammit, why couldn't she smell like ass and toxic jism instead of a delicious dessert?

"I'm fine, I'm fine," I tell her between coughs, subtly scooting a little bit away from her on the bench.

Her hand drops from my back and she smiles. "It's good to know I'm not the only one who almost chokes to death at just the mention of that guy's name. If you aren't following him on Facebook, you should, just to see what asshole thing he'll say next."

She laughs and if I wasn't the dickhead in question, I'd probably laugh right along with her. Molly turns to face me on the bench, tucking one leg up underneath her. My eyes glance down to her flat stomach and I try picturing it all ginormous and gross with arms and legs kicking through the skin trying to claw their way out, instead of how her laugh makes my dick tingle and how if I told her I'm the one saying asshole things on Facebook she'd give me one of those left hook kicks to the nut sack instead of another smile.

"Sorry, I know I'm being weird. Evading your questions, changing the subject, and talking about some idiot on Facebook that pissed me off," she explains. "I can't lie to you when you're being so honest and nice."

Honesty is my middle name. Right after Lying Dickhead Asshole.

She looks away for a minute, blows out a huge breath, and then turns her head back to me, nervously chewing on her bottom lip.

"Marco, I'm not pregnant."

Now my eyes move to the general region of her crotch area, and I wonder if I should have paid better attention in health class since I'm guessing she must have lost the baby somewhere between Third Street and the second refill of our drinks, and I had no idea it could happen so fast and without my knowledge.

"Um, do you need to go to the hospital or something?" I ask lamely. "Boiling water or clean towels...I could flag down the waitress."

I don't know much about losing a baby, but I'm guessing it's not as simple as losing your car keys and she probably needs medical assistance at the very least. And why do they call it *losing* a baby? You didn't misplace it. I'm pretty sure you know where that thing is at all times.

Molly laughs again and shakes her head, and I'm a little surprised she isn't more torn up about this. I cried when I lost my favorite star frosting tip. I mean, allegedly. Like I'd really cry over a little piece of stainless steel I found by chance at a garage sale three years ago that made the perfect fleur-de-lis I haven't been able to recreate with another tip since it disappeared months ago.

"I didn't lose the baby, Marco. I was never pregnant to begin with."

Her words make my mouth drop open and save me from the embarrassment of telling her the tears in my eyes are from allergies and not a frosting tip whose loss I can neither confirm nor deny still haunts me to this day.

"I'm sorry. I should have told you the truth as soon as you offered to help me. I'm not pregnant, and I understand if you hate me for lying to you," she tells me sadly.

All thoughts of the perfect fleur-de-lis fly from my brain and it's all I can do not to pinch myself to see if I'm dreaming.

"Come again?" I whisper.

No, really. I'm pretty sure I just came in my pants when you said you weren't pregnant and I'd like to do that again, please.

"I'm not pregnant and I never was. I was lying for Charlotte," she explains. "She's getting married in a month and just found out she's pregnant and it's this whole big mess I got roped into because she doesn't want her fiancé...never mind. It's not important. It's my mess to deal with and I'm sorry you got pulled into it."

I can hear sadness in her voice and I feel bad she thinks I'd hate her over something that just made me the happiest man on the earth. I can still fantasize about having sex with her without feeling gross. I can still

32

have sex with her without worrying another man's fetus is giving my penis the side-eye.

Finally pulling my eyes away from her crotch where a baby didn't somehow escape between courses, past her flat stomach I no longer have to worry about alien limbs trying to claw out of, taking a moment to pause on her tits and only feeling a little ashamed that the one thing I might have enjoyed about this entire shit show is seeing them get huge from the douchebag fetus (because that was something I definitely paid attention to in health class), my eyes finally land on her face.

"So, what you're telling me is I can ask you out on a date now and not feel weird about you carrying another man's child?" I ask happily.

She raises her eyebrow and glares at me. "Seriously? That's all you got out of my confession?"

I quickly backpedal, realizing I still need a way for her to see I'm a good guy and only pretend to be a dick online to sell more cookbooks. I can't tell her I'm Alfanso D. until she knows the D. stands for something much better than dickhead. Like decent, dependable, desirable, daring, and hopefully delicious (pineapple dump cake jizz, here I come!).

"What I meant to say is, I could never hate you for doing something so selfless for your sister," I explain, doing my best to let the whole decent and dependable part shine. "How long are you supposed to help her out with this?"

Molly rolls her eyes and turns away from me, flopping her body against the seat back. "Just until the wedding. So roughly four weeks. It's not *that* long I guess, but it's an entire month of my family being disappointed and ashamed of *me* instead of her. I mean, my family is cool and understanding and they wouldn't come right out and tell me any of this, but I know they'll feel it deep down inside whenever they look at me. This is supposed to be the best time of my life. I just graduated and I have my whole life ahead of me, and instead of celebrating, I'm going home to lie to my family. I keep trying to tell myself it's for a good cause. I'm helping my sister, as selfish as she is, get her shit together and figure out a way to break the news to her fiancé so they can live a long, happy life together. Right now, it doesn't feel like a good idea thinking about what will happen when I walk in that door."

Now that I know there's no chance of her pregnant-puking on me, and I don't have to fight the delectable smell of her skin and how it makes me want to lick every inch of it, I slide across the bench until our thighs are touching. A month is perfect. It's plenty of time for me to charm the pants off of her and hopefully *take* the pants off of her, blinding her with passion and bedroom skills until she has no other choice but to fall for me AND Alfanso D.

"I'm still in, if you are," I tell her softly, leaning in until her long, dark hair tickles my nose and I can take a big, completely innocent inhale of her scent.

"Did you just sniff my hair?" she asks softly, her face turning towards me and our noses are almost touching since I moved even closer while I got a whiff.

"Yes, yes I did smell your hair, and I'm not ashamed to admit it," I inform her, hoping she'll see this as *daring* that I didn't cover up my obsession with her sweet fragrance. "I've noticed you always smell like cinnamon and apples and I like it."

She runs her hand nervously through her hair and I watch as the cutest blush highlights her cheeks.

"It's an essential oil I use for stress. Apple cinnamon oil. You're supposed to put it on the inside of your wrists and the back of your neck to relieve stress and anxiety," she rambles. "I took to bathing in it the last two years of school just so I wouldn't lose my mind."

I stare into her eyes and smile when I see the color on her cheeks deepen and she laughs uncomfortably, pulling her face back from mine and scooting away from me this time. She shakes her head and huffs in annoyance.

"Stop distracting me with your stupid dimples and tell me if I heard you correctly a minute ago, or if you've been sneaking hits of crack under the table," she speaks, a little snark mixed in with her words.

I've caught a few glimpses of her fiery attitude over the past couple of years when she didn't know I was watching, and it's something I looked forward to seeing and hearing whenever I was around her. I like a woman who speaks her mind and doesn't get all giggly and shy with a guy. I like a little ball-busting from a woman, as long as it doesn't result in the *actual* busting of balls because I kind of need those things to live.

"Did you really tell me you're still in if I am?" she continues, looking at me like I've lost my mind.

I probably have. I'm sure I lost it somewhere after the meatloaf and before I found out she didn't really lose a baby in between the seat cushions and realized she was no longer chock full of infested, smelly-ass sperm from some no-name douchebag I'd no longer have to hire someone else to beat up.

"I did, and I am," I reiterate. "I have two sisters myself that drive me insane, but I'd still do anything for them. If you want a baby daddy to take some of the heat off of you, I'm am ready, willing, and able to be your baby daddy."

She shakes her head rapidly back and forth. "I can't let you do that, Marco. I know I said my family is cool and understanding, but they're straight up insane. You have no idea what you'd be walking into with them. Hell, I've known them my entire life and *I* don't even have a clue."

Unable to help myself, I reach up and brush her hair off of her shoulders, mentally sending words of warning to my dick that now is NOT the time to jump around with his hands in the air when I find out her hair is as silky and soft as I thought it would be.

"Molly, I want to do this. Believe me, my family is certifiable," I tell her with a laugh. "There is nothing I haven't seen or heard before when it comes to family. I can handle whatever they dish out."

For a second there she looked like she might bite off my hand when I touched her, and I'm not gonna lie, that it turned me on. My mind starts churning out ideas of adding a little BDSM to the next cookbook, maybe some light whipping while your partner whisks egg whites into cream...

"You don't have to do something like this just because you feel sorry for me," she says in irritation, pulling my head out of the gutter where Molly was wearing a black leather apron and nothing else while I held a riding crop in my hand.

"Did you miss the part where I told you I like you?" I ask her, realizing she thinks I'm still offering to help her out of some sort of guilt. "I *really* like you, Molly, and I'd like to spend more time with you. If that means I have to be the fake sperm donor to your fake baby, then so be it."

I wisely leave out the part where my dick is now handing out "It's not a boy OR a girl" cigars to my balls in celebration that they still have a chance with this girl.

"You have no idea what you're agreeing to...." she tells me, trailing off as she scrunches up her face while she thinks it over.

The waitress drops off our check and I leave Molly to her thoughts as I pull out my wallet and count enough for the bill and a hefty tip, even if I'm still pissed about them not having apple pie. Smelling Molly's hair cured me of my need for it anyway.

Pushing against Molly's hip with my own to get her to move out of the booth, she slides out and stands next to the table to wait for me to follow. Returning my wallet to my back pocket, I grab her hand and slide my fingers through hers, giving her hand a reassuring squeeze.

"Come on, let's go tell your family the happy news." I smile, tugging her towards the door. "I can practice my apologetic looks and fake happiness over this pretend blessing on the ride over and you can tell me more about your family."

When we get out to the parking lot, I add a little more decency to the D. in my name by holding the passenger door open for her, quickly realizing I might have pushed it a little too far when I made a grand, sweeping gesture with my arm and called her *m'lady*, going by the annoyed snort and eye roll she gave me.

Making a mental note that she doesn't seem to like being treated like a princess, I round the hood of the car and get in behind the wheel, looking over at her as I pull my car keys out of my front pocket.

"So, what's the first thing I should know about your family?" I ask, sticking the keys in the ignition.

"Don't do all that mushy, girly stuff like hold my hand or open doors," she begins. "My family will know you're lying right away because I'm not into all that PDA shit," she begins. "When my dad starts cracking his knuckles and talking about how he trained as a kickboxer for twenty years, don't show any signs of weakness. But if he gets his gun out of the hall closet, run."

Silence fills the car for a few moments until a high-pitch, screeching noise hits my ears and I realize my fingers are still clutched tightly to the key in the ignition and I've continued to turn it in a daze even though it started twenty seconds ago.

"Heh, heh," I laugh uncomfortably, yanking my hand away from the key to clutch the steering wheel. "That's hilarious, Molly. Good work trying to scare me out of doing this."

She laughs as I put the car in gear and pull out of the parking lot, her laughter letting me know she really *was* kidding and her father isn't going to try and kill me.

"You can't blame me for trying," she says with a shrug as I pull out into traffic and head in the direction she points. "My dad's never taken a kickboxing class in his life, so you don't have to worry about that."

Well, that's good to know. If I couldn't fight that little shit, Tommy Knittle, there's no way I could take on a pissed off father who thinks I knocked up his little girl. I'm a baker, not a fighter.

We both share a laugh until she suddenly stops and looks over at me. "But seriously, you can run, right? Because he really does have a gun."

I can still bake with a gunshot wound, right?

Chapter 5

— Thug Mug —
Molly

AS MARCO FOLLOWS my directions home, I throw out a few random facts about my family on the way, doing my best not to freak him out too much. I mean, aside from the whole gun thing, but I feel like I would have done him a disservice by leaving that part out. It's bad enough I let him think I was pregnant, even if was only for thirty minutes tops before my conscience got the best of me. I don't want him to be completely blindsided by my family when he's doing something so amazing for me, but maybe I said too much. He stopped talking and started looking like he might throw up about ten miles ago. Maybe telling him about how my Uncle Drew and Aunt Jenny never shut up about their sex life is where I lost him. Or it could have been when I tried to explain what a Brony is and promised him I'd never let Ava and her boyfriend Tyler force him to wear a horse tail. It was probably when I said that stupid shit about not liking PDA. Normally, I cringe if a guy tries to kiss me or hold my hand in public, but when Marco does it I want to rip his clothes off. Which is why it's probably for the best that he stop doing it altogether. My family doesn't need another reason to be freaked out.

"Turn left at the next stop sign," I tell him, twisting my neck to stare at his profile as he flips on the blinker and slows to a stop.

He's so good looking it's almost sickening. With his Italian genes that give him a gorgeous olive complexion, thick dark brown hair he keeps short on the sides with a messy spike on top, and so many muscles it's a wonder he doesn't bust out of every shirt he puts on, it's very hard not to drool in his presence. The fact that he told me he *likes* me should make me feel better that my crush isn't one-sided, but it just makes everything worse. It makes me act like a *girl* around him – a stupid, giggly, shy girl who forgets how to speak when he smiles at her. I might be known as the quiet one in the family, but I've never been shy until I met Marco Desoto. Now, not only do I have to worry about what's going to happen with my family in the next couple of weeks and if I'll be able to pull this whole thing off, I have to worry about Marco witnessing all of it and hoping he still likes me when it's over.

My phone vibrates in my hand and I stop gawking at Marco long enough to look down and see I have a Facebook notification. Opening the app, I laugh out loud when I see what the notification says and who it's from.

"What's so funny?" Marco asks, taking his eyes off the road long enough to see that I'm looking at my phone.

Since he's finally talking again, and no longer looks like he's going to yak all over the dashboard, I figure I might as well share this with him and give him a good laugh to ease the tension of what's about to happen.

"So, remember that douchebag I mentioned at the diner? Alfanso D., the supposed cookbook author? I called him out in front of all of his adoring fans, and he just replied to my comment."

"HE WHAT?!" Marco shouts, the car swerving off the berm and onto the gravel before he hastily rights the wheel and gets us back onto the road.

He gives me a quick look of apology and mutters something about a cat in the road before continuing. "There's no way he replied. Are you sure? Maybe you're confused."

I laugh, wondering why the hell he looks so freaked out when we're not even talking about my family, but some idiot on Facebook.

"I'm definitely not confused, and yes, I'm sure he replied. Here, listen to this," I tell him, clearing my throat and reading the pathetic comment. "'Dearest Molly, I am deeply sorry if anything I said angered you. Please accept my apology and know I will do my best not to make such offensive comments going forward.'"

It's even funnier reading it out loud so I do it one more time, but make my voice high-pitch and very feminine this time.

"There's no way this guy wrote that thing himself. I bet the comment I made about cutting the cord from his mommy made him go running right to the poor woman and he made *her* type this," I chuckle.

"His mother tries to text people using the TV remote. I doubt she'd know her way around Facebook," Marco mutters.

I look at him questioningly and he laughs. "I mean, I'm *assuming* that's how his mother is. You know, because he's a douchebag and all that…"

Figuring he's probably right and that the mother of Alfanso Douchebag has got to be as dumb as *he* is, I point out the next street Marco needs to turn down and which house is mine before looking back at my phone.

"He even put a heart and smiley face emoji at the end of his reply. How sad is that?" I ask. "This guy definitely has a small penis. Or no penis at all."

Marco pulls the car to the curb, mumbling under his breath so quietly I can barely hear what he says. The only words I catch are *anaconda penis* and something about *sisters wishing they'd never been born*, but before I can ask him to repeat himself, I look up and realize we're in front of my house. My hands start to sweat and my stomach flip-flops all over the place as he turns off the ignition and we sit in silence.

"Deep breaths, it's going to be fine," Marco reassures me as he pockets his keys. "I'm going to be right here the whole time. You're going to do great, they're going to believe every word you say, and they're going to surprise you by being happy and supportive and making this a hell of a lot easier on you."

I do what he says and take a few deep, calming breaths. I just need to keep my eye on the prize. A whole new set of baking utensils, a KitchenAid mixer, and ten percent of Charlotte and Gavin's wedding money. That will be more than enough for a deposit on my own apartment so I can move out of my parent's home and finally have some privacy. Privacy that will hopefully include a lot of naked time with the man next to me, as long as he hasn't changed his name and fled the country after dealing with my insane family for the next few weeks.

"And if things start to heat up, I'll just tell them about my incredibly huge penis, and how I'm without a doubt decent, dependable, desirable, daring and delicious," he says with a smile, leaning across the console to give me a quick peck on the cheek.

He's out of the car and around to my side, holding my door open for me before I can do something stupid like cradle my cheek in my hand and vow to never wash it again after he kissed it.

"Didn't I tell you to stop doing stuff like that?" I growl, pretending like I'm annoyed instead of two seconds away from asking him to take his pants off on the front lawn.

"Well, stop having such a kissable cheek then," he replies easily.

Marco continues to tell me how everything will be fine as we make our way up the sidewalk and onto the porch. I start to feel a bit more confident until I open the front door. The quiet peacefulness of the neighborhood outside is immediately ruined as we step into the foyer and the sounds of screaming, arguing, and cursing coming from the living room explode through the house.

"What in the hell?" I murmur as I start to move down the hall to the direction of the noise, the sound of Marco's shoes on the hardwood echoing behind me as he quietly follows.

When we're a few feet from the living room and the noise has reached ear-piercing level, Charlotte suddenly flies out of the room and around the corner, sliding across the floor in her stocking feet and quickly latching onto my arms to stop herself from slamming into me.

"What is going on in there?" I ask her when I can finally make out one of the shouting voices and it's my mother's, who just told someone to *"Shut the fuck up before I fucking make you shut the fucking fuck up, you fucking fuck!"*

Not her cleverest of curses, but certainly not one I haven't heard before.

"What are you doing here?" Charlotte whispers frantically. "I sent you a text! Didn't you get my text?!"

The shouting in the other room goes back to blending all together into one big noise as I pull my phone out of my back pocket and see I did indeed miss a text from Charlotte.

"Sorry, we were talking on the ride over and I missed it. Oh my gosh, wait until I tell you about the douchebag who—" I stop mid sentence when I open up the missed text and see what has Charlotte in such a panic and World War III happening in our living room.

THEY KNOW! OMG THEY KNOW! TXT ME ASAP!

I look up at Charlotte in sympathy and awkwardly pat her shoulder. "I'm sorry. Obviously the adults aren't taking it very well, but what did Gavin say? Are you guys okay?"

She winces and shakes her head back and forth. "No! They know about YOU, not about me!"

"Would you guys just shut the hell up so I can think? Drew, go get my gun. And the brass knuckles. Oh, for fuck's sake, don't look at me like that. A coffee cup with brass knuckles as the handle does too count as actual brass knuckles, so you can fuck right off."

My dad's voice is loud and clear over everyone else's this time, and I hear Marco whimper softly behind me. I wish I had time to remind him again that my dad's bark is usually worse than his bite, but I have more pressing concerns right now.

"What do you mean they know? How in the hell did they find out?" I whisper-shout as Charlotte suddenly realizes Marco is standing behind me.

Her eyes widen and she not-so-subtly jerks her head in his direction before moving her face closer to mine.

"Oes-day e-hay now-kay?" she mumbles, still shooting worried glances over my shoulder.

"Does he know?" Marco asks in confusion. "Does who know what?"

Charlotte gasps. "He knew what I said!"

"You spoke in Pig Latin, Charlotte," I say with a roll of my eyes. "That's not exactly a foreign language no one understands. And yes, he knows everything."

She clutches my upper arms tightly, jerking my body with each of her words. "Why would you tell him?! Before you know it, the whole world will know!"

"I am not afraid to smack a pregnant chick, so let go of my arms," I threaten through my gritted teeth, shrugging out of her tight hold on me. "In case you're forgetting, this is my life too, and I will tell whomever I want, especially the guy agreeing to be your baby's fake baby daddy that I'm now pretending to carry."

Can this get anymore confusing???

"Can we get back to a more pressing matter right now?" I continue once Charlotte has the decency to look sorry for being an asshole to someone going through a hell of a lot of trouble to help save her marriage. "How did mom and dad find out already?"

Charlotte winces and shrugs.

"I told Gavin not to say anything, but I guess he mentioned it to Tyler, and you know Tyler can't keep his mouth shut so he told Ava and she called mom and dad, thinking they already knew!" Charlotte quickly spits the words out in one breath. "But hey, look at it this way, at least you don't have to come right out and tell them, and that's the worst part!"

A bright smile lights up her face, and if she wasn't pregnant, I'd punch her right in the ovaries.

"Really, Charlotte? THAT'S the worst part?" I scoff. "Do you even hear the shit coming out of that room right now?"

"I don't care if it's been a while and I am NOT too old for Fight Club," my mother yells at someone. *"Claire, get over here and punch me in the stomach so I can get warmed up for that asshole responsible for this shit."*

My eyes widen in fear. I've heard stories about my mom and Aunt Claire's Fight Club and it isn't pretty. Forget having Marco fear my dad's gun, he really needs to fear my mother's fists.

"It will be fine once you get in there and tell them everything," Charlotte reassures me. "They still think you got pregnant by a loser who walked away. I tried explaining how that was a misunderstanding, but they won't stop screaming long enough to listen to me."

Charlotte looks over my shoulder and smiles. "Besides, I'm sure as soon as they meet Marco and see how sweet and nice he is, they'll forget all about wanting to kill him."

Marco puts his hands on my hips and his face next to my ear, the heat from his body against my back making my brain short-circuit.

"So, I'm rethinking that whole talk-about-my-huge-penis idea, and I've decided crying might be the best way to go," he informs me. "They wouldn't hit a guy who's crying, right?"

Sounds of a scuffle and something falling off a table and thumping to the floor comes from the living room.

"Are you CRYING? There's no crying in Fight Club!" my mother yells.

"That HURT, you dick-nose slut-box! I HAD CANCER!" Aunt Claire responds.

"Oh, fuck right off! You HAD cancer, you don't have it anymore and you should be able to take a punch, you pussy!" my mother shouts back.

Marco gasps and his hands fall from my hips. "Jesus Christ. They hit people with cancer? I'm a dead man."

He starts pacing nervously behind me and I ignore him, strapping on the set of balls I'm going to need to make it through this without killing my sister.

"Marco, what's the going rate for a convection rack oven?" I ask, talk of anything that involves baking taking his mind off of his impending doom.

He stops pacing and comes to stand next to me, looking down at me while he contemplates my question as Charlotte looks back and forth between us in confusion.

"For a good rack oven? I'd say around three grand, give or take," he tells me as I look back at Charlotte and put my hands on my hips.

"All the baking utensils at the shower, the KitchenAid mixer, ten percent of your wedding profits, AND a three thousand dollar bonus that you will hand over before you leave here tonight," I demand.

Marco whistles and Charlotte's narrows her eyes at me.

"Three thousand? Are you kidding me? Where in the hell am I

supposed to get three thousand dollars TODAY?" Charlotte asks in irritation.

"Hey, Marco, how much do you think an ice sculpture of a heart with two doves kissing on top of it costs?" I ask casually.

Charlotte gasps and her hand flies up to her chest. "You wouldn't?!"

I've heard Charlotte and my mom talking about that stupid ice sculpture for months and how proud Charlotte was that she saved the money herself so our parents would have one less thing to pay for.

"Would you rather have a block of ice at your reception that people are going to dare each other to lick all night long after they start drinking, or a reception that actually has a groom in attendance who didn't freak out about being a father and head for the hills?" I demand.

"What kind of wedding receptions have *you* been attending lately?" Marco asks in wonder.

Charlotte stomps her foot and crosses her arms in front of her with an angry huff. "FINE! I'll write you a check later. But I don't want to hear one complaint out of you for the next four weeks."

I make a crisscross over my heart with my finger and then hold my hand up. "Cross my heart. I'll be a better fake pregnant girl than a slutty college co-ed trying to trap her boyfriend into not breaking up with her."

Charlotte rolls her eyes, turns and stomps back into the chaos of the living room.

"If this works and we both make it out alive in a month, you can have all that extra stuff she promised me. It's the least you deserve for not running right back out the door as soon as we got in here," I tell Marco as he tries to grab my hand, but I quickly jerk it away and roll my eyes at him as we head towards the shouting. "I was going to use the extra money to get an apartment, but I don't care about ever moving out of this house as long as I have that rack oven."

Marco laughs as we pause in the doorway of the living room and takes in the scene in front of us. My mom and Aunt Claire are over by the couch trading punches to the stomach, Uncle Drew is sitting on the couch staring at them with a bowl of popcorn in his lap, Aunt Jenny is sitting on the arm of the couch filing her nails, and Uncle Carter is pacing in front of the fireplace. I find my dad sitting in a chair next to the fireplace, holding his hand out in front of him and admiring the brass knuckle coffee mug hanging from his fingers that says "Thug Mug" on it.

"If I'm still breathing in the next twenty minutes, you can keep it all," Marco whispers, finally responding to my offer of letting him have everything I'd negotiated from Charlotte. "The only thing I want in return is a promise that whatever happens at the end of these four weeks, you'll keep an open mind no matter what I say to you."

His words confuse me, but I'm so happy and shocked he still wants to go through with this that nothing else matters right now.

"I'd also like for you to remember at the end of these four weeks how brave it was of me to take a bullet for you and your unborn fake baby," he finishes, flashing me that damn dimpled smile that turns me into an idiot.

Instead of blushing and giggling, I go with the snark that makes me comfortable.

"No one is going to shoot you," I whisper back to him with another roll of my eyes.

"Fine, maybe I won't be taking a bullet tonight," he concedes, "but I'm pretty sure your dad plans on shoving that Thug Mug into my skull, and I can guarantee you it's not going to be pleasant."

I glare at Marco and his dramatics, refusing to let him know that everything he says just makes him look even more adorable and sweet in my eyes. I take another glance around the room, realizing we still haven't been spotted in the doorway when Gavin suddenly jumps out from the other side of the wall where he must've been lurking. A flash of panic rushes through me, wondering if he overheard Marco's comment about my unborn fake baby, but it's pretty clear Gavin is still in the dark as soon as he opens his mouth.

"So, this is the guy," Gavin states loudly, punching his fist repeatedly into his opposite palm as he tries to look intimidating.

His voice causes every head in the room to jerk in our direction, including my mother's, which unfortunately happens at the exact moment whens Aunt Claire pulls her arm back and slams her fist into mom's stomach.

"Wow! That was a nice roundhouse punch, Mrs. Gilmore!" Marco shouts happily across the room as my mother clutches her waist and drops to her knees.

"Roundhouse *kick*, left hook *punch*!" I remind him out of the corner of my mouth. "And the woman jumping up and down in victory is *not* my mother. The one on the floor groaning in pain is!"

Marco winces as my mother starts crawling on all fours across the room towards us, smacking Charlotte's hand away when she rushes over to her and tries to help her up.

Leaning closer to Marco's side, I figure it's probably best to just introduce him and get it over with, and quickly, before my mother makes it over to us and starts biting his ankles or something.

"Everyone, I'd like you to meet my...um..." I pause in a panic, realizing Marco and I never discussed what he'd be in this whole charade. Friend, boyfriend, nice guy who got me pretend pregnant who doesn't want a relationship, but wants to be in the pretend baby's life?

"Boyfriend," Marco finishes, smiling down at me. "I'm Molly's boyfriend."

Gavin continues punching his palm while he looks Marco over from head to toe. "And does this *boyfriend* have a name?"

Tearing my eyes away from Marco's sweet smile, I glare at Gavin and send him a silent warning to back the fuck down because no one is going to believe he could beat up a guy twice his size, even if the poor guy keeps confusing fight terms.

"Yes, he has a name," I inform Gavin through clenched teeth before looking away from him to address the rest of the room.

I paste a happy smile on my face and point in Marco's direction. "Everyone, this is Marco."

Uncle Drew jumps up from the couch so fast that his bowl of popcorn goes flying, dumping the entire thing all over the floor. He kicks the bowl and some of the popcorn out of the way to bounce back and forth on the balls of his feet.

"Honey, do you have to pee?" Aunt Jenny asks as she gets up from the arm of the couch and puts a worried hand on his elbow.

"I'm sorry, I'm usually better prepared for situations like this," Uncle Drew mutters, ignoring my aunt and smiling so big and with so much excitement he looks like a kid on Christmas morning. "Could you just tell us what his name is, one more time?"

Marco and I share a confused look, but I just shrug. I stopped trying to figure out my Uncle Drew a long time ago, and really, he'll be the easiest person in this room to deal with, so I don't even care about the point of this right now.

I give Marco's arm a squeeze to let him know it's okay to speak and unfortunately, he does.

"Marco."

"POLO!" Uncle Drew screams, throwing both of his arms up in victory. "Oh, my God, this is the best day EVER!"

Everyone turns and shoots him a dirty look. He drops his arms, bends down, and grabs a handful of spilled popcorn from the floor, shoving it into his mouth as he stands back up.

"You know, without the whole *Molly-is-knocked-up-by-some-dude-we've-never-met-before* thing," Uncle Drew says with a shrug as he licks popcorn salt from his fingers.

Chapter 6

- Cream Puff Balls -
Marco

"SO, ANYWAY, THIS is my boyfriend, Marco—"

"POLO!" the guy munching on popcorn shouts again, cutting her off.

I try not to roll my eyes because going by the description Molly gave me in the car, I'm guessing he's her Uncle Drew, and after what she told me he can do with a cheese grater, waffle iron, and a two pound bag of Skittles, I'm thinking he could be a lot of help with this next cookbook. Also, it's hard to be irritated when my penis is happy after hearing Molly call me her boyfriend. It's too conflicting and it's always best to go with whatever emotion my penis wants, and my penis wants me to be happy, dammit.

Molly grabs my arm and starts squeezing it so hard I'm not sure if it means I should speak or let her do the talking for now. I'm too busy watching her mother continue to crawl across the floor with her hair draped down over her face like that freaky little girl in the movie *The Ring*, while eyeing the coffee mug in her dad's hands that he's now puffing his breath on and then buffing against his chest. I'm sure it will feel so much better smashing into my skull if it shines.

"Desoto," Molly continues, giving them my last name and wisely ignoring her Uncle Drew. "We've been dating for…"

"Six months," I finish for her when she pauses, figuring six months

49

sounds like a good number. Not too short where they'll think I defiled their little girl on the first date, and not too long where they'll think we're in a really serious relationship and drag us to the courthouse, demanding we get married immediately.

"Oh, aren't they just the cutest thing, finishing each other's sentences like that?!" Charlotte asks happily, trying to get everyone's minds off of all the different ways they could kill me and make it look like an accident.

The woman I mistook for Molly's mother walks across the room, sidestepping the real Mrs. Gilmore as she pauses on her hands and knees in the middle of the room to catch her breath from all that crawling.

She stands in front of me and holds out her hand. "I'm Claire Ellis, Molly's aunt. It's nice to meet you, Marco."

"POLO!" Uncle Drew shouts again and the room lets out a collective groan. "I'm sorry! I just can't help myself. It's like a sickness."

Aunt Claire gives me an apologetic smile and a quick reassuring squeeze of my hand before letting go. She seems really sweet and nice and not at all scary like Molly warned me in the car. Some of the tension immediately leaves my body, and I decide the best course of action right now is to suck up to someone who seems to be on my side and hopefully, the rest of these people will follow.

"Claire Ellis," I repeat, returning her smile. "I thought you looked familiar. I can't believe Molly never told me she had such a famous and talented aunt."

I quickly realize I'm on the right track when Molly's death grip on my arm loosens and I see the appreciative smile on her aunt's face. I don't even have to pretend how cool it is to find out Molly is related to THE Claire Ellis. We use several of her recipes in our classes at school, and there's even a chapter in one of the first-year textbooks on business management about how she went from being a single mother and waitress to co-owning one of the largest business chains in the United States.

"You're one of the reasons I became a pastry chef," I boast proudly, hoping it'll win me more brownie points. "My mother bought me your first cookbook for Christmas, I can't even remember how long ago now, and your tip about chilling eggs before separating them changed my life."

She laughs, her smile widening as she listens and basks in the glory of every compliment I throw at her like it's my job.

"That is so sweet of you to say," Claire tells me before giving Molly a wink. "Handsome, a pastry chef, *and* an outstanding suck-up. Looks like you picked a good one, Molls."

Molly rests her cheek against my shoulder, forgetting about her no PDA rule, and I can practically feel the happiness and pride radiating off of her.

Yeah, that's right Mr. Thug Mug over there, I'm good at this shit so pay attention! You too, Mrs. Ankle Biter trying not to have a heart attack on the carpet. Your best friend thinks I'm a good one! Back off, haters, I'm on a roll.

To firmly secure my excellent standing with Molly's Aunt, I give her one last, perfect compliment I know she'll appreciate, holding my hand out to her for another shake to seal the deal.

"Seriously, though. It's an honor to meet you, ma'am."

There's a gasp from someone in the room, but I have no idea who it came from or why.

"Awwwww, shit," Molly mutters, lifting her head from my shoulder.

The guy standing to the side, who I think is Gavin and just moments ago looked like he wanted to pummel my face, suddenly looks like he fears for his life as he begins backing away. With a quick glance around, I realize *everyone* has backed away as far as possible and they're all studying different objects in the room like they've never seen them before. Uncle Drew has dropped to the ground and rolled under the coffee table to stare at the underside of the damn thing, and even Molly's dad has his head stuck up the chimney, looking all around the inside like he expects to find a nest of birds in there.

When my eyes make it back to Molly's aunt's face, I realize the smile is completely gone and I'm still standing here holding my hand out that she's refusing to take for some reason.

What in the hell did I do wrong?

"Forget everything I said about my dad," Molly whispers. "You should probably start running now."

Right when I start to drop my hand and apologize for God-knows-what, Claire's smile suddenly reappears and she grabs my hand, squeezing it so hard I can feel my bones pop and rub together. I start to wonder if I imagined what just happened when Claire yanks me towards her so forcefully that I stumble and catch myself right before I slam into her.

"Wow, you are curiously strong," I mutter as she leans her face so close to mine I can count each individual eye lash.

"You seem like a nice guy, Marco—"

"POLO!" Uncle Drew shouts from under the coffee table.

Claire continues in a low, threatening voice, like she didn't even hear him. "But if you ever call me *ma'am* again, I will chop off your testicles and use them as cream puffs."

My formerly happy penis shrivels up in fear, taking my balls with him.

Claire gives me a big smile that no longer comforts me, and I have a feeling I'll be seeing this smile in my nightmares in the coming days, waking up in a cold sweat and clutching my balls.

She drops my hand and turns away, walking over to Molly's mom. "Get up, fuck-face. I didn't hit you that hard."

Claire grabs Molly's mom's elbow and hauls her up from the floor.

"Kiss my ass, twat-licker!" her mom replies, yanking her arm out of Claire's grasp, pushing her hair out of her face and straightening her clothes. "I'll have you know I got carded buying wine the other day. The cashier told me he thought for sure I was only twenty."

Claire snorts. "Yeah, maybe in dog years. Don't worry, as soon as I buy you a *Worlds Greatest Nana* sweatshirt, no one will ever mistake you for being anything but old as fuck."

Right when I think I can relax and have a few seconds without any attention on me while these two are busy bickering, everyone in the room suddenly grows balls again, crawling out from under tables and pulling their heads out of chimneys to give me the evil-eye now that Claire has mentioned the elephant in the room.

"Wait, did we decide on Nana, Granny, or Mee-Maw?" Claire asks, poking the bear that is Molly's mom even harder. "Personally, I think Granny suits you. Granny Liz has a nice ring to it."

Newly-crowned Granny Liz sticks her finger right in Great-Aunt Claire's face, glaring at her without saying anything for a few seconds.

"I'll deal with you later," she finally threatens with a growl, flicking the tip of Claire's nose before turning and stalking across the room to stand in front of me.

She crosses her arms over her chest and taps her foot against the ground, obviously waiting for me to speak first. After the mistake I made with Aunt Claire, I know I need to step my game up the next time I open my mouth. This is Molly's *mom*. I cannot piss off the mother of the woman I want to date or say anything stupid that will come back to haunt me even after everyone finds out the truth.

Be smart, be cool. You've totally got this, Marco.

"You're really pretty and young and don't look like a grandma at all. I'm sorry I made you a grandma when you're so young and pretty and did I mention young? It was an accident, I swear. I mean, no, not an accident because this is kind of a happy thing and an accident is usually a bad thing where people die or bleed profusely and well, I guess there will probably be blood from what I remember of those high school health class videos but I'm pretty sure no one will die unless you or your husband decide to kill me and can I just say if I go missing my family would probably notice when I didn't show up for Sunday dinner and if I miss a Sunday dinner, my mother would find where you buried my body and dig it up just to kill me again for missing dinner. Please, please don't kill me and then make my mother kill me again because she'll probably use a wooden spoon to beat me and that kind of thing will take a really long time to kill me and I don't do very well with pain and—"

I feel a smack against the back of my head, cutting off the shit I couldn't stop spewing, and I jump in fear wondering if my mother is somehow here and I really am about to die.

"I have a big penis, and I think I'm going to cry," I mumble.

That earns me another smack to the back of my head and I realize

Molly is the one channeling my mother when this time, she adds a threat to the smack.

"Stop talking. Please, for the love of GOD, stop talking," she whispers loudly.

"Mom, I'm so sorry for—"

Molly doesn't have a chance to finish her apology because her mother suddenly bursts into tears, moves away from me and wraps her arms around her daughter.

"I love you, Molls. Everything is going to be okay, even if you've been impregnated by an idiot," her mother sniffles, rocking them both back and forth. "At least he's pretty and you'll have a pretty baby."

I feel like I should take offense to that statement, but I wisely keep my mouth shut this time since I'm still feeling lightheaded after that long, run-on sentence of pure dog shit.

"So, is it okay for me to be happy about this now?" the woman who I guess to be Aunt Jenny shouts from across the room.

I'm assuming that's Aunt Jenny since Molly told me a little bit about the woman in the car, and judging by the fact that she's the only one in the room still pretending to be engrossed in something else, and that something else being a spot on the wall she's had her nose pressed up against since I first made the mistake of using the word *ma'am* with Aunt Claire, I'm going to go out on a limb here and say I'm right.

"I can't handle all of the yelling and fighting, it's messing with my Aurora," she complains, turning away from the wall and rubbing her nose.

"I think you mean *aura*," Charlotte informs her.

"No, it's *Aurora*. She's the one in charge of my chalks, which are the centers of spiritual power in my body. If Aurora is upset, all of my chalks are upset, and then my day is just ruined. *Aura*," she scoffs. "That's not even the name of a real person, Charlotte."

Yep, that's definitely Aunt Jenny.

"Get used to it, pretty boy," Molly's mom advises as she continues holding tightly to her daughter, but finally gives me a smile. "It's best to just let Jenny talk. She'll tire herself out eventually."

I let out a sigh of relief, hoping she's forgiven me for everything I said and what I allegedly but not really did to her daughter, praying it will help with her husband, who has gone back to shining his Thug Mug as he casually saunters over to one of the windows and glances outside.

"That your car out there parked by the curb?" he finally speaks without turning around.

Molly and her mother move out of their embrace, but keep one arm around each other's waist as they look over at Molly's father.

"Um, yes. Yes, sir, it is," I reply, hoping to God he doesn't have the same aversion to *sir* that Aunt Claire has to *ma'am*.

"GT Mustang Fastback, manual transmission with a five-point-oh-liter V6 engine?" he asks quietly.

The man definitely knows his cars and described my baby to a T just by looking at her parked on the street. I saved up for two years to buy that car and she is the most important thing in my life, after my mother and sisters, of course. Oh, and I guess this pretend baby that I'm the pretend father of. That should probably go somewhere towards the top of the list I suppose.

"That's correct, sir," I confirm, starting to get a little nervous that he might be having thoughts about bashing in my car's skull instead of my own.

He finally turns away from the window and thankfully sets the Thug Mug down on the table next to the couch.

"Drew, Carter, how about we take Marco—"

"POLO!" Drew quickly screams happily.

Molly's dad purses his lips in annoyance at the interruption, letting out a sigh before continuing.

"How about we take Marco-I-Swear-To-Fuck-If-You-Say-Polo-One-More-Fucking-Time-I-Will-Shove-My-Foot-Up-Your-Ass, for a little drive?" he asks, glaring at Drew as he turns my name into one long curse word.

"Jim, everything's fine, honey," Molly's mom tells him. "There's no need to do anything stupid."

Jim smiles at her. "We're not going to do anything stupid. Are we, boys?"

Drew and Carter walk up to either side of him and all three of them smile at me. Three evil smiles that don't quite reach their eyes and obviously scream, "We're going to fuck this Marco Polo asshole up until his face looks like raw hamburger meat and he no longer has the use of his legs."

What the hell am I doing? Is some hot chick I've fantasized about really worth all of this? I can't believe I actually thought MY family was crazy. They look like the damn Brady Bunch compared to these people.

I look away from the evil triplets long enough to glance at Molly. Her smile is so big it takes my breath away and that's all it takes for me to realize she's worth it. No woman has ever made me want to jump through hoops just to get her to smile. I've never felt so tied up in knots around anyone like I feel whenever Molly looks at me. Call it a gut feeling, call it plain old stupidity, but whatever it is, I'm not about to give up now. I knew the moment she told me she wasn't really pregnant and I thought my heart would burst out of my chest that I would do whatever it takes to see where this thing goes. I want to know everything about her, even if it means dealing with her insane family. What's a little blood in my urine and drinking my food through a straw as long as she's there to give me sponge baths?

"Keys?" Drew asks, holding his hands out.

I tell myself everything will work out in the end as I pull the keys to my baby out of my front pocket and toss them across the room to Drew. As soon as he catches them, he runs towards me, ramming into my shoulder as he races through the doorway of the living room and down the hall behind us.

"SHOTGUN, BITCHES!" he shouts right as the front door slams closed behind him.

"Carter, don't you *dare* let him shoot any guns while he's driving!" Jenny warns.

Carter walks over to her and pats her on the head like a puppy without saying anything. He then makes his way to Claire, giving her a kiss on the cheek.

"Don't wait up, honey," he tells her with a smile as she runs her palms down the front of his chest.

"Please try not to get any blood on this shirt. Blood stains are such a bitch to get out," she informs him with a sigh.

Everyone seems to think this is funny and they all laugh. I don't find this funny at all. It's so NOT funny that I think a little pee might have come out of me.

Carter casually sticks his hands in his pockets and whistles jovially as he too rams his shoulder into mine when he walks through the doorway and down the hall to the front door.

Molly pulls away from her mother and rushes in front of me when her father starts to make his way in this direction, and there's no sense in denying it, I'm pretty positive I'm going to pee my pants.

"Daddy, don't hurt him," she warns, blocking him from me and throwing both her hands up in the air to stop him from coming any closer.

"I'm not going to hurt him, Molls," he promises softly with a smile that's faker than the baby I didn't knock Molly up with. "Marco Polo here has nothing to worry about, aside from the fact that the man who currently has the keys to his brand new Mustang felt the need to call shotgun just to make sure he sat in the front seat."

I forget all about my own well-being and hope my car insurance policy covers three lunatics who purposefully slam a vehicle into every tree they encounter before shoving it over a cliff.

Jim kisses the top of Molly's head, lingering there for a few seconds before telling her softly that he loves her no matter what. Charlotte starts sobbing loudly from across the room, breaking up the heartfelt moment with huge sniffles and gasping breaths.

When Jim pulls away from Molly and looks over at Charlotte with a raised eyebrow at her outburst, she quickly puts a big smile on her face and waves away his concerned look.

"It's fine, I'm fine, no big deal," she says with a hiccup and a smile. "I'm just so happy you still love Molly, even if she screwed up and made a huge mistake that will probably ruin her life, because she's going to really need you to love her when she gets fat and ugly and no one else will love her anymore!"

She starts crying louder this time and Gavin rushes across the room to console her. Molly doesn't have any reason to worry about *our* ability to pull this off since it looks like it will only be a matter of time before Charlotte completely cracks and ruins her own stupid plan.

While Molly and her mother are busy watching Charlotte lose her shit, Jim takes that opportunity to sneak around Molly and her attempt to protect me from bodily harm. He slings his arm around my shoulders casually and leads me quietly away from the women and Gavin.

Maybe he really is all talk, just like Molly told me. I mean, he wouldn't really hurt the fake father of his fake unborn grandchild, would he?

"Um, I'm sure you already know this, sir, but my car isn't really big enough for four large men," I tell him as he opens the front door and we walk through it together.

He takes his arm off my shoulders to pat me on the back good-naturedly, giving me a friendly smile.

"Oh, that's not going to be a problem at all," he says with a chuckle.

His good humor is contagious, and I laugh along with him as we make our way down the steps of the front porch and across the lawn to my car. I try not to cringe when I see Drew sitting on the open window ledge of the driver's side door with his feet inside the vehicle and his fists pounding on the roof to the beat of the rock song he has playing loud enough to shake the entire car.

"Let's go, fuckers!" Drew shouts to us over the music. "Happy hour at the strip club is over in thirty minutes, and then I'll have to pay full price for lap dances. Ain't nobody got time for full-price lap dances!"

Jim puts his hand on my shoulder and leads me to the back of the car, rapping his knuckles against the top of the trunk twice, and I see Carter through the back windshield lean in between the two front seats from his spot in the back. The trunk suddenly pops open and Jim gives me another big smile.

"Nope, no trouble at all with this small, fancy car of yours," Jim tells me as he grabs the edge of the trunk lid and lifts it open wide. "We'll all fit just fine because your daughter-impregnating ass is riding in the trunk."

With a hard shove from both hands against my back, I fly face-first into my own trunk and the lid quickly slams shut on top of me.

"Hold on tight, asshole, it's going to be a bumpy ride!" Jim's muffled voice shouts through the closed trunk as he laughs at his own joke.

I hear a car door slam and my engine rumbles to life through the trunk. My body slams against the inside as we take off like a shot, the squeal of tires against the street punctuating how fast we're going.

Molly's mom might not be very good at removing blood stains from clothing, but I hope to God she knows how to get the smell of urine out of the trunk of a car.

Chapter 7

– Meat Sweats –

Molly

"MOLLY, STOP STARING out the window, he'll be fine. I'm sure your father will wait until after the baby's born to kill him," my mother says with a laugh as I move away from the kitchen window where I've spent the last twenty minutes silently brooding.

"Very funny," I tell her as I lean against the edge of the kitchen sink and watch her rapidly move around the island in the middle of the kitchen. My mom likes to feed people whenever there's a tragedy, and going by the sheer volume of cold cut sandwiches she's been putting together since the guys left, she's preparing for the end of the world.

"It's the least your father can do," she continues as she slathers mustard on sandwich number thirty-seven. "Maybe the baby won't even look like Marco and it turns out to be someone else's. Then he's just gone and killed a man for no reason."

Aunt Claire laughs and I shoot her a dirty look before aiming it in my mother's direction. "Seriously, mom? Did you just insinuate that I'm a slut?"

"If it looks like a slut and quacks like a slut!" Aunt Jenny pipes up from the kitchen table.

"Oh, don't give me that look, young lady," mom warns. "I never said the word *slut*. It's not like you got drunk and knocked up at a frat party and never got the guy's name until four years later."

"Heeeeeeeey!" Aunt Claire yells, from her seat next to Aunt Jenny.

Mom sets her mustard-covered knife on the counter and glances over at Aunt Claire.

"Really?" she deadpans.

Aunt Claire sighs. "Okay, yeah, that was kind of slutty. Carry on."

Mom goes back to her work, moving from turkey sandwiches to salami.

"I'm just saying, Molly, we don't know this guy, nor did we have any idea you were even dating someone. Forgive me for being a little suspicious about your sexual activity."

I shudder, grabbing the sandwich she just finished and tossed on top of the giant pile. "Please, never say the words *sexual activity* again."

The funniest part about this entire mess is that I have no sexual activity for her to be suspicious of. I wonder if she'd go easier on me if I told her I'm the world's first official pregnant virgin. Well, aside from that whole mother of God thing, but that happened a long time ago, and I'm pretty sure it's a bit more rare in this day and age.

Figuring I should just shovel food in my mouth before I'm tempted to say something I shouldn't, I wrap my lips around the sandwich filled with lettuce, cheese and extra salami, just the way I like it. As soon as my teeth sink into the bread, the sandwich is smacked out of my hand and it goes flying across the kitchen.

"WHAT THE HELL ARE YOU DOING?" Charlotte yells, wiping bread crumbs off of her sandwich-smacking hands.

"What am *I* doing? What are *you* doing? I was going to eat that!" I argue, staring longingly at my sandwich scattered across the floor.

I barely ate two bites of my spaghetti at dinner with Marco earlier because my stomach was tied in knots and every forkful of pasta I tried to choke down threatened to come right back up.

"You can't eat lunchmeat, Molly!" Charlotte scolds with a huff. "Everyone knows you can't eat lunchmeat."

I didn't know I can't eat lunchmeat. Since when did this become a rule around here?

I really think this pregnancy has made my sister lose her mind completely so I grab another sandwich from the pile and ignore her.

"I'm starving. Go away," I mutter.

Charlotte rips the sandwich right out of my hands and starts to shake it in front of my face, meat and lettuce falling out of the bread and onto the counter.

"Pregnant women can't eat lunchmeat. Everyone knows it can cause Listeriosis," Charlotte complains.

"Isn't that the stuff you wash your mouth with?" Aunt Jenny asks.

"Sweet mother of pearl..." Aunt Claire mutters.

Charlotte's face quickly changes from irritation to revulsion as she stares at the parts of the sandwich still clutched in her hand. She swallows thickly, but manages to keep talking. "Lunchmeat is dangerous. And smells. And....smells like...meat."

She stops mid-sentence, shooting a look of panic at me. "You look sick, Molly. Are you going to throw up?"

I look at her like she's as insane as I believe her to be and shake my head. "Uh, no. I'm fine."

"No, you really look sick. You should go to the bathroom right now."

She's still holding the sandwich in her hand, but now she's fisting it into a ball and I can see beads of sweat dotting her forehead.

Awwwww shit.

"You know, now that you mention it, I'm feeling a little pukey," I announce, quickly pressing my hand to my stomach. "Uuughhh, yeah, definitely gonna throw up."

Charlotte nods, still holding the mangled mess of a sandwich in one hand while she grabs my hand with the other. "I should go with you and hold your hair back just in case."

"Yes, yes, wise decision. Wouldn't want to get puke in my hair," I laugh awkwardly before realizing I probably wouldn't be laughing if I really felt like throwing up. I quickly change my laugh to a groan as Charlotte drags me from the kitchen while our mom and aunts stare at us wordlessly.

"Don't use the Listeriosis on the bathroom sink after you throw up, Molly! I have a mint you can use instead," Aunt Jenny shouts after us as we race out of the room and down the hall to the bathroom.

As soon as I shut the door behind us, Charlotte drops to her knees in front of the toilet and tosses not only her cookies, but from the looks of it, everything she's eaten in the past week. I don't know how one person can have so much bile in their body, and now I really am starting to feel sick listening to the sounds that are coming out of her as well as the smell of vomit that quickly fills the small space.

"Oh, my God, what did you eat?!" I complain, covering my nose with my hand.

"The salami! It smells so bad! Like meat!" she cries in between heaves.

"Then why are you still holding it in your hand?!" I screech.

"I DON'T KNOW!" she cries, leaning her head closer to the bowl as more vomit comes flying out.

A knock at the door makes me jump and Charlotte choke in the middle of a gag.

"Everything okay in there?" mom asks softly.

Charlotte groans loudly and I quickly cover it up with an even louder groan.

"UUUUGGHHHHHHH, so sick!" I yell through the door. "Be out in a minute!"

Moving behind Charlotte, I hold my breath while grabbing onto her hair and hold it away from the toilet while she continues throwing up. "You will be done soon, right? Good God, woman. How does someone so small have that much puke in her?!"

She rests her head on the arm draped over the toilet seat and sighs.

"I'll just make you some soup to settle your stomach when you're finished," mom says through the door.

"Oh, no," I whisper as I hear her footsteps moving her away from the bathroom.

"SOUP!" Charlotte wails, moving her head back over the bowl and gagging even harder.

"Don't worry, I'll eat it in another room or something," I promise.

Five minutes later, after Charlotte cleaned herself up while I messed up my hair and splashed water all over myself to look like a recent puke victim, we walk back into the kitchen where my mother has wisely hidden all of the sandwiches and bags of lunchmeat.

"So, no one answered me before when I asked if we can be happy about this now. So, can we?" Aunt Jenny asks.

Mom shrugs and gives me a small smile. "Sure, Jenny. I guess we can be happy about this as long as Molly is happy."

Charlotte wraps her arm around my shoulder and gives me a squeeze. "Molly is very happy. She's just scared and nervous and worried, but she's so happy."

"Thank you for telling us how Molly feels," Mom laughs. "How about we let Molly tell us?"

I stare at everyone dumbly as they wait for me to say something.

"Um, yeah. What she said," I reply with a forced smile.

"Sweet! Pound sign, Molly's pregnant!" Aunt Jenny cheers, holding her fist out for someone to "pound."

"Don't you mean *hashtag*?" Aunt Claire asks.

"No. It's pound sign. Twitter stole it from math," Aunt Jenny replies with a roll of her eyes.

"Wow, I actually can't argue with that," Aunt Claire says with a shrug, giving in and pounding her fist to Aunt Jenny's.

"Alright, who wants chicken noodle soup?" Mom asks happily, holding up a can of Campbell's.

"Oh, God. Molly's going to be sick again!" Charlotte yells, grabbing my hand and dragging me back out of the kitchen.

Chapter 8

– Bag of Dicks –

Marco

"I CAN'T BELIEVE I missed half-price lap dances," I hear Drew grumble as I make my way into the house a few minutes after everyone else.

My shoes squeak and squish against the floor as I go, and thankfully, the women seem to be more interested in what Drew is saying than what I look like and I can stand in the doorway of the kitchen unnoticed.

"You guys went to a strip club? Are you kidding me?" Molly's mom complains.

"Do you see stripper glitter on my face? Do I smell like desperation and bad life choices?" Drew asks, pausing to lift his arm & smell his pits. "Wait, don't answer that."

"We didn't go to a strip club; don't worry," Molly's dad reassures her, walking over to the fridge and opening the door. "Ooooh, you made sandwiches!"

I see Charlotte slide against the wall in my direction, quickly covering her mouth when Jim brings the plate, heaping with sandwiches, out of the fridge and sets them in the middle of the island. Gavin moves to her side and puts his arm around her, quietly asking if she's okay.

"The meat," she whispers with a shell-shocked look in her eyes. "Uh, Molly can't stand the smell of meat and she threw up earlier.

65

Seeing the sandwiches again just made me think of all that puke."

I feel a hand on my arm and look away from the couple to see Molly staring at me in confusion.

"Why are you all wet?" she asks, taking in my wrinkled, damp t-shirt I wrung out and put back on and my jeans that are now dripping onto the kitchen floor.

I notice her wet, gnarled mess of hair hanging around her face that is also dripping with water and return her own question. "Why are YOU all wet?"

"She had the meat sweats," Jenny informs me, giving Molly a pat on the back as she walks behind her and over to Drew.

"What the hell are meat sweats?"

Molly winces, pushing a clump of hair out of her eyes. "I really don't want to talk about the meat sweats."

I force myself to keep my eyes off of Charlotte even though I can see out of the corner of them that she's got her back pressed up against a wall next to us, watching her father nervously as he takes a big bite out of a salami sandwich.

"I really like salami, too," Molly mutters sadly before looking back at me. "But seriously, why are you all wet?"

Drew and Carter start laughing as they each grab a sandwich from the insanely large pile from the plate on the counter.

Molly leans in close to me and sniffs. "And why do you kind of smell like pee?"

I groan and throw my hands in the air, shooting an annoyed look at the three men now giggling like little girls. Little asshole girls. "You guys said the smell was gone!"

"It's not our fault you couldn't handle the low pressure hot wax," Drew says through a mouthful of food. "If I can handle a little candle wax on my balls every third Friday, you can handle a hot wax treatment on your undercarriage."

"I really don't want to know what you're talking about, but I'd still like to know why Marco is all wet," Molly informs him, wisely choosing not to comment on the candle wax on the balls subject. I learned much more about Drew's balls tonight than I ever needed to know, thank you very much.

"You can't get clean going through a car wash if you're in the trunk. Obviously riding on the hood made more sense," Jim smirks.

"Jim Gilmore!" Liz scolds.

"What? We had to get the pee smell off of him somehow."

So much for thinking this night couldn't get any more uncomfortable after Drew felt the need to show me the scars on his balls from when he let Jenny shave them.

"Do you want to talk about the pee smell?" Molly asks me.

"Do you want to talk about the meat sweats?" I fire back.

"So, what else did you guys do?" she asks, looking away from me and back to the guys.

"Marco, why don't you take her and the rest of these lovely ladies outside and show them what else we did?" Carter suggests.

I forget about my embarrassment over the whole pee situation and get excited all over again about what we did. Grabbing Molly's hand, I pull her towards the front door while the rest of the women follow behind, leaving the men in the kitchen to stuff their faces.

"Wait until you see it, Molly. It's the coolest thing in the world!"

"It sounds like you had a good time. And there aren't any noticeable bruises on your face, so that's a plus," she tells me.

"Aside from the incident in the trunk that we are never to speak of, and the scalding hot water from the car wash, I had a good time. Although you could've warned me that your Uncle Drew likes to whip his balls out in public."

She shrugs. "He only shows them to people he likes, so that's a good sign."

I press my hand to the small of her back, guiding her outside and down the steps of the front porch, stopping in the yard and pointing proudly to the curb.

"Well, what do you think?"

Molly stares out at the street, my new beauty perfectly spotlighted under one of the blazing street lamps right in front of it.

"What do I think about what?" Molly asks, looking everywhere but at the lovely little lady in front of her house.

"Do you not see what's parked right in front of you?" I ask with a laugh.

"I see a mom van. Where's your Mustang?"

Claire walks around us to check out my new set of wheels with Liz, Jenny, and Charlotte following right behind her. "Oh, my God, did you buy a minivan?"

I scoff and put my hands on my hips.

"It's not a mom van OR a minivan. That is a state-of-the-art, safest thing with four wheels, family car," I announce proudly as the four other women walk around the brand new red, Chrysler Town and Country.

"I repeat, where is your Mustang?" Molly asks, not sounding anywhere near as excited as I thought she'd be.

"The guys told me it wasn't safe or practical for a family man," I explain. "It didn't even have the proper hook-up in the backseat for the six-point harness system car seat or side airbags, and we can't have our baby riding around in a death trap like that."

I realize as soon as the words leave my mouth that I sound crazier than anyone in Molly's family. I'm a twenty-four-year-old single dude helping the woman I want to sleep with fake a pregnancy. It does not require trading in my chick-magnet Mustang for a mom-magnet van, but it was peer-pressure, dammit! I couldn't exactly refuse to trade in the Mustang for a family car with Molly's dad and uncles cracking their knuckles and staring me down. Besides, this thing has plenty of room, and I didn't have to ride in the trunk on the way home.

"Wow, it has built-in DVD players in the seat backs!" Claire shouts to us as she slides open the side passenger door and sticks her head inside.

"Marco, how much alcohol did my dad and uncles give you? Do you feel strange or lightheaded? Is there a tingling in your arms and legs? They could have roofied you," Molly tells me nervously. "Never leave your drink unattended around them, wasn't that one of my warnings on our way over here earlier?"

I laugh, patting her softly on the back. "I'm not drunk and I haven't been roofied. I traded in the Mustang for safety reasons."

"Are you forgetting the one little fact that you aren't going to be a family man?" she whispers. "You don't need a mom-mobile with a six-point whatever or extra air bags. Did they hypnotize you? What's your name? What year is it?"

She leans up on her tip toes and uses the pad of her fingers to pry my eyes open wide so she can stare into them.

Even after the pretend meat sweats or whatever the hell happened to her while I was gone, she still smells like apple pie and I smell like I pissed my pants. Which I will neither confirm nor deny happened after Drew drove to an abandoned parking lot, did a hundred donuts at roughly ninety miles an hour, and then from my fetal position in the trunk, I heard the guys screaming about Drew playing chicken with an oncoming semi and how he'd never be able to jump the gap in the bridge at such a slow speed. How was I supposed to know they were fucking with me when I was trapped in a dark trunk?

"It's not my fault and it happens to everyone!" I shout, realizing I said that out loud by mistake.

"You've definitely been hypnotized," Molly says with a slow shake of her head. "I know it sounds weird, but my Uncle Drew learned how to do it on the Internet. No one believed it until Aunt Jenny volunteered to let him do it to her. Whenever he said the word *moist* she'd bark like a dog and try to shit on the carpet. It wasn't pretty."

She drops her hands from my face and I'm surprised I'm not even shocked by the things I continue to find out about her family at this point. Claire, Jenny, Charlotte, and Liz are all busy looking in the front seat and talking about the GPS and other bells and whistles and luckily can't hear us.

"Is that a car seat in the back?" Molly asks in shock.

"We went to Babies R Us after the dealership and the guys all chipped in. Wasn't that nice of them?" I tell her excitedly as I push the sliding back door open wider. "We went to the fire station after so one of the firemen could properly install it. I had no idea you couldn't just buckle one of those things in and call it a day."

Molly grabs both of my arms and turns me around to face her. "I knew it. My family made you lose your mind. I thought you'd be able to make it out unscathed in four weeks, but I was wrong."

I laugh and shake my head at her. "I know it's crazy, but I didn't lose my mind. That Mustang really was impractical."

"It was not impractical for a single, twenty-four-year-old guy who is NOT going to be a father," she whispers, echoing my earlier thoughts.

"Well, maybe I am going to be a father. I've been thinking about getting a puppy for a while now and I'm going to need something safe to transport him in," I explain.

"I don't think a puppy needs a mom-van," Molly laughs with a shake of her head.

The puppy thing was a stupid, spur-of-the moment answer to try and explain away how crazy I'm behaving just because I'm afraid of a few guys twice my age and twice my size, but hearing her laugh makes me go with it.

"You can't be too safe with puppies, Molly, and stop calling it a mom-van. It's a Town and Country which sounds much more manly," I inform her. "The puppy can be nice and safe while we cruise around town AND he can watch Animal Planet on the built in DVD player that also has a satellite cable hook-up."

Molly stares at me with a smile and I'm not sure if it's because she still thinks I'm crazy or because I did something so *decent* and *dependable* to try and score more points for that dipshit Alfanso D. I know trading in my Mustang is the most insane thing in the world and I probably *have* started losing my mind after only a few hours with the men in Molly's family, but after the first half hour of torture when they finally let me out of the trunk, they taught me a hell of a lot.

Like how having a child is the most important thing you will ever do in your life. And how it makes you grow up fast and changes your entire view on life. How it's scary and nerve wracking and the hardest job you'll ever have, but it's also the most rewarding. I had to grow up a lot after my father died, but I've still spent the last few years refusing to settle down and jumping from one girl to the next because I thought that's what I needed to do to be happy. Spending one day with Molly and her family has made me see there is a lot more to life than that and it makes me want more.

Jesus, maybe I really have gone insane.

"Good choice on the leather seats," Claire says with approval as the women all move out of the front seat and over to us. "Cloth seats are a bitch to get amniotic fluid out of."

"Amni-what?" I ask in confusion.

"Amniotic fluid," Liz repeats. "It's a yellowish liquid that surrounds the baby and gets all over the fucking place when your water breaks. Leather seats will be a plus if it happens while Molly's in the car. You can just wipe the stuff right off."

I nod, my eyes glazing over with thoughts of yellow, pee-like liquid pouring out of someone and getting all over my new seats.

"Plenty of leg room too, in case she goes into labor in the car and you have to pull over on the side of the road and deliver the baby yourself," Claire adds.

Liz nods and it's a good thing Charlotte is standing behind them and they can't see the deer-in-the-headlights look in her eyes.

Claire smacks her hand a couple of times against the side of the van. "This baby definitely has enough room for Molly to spread her legs and push that baby out into your hands. You should probably throw a couple of towels in the back to clean up all the blood and the afterbirth."

"Don't forget the poop," Liz adds. "There's always a chance she'll shit all over the place pushing that thing out."

I know none of these things are really going to happen in my new vehicle, and definitely not to Molly, but that doesn't stop my brain from seeing it all, clear as day and want to run down the street screaming at the top of my lungs.

Charlotte looks like she's going to start crying and it would appear that I might get to see what these meat sweats are, going by the disgusted look on Molly's face as her mother and aunt continue talking about bloody placentas and other things I would've been able to continue living out the rest of my days knowing nothing about, but I need to get out of here. It would probably be best if I go back inside the house and get away from all this womanly talk before I never want to have sex again.

"I think I hear Drew calling my name," I suddenly announce, cutting of Claire when she starts talking about people who eat placentas for the nutrients and vitamins.

Dropping a kiss on Molly's cheek and ignoring the dirty look she shoots me for PDA'ing her, I back away as quickly as I can. She watches me go with a look of annoyance on her face that I'm making an escape while she's stuck out here listening to her aunt rattle off placenta recipes. I realize she'll probably kick my ass for the easy and natural way I kissed her cheek in front of her family, like it was something I do all the time in the six months we've been fake-dating. Just like trading in my Mustang, I know it's crazy, but it feels right. I can't explain how after only spending a few hours with her I feel like I've known her forever instead of just fantasizing about her for two years from a distance. I didn't even think about kissing her cheek, I just did it automatically, her aversion to public displays of affection be damned.

When I'm halfway across the yard and the older women start talking again, I see Molly mutter the words "*chicken shit,*" and I laugh, giving her a wink before turning around and jogging up the steps and back into the house.

After all the gross childbirth talk and girly feelings I've been having all evening, I need some intelligent, manly conversation. I need to talk about something intellectual and macho like politics or war.

"You cannot justify your reasoning because of an article you read online," I hear Carter complain as I enter the house and head towards the living room where the voices are traveling from.

"The facts are right in front of you, man. You can't shut down my theory just because you don't share the same views as I do," Jim argues.

Perfect! Just what I was looking for. A nice, civilized manly discussion that has nothing to do with the goo that comes out of a woman when she gives birth or anything else that will make me vomit.

"I'm telling you, I've seen the stats and maybe I'm in the minority here, but I'm going to have to side with Carter on this one," Drew says with a sigh as I enter the room and find them seated around the coffee table.

"Perfect timing, Marco Polo," Drew greets me with a smile. "You can settle this debate once and for all."

I drop into the remaining empty chair and lean forward, resting my elbows on my knees and clasping my hands together between them.

"Lay it on me. What's the topic? Presidential candidates? War climate?" I ask.

Drew looks at me like I've grown two heads. "Uh, no. We're talking dicks."

"Bag of dicks, to be precise," Jim adds.

I sit up slowly, wondering if I should walk back out of the room and pretend like I was never here.

"I'm sure you've heard the expression 'eat a bag of dicks', correct?" Carter questions seriously.

Drew rolls his eyes when I continue to sit here, planning my escape without answering the question.

"You know, like, 'Eat a bag of dicks, you piece of shit!'" Drew yells in an angry voice. "Tell me you've heard it or I'm going to seriously regret giving you the privilege of seeing my amazing balls."

Not wanting him to mention those bald, wrinkly, scarred pieces of flesh again, I nod in agreement. "Yeah, sure. I've heard the phrase. Why?"

"We need you to settle this argument once and for all," Jim states.

"Okaaaaaay," I drag the word out cautiously and a little bit in fear.

"I mean, how big of a bag are we talking here? Like, Ziploc baggie or Hefty garbage bag? Because size really does matter when it comes to eating dicks," Drew states.

"That is false and you know it!" Carter argues. "Eating a bag of dicks is eating a bag of dicks whether you eat ten or a hundred and ten. You're still eating dicks!"

Jim nods, his face a mask of complete seriousness. "And if size really does matter, is this bag of dicks hot-dog-sized dicks, or cocktail-weenie dicks? Because I think I could handle a bag of cocktail weenies, no problem."

"Of course you could, cock sucker," Drew laughs. "We all know how much you like to gobble up those dicks. Nom, nom, nom!"

Carter lifts his hand and silently gives him the finger.

"I think it makes much more sense if people would just say 'Eat a dick', rather than an *entire bag* of dicks," Jim says with a sigh. "It would cut down on so much confusion, and then we wouldn't even be having this debate. Marco, what are your thoughts on the situation?"

I think I'd rather be talking about placentas right now.

Chapter 9

– Pee Hand –

Molly

"I'M SORRY, MINIVAN means WHAT? And how do you even know this?" Charlotte asks loudly.

A few people in the waiting room look in our direction and mom shushes us. I lean in closer to Charlotte, speaking as softly as I can.

"When I walked back into the house the other night, I heard Uncle Drew explaining it to Marco. I can't even repeat it, just look it up on Urban Dictionary," I explain.

Of course she immediately pulls her phone out of her purse, goes to that stupid website, and starts reading the definition out loud.

"The act of putting two fingers in the vagina and a fist up the ass. Called the *minivan* because you can fit two in the front and five in the back."

I shudder just imagining it, and Charlotte can't decide between being disgusted along with me or laughing, the noise she makes coming out as some sort of gag-snort-cough that makes everyone look at us again.

"Sorry!" she apologizes loudly. "Just discussing minivans and their amazing rear capacity!"

I smack her in the arm and she tucks her phone back in her purse, still laughing.

"That still doesn't explain why dad, Uncle Carter, and Uncle Drew keep calling Marco, *Mo* and then laughing like idiots the rest of the night," she says in confusion as she turns to face me.

I sigh, thinking about all the abuse Marco took the other night and realizing it's probably why he hasn't called since then.

"Not *Mo*, like the name. M. O. – *M* period, *O* period, for Minivan Operator."

Charlotte giggles and I glance down at my phone instead of punching her for laughing at poor Marco. This is the hundredth time I've checked my phone today and I try not to feel like an idiot for doing so when I don't see any new messages or missed calls. I will not be like one of those stupid girls who powers the phone off and on just to make sure it's working. And not because I already called Charlotte four times in the last half hour and made her call me twice to confirm I can in fact still receive incoming calls, but because I have more dignity than that, dammit.

It's bad enough I have that whole minivan fisting image in my head, now I have to deal with anxiety about not hearing from Marco since the text he sent me yesterday morning, the day after the strangest day of my life that ended with my dad and uncles daring Marco to eat a quart-sized Ziploc bag of hot dogs in under a minute to prove some point I didn't even want to ask about. On top of not hearing from him since he texted me to say he now knew what the meat sweats were and he'd been puking up hot dogs since he got home from my house, I've been forced to go to the doctor to confirm my fake pregnancy.

"I can't believe it's taking this long," Mom complains as she flips through an old magazine. "When I called to make the appointment they told me they had a bunch of cancellations and could get you right in today."

Yes, my wonderful, loving mother took it upon herself to call up the doctor and make an appointment for me without my knowledge, informing me when I woke up this morning that I had fifteen minutes to get dressed and get out the door. Thank God Charlotte answered her phone on the first ring as I raced around my bedroom getting dressed and trying not to panic. She got to the doctor's office before we did and mom only seemed a little bit surprised when I told her I asked Charlotte to come for moral support.

"He'll call, don't worry," Charlotte whispers while I stare in annoyance at my phone.

I quickly shove it into my front pant's pocket and roll my eyes. "I have no idea what you're talking about."

Charlotte snickers. "Nice try. You might be pretty good faking a pregnancy, but you suck faking noninterest in a guy."

I glance nervously at Mom sitting across from us and see she's still engrossed in the magazine, not paying any attention to us or preparing to ask a hundred questions about what we're whispering about. She's got to wonder why Charlotte and I are suddenly spending more time together considering we've never kept it a secret that we haven't been able to stand each other for most of our lives. Even though I've always felt like an outsider with my two sisters and have nothing in common with them, I've always been a little closer to Ava. She has the same sarcastic, brash attitude that I do and it's just easier to talk to her than Charlotte. I have no idea why our mother hasn't asked why Charlotte is the one I called for the supposed moral support today, but I guess I should be glad that it's one less thing I have to lie about.

"I'm not faking noninterest in Marco," I tell Charlotte. "I just don't want to be one of those girls who drops everything for a guy and acts stupid whenever he's around. This isn't exactly how I pictured us together the first time he finally noticed me and it's confusing and weird and I don't like it."

Charlotte laughs softly and shakes her head at me. "I'm pretty sure this is not the first time he's noticed you. He definitely has much stronger feelings for you than you realize. No guy would go through all of the shit he's gone through in one day for a girl he just 'likes'. You need to have more faith in yourself, Molls. You're smart and beautiful and talented. If he hasn't noticed those things long before now, he never would have set foot in Mom and Dad's house the other day, let alone put up with all that torture from Dad and the guys."

I'm pretty sure I still remember the last time my sister said anything this nice to me. I was seven and she was nine; it was the first day of school and mom forced me to wear this frilly pink dress that I hated. Charlotte stared for a few seconds and then said, "It's fine. You don't look *that* gross."

These compliments throw me for a loop, and it's not until Mom gets up from her chair and leans across the coffee table to tap my knee, that I realize the nurse was calling my name.

"Molly Gilmore?"

I raise my hand meekly and the nurse smiles. "You can come on back. You're family is welcome to join you."

Shit! How the hell do we keep Mom out of the room?

Before I can go into a full-blown panic trying to come up with a plausible reason to give my mother on why she needs to be blindfolded and wear earplugs, Charlotte quickly speaks up.

"Mom, if you don't mind, can I go back with Molly alone?" she asks so sweetly that I start to wonder if that baby inside of her has some sort of magical powers. "It's just…I know I haven't been the best sister to her growing up, and I'd really like to do something important like this with her, just the two of us."

Mom practically melts into a puddle of goo right on the floor of the waiting room, her eyes filling with tears as she looks back and forth between the two of us.

"I've been waiting twenty years for you two to stop being assholes to each other and all it took was one of you getting knocked up," she sniffles. "If only getting pregnant when you're a teenager wasn't frowned upon, we could have solved this problem years ago."

The nurse gives her a funny look and Mom rolls her eyes. "Oh, don't judge me. *You* try giving birth to three spawns of Satan who constantly try to kill each other."

With those parting words to the shocked nurse, Mom wipes a stray tear from her cheek and waves us away, sitting back down in her chair and grabbing the magazine she previously tossed onto the coffee table.

Charlotte and I leave her in the waiting room and follow the nurse down the hall. She weighs me on the scale in the hallway and takes my temperature with an ear thermometer before leading us further down the hall, pushing open a door and handing me a small plastic cup with an orange lid.

"I just need you to give us a urine sample. I'll be right over there at the nurse's station so you can bring it out when you're finished," she explains with a smile before looking at Charlotte. "If you'd like to come with me, I can show you to the exam room and you can wait for her to finish."

I quickly grab Charlotte's arm and the cup from the nurse.

"It's okay, she can come in with me. I need her to hold the cup for me," I blurt without thinking.

The nurse gives me a quizzical look, and I laugh nervously. "I'm a little freaked out and my hands are shaking and if I try and hold the cup I'll probably pee all over the place so I need someone with steady hands and Charlotte's are rock steady. She'll make sure the pee goes where it needs to go."

Charlotte nods, confirming my crazy explanation and then pulls me into the bathroom, slamming the door closed in the poor, confused nurse's face.

I hand her the little plastic cup and lean against the wall, bending forward with my hands on my knees to take a few calming breaths while Charlotte goes to work.

"I think I'm going to hyperventilate," I tell her. "Do you think I could go to jail for insurance fraud from filling out all those medical forms when we got here? I can't go to jail; I'd never survive. In theory I feel like I have enough balls to make someone my bitch, but I don't know if I could actually do it. I can make an amazing sugar display, but I don't know if that will translate well when I need to make a toothbrush shank."

I realize I'm rambling and it suddenly occurs to me that I might not be as different from my sisters as I always thought considering I'm acting just as insane as they usually do. None of this makes me feel any better about what is happening right now.

"You're not going to jail. Stop freaking out or you're going to make me freak out, and it's not good for the baby," Charlotte tells me as she flushes the toilet and washes her hands. "Personally, I think you'd make a great badass in jail. You'd have plenty of bitches offering to make toothbrush shanks for you."

I stand up and scowl at her. "You're not helping."

She picks up her cup of pee, walks over to me, and holds it out in front of her.

"Eeeew, get that thing away from me," I complain, scrunching up my nose.

"You have to take it out there to the nurse. Technically, this is your pee," she reminds me.

With a sigh, I tentatively reach out and take the cup from her, trying not to drop it as soon as my hands wrap around it. Charlotte opens the bathroom door and I walk as slowly as I can behind her, holding the cup out as far away from me as possible.

"Oh, my God, it's so warm," I whisper in disgust. "And why does my hand feel wet?"

Charlotte glares at me over her shoulder as we make our way down the hall to the nurse's station.

"I might have dribbled a little down the sides, it's fine," she whispers back to me like it's no big deal.

"I have your pee on my hands?!" I hiss a little too loudly and she stops quickly, almost causing me to slam into her with my pee-covered hands holding her warm cup of pee.

"Will you keep your voice down?" she scolds quietly. "It's just a couple tiny drops of liquid. Just pretend it's water."

"But it's *not* water, it's your warm, wet pee! And it's touching me!" I reply, wondering if I'll ever be able to look at my hand again and not picture Charlotte pissing all over it like a dog marking its territory. "I cook with this hand, and now it's a pee hand! You had one job to do— piss in a fucking cup without getting pee on my hand. This is why we can't have nice things, Charlotte, because you piss all over everything, and now I smell like pee!"

She rolls her eyes and grabs my wrist holding the cup, dragging me the rest of the way down the hall to the waiting nurse. I sigh in relief when the nurse takes the cup from my hand and tells us to head right across the hall to examine room number four, letting me know she'll be in as soon as she processes the urine sample.

I run to the room without saying a word, racing to the sink in the small room and start scrubbing my hand as Charlotte follows me and closes the door behind her.

When I'm satisfied that there are no lingering traces of Charlotte pee on my skin, I dry my hands, and the door opens right as I'm throwing away the paper towel.

"Okay, Molly, I just need you to get fully undressed and put on the paper robe on the exam table," she explains as she walks to the table and starts pulling the stirrups out of their hiding spots inside it.

I shoot a worried look at my sister and she just shrugs, her expression mirroring my own as we watch the nurse move to a side table and start extracting things out of the drawers.

"Um, I thought I'd just be peeing in a cup today," I mutter.

The nurse turns around and Charlotte and I both gasp loudly when we see the world's biggest vibrator in the nurse's hand. And that's saying a lot considering my mother owns one of the largest sex toy stores in the world and I've been around those things since birth. I still have nightmares about Chocolate Thunder.

"What the hell is that for?" I ask, pointing at the huge, white phallic object in her hand that the nurse is busy putting an equally huge condom over top of.

She laughs sympathetically.

"It's an internal ultrasound wand. According to the date of your last period you put on the medical form, you're not very far along in your pregnancy. Ultrasounds done on the stomach won't be very accurate at this point, so the doctor will use this internally to get a better reading," she says with a smile.

"That thing has to go inside me?!" I screech loudly.

"Believe me, it looks much worse than it actually is," she explains. "It's really no different than having sex, maybe just a tad more uncomfortable, but it won't hurt."

I'm willing to do a lot of things for a KitchenAid mixer and money for an apartment, but having a tree stump shoved up my vagina is not one of them.

While I try my best not to hyperventilate again, the nurse finishes setting everything up for the doctor and leaves Charlotte and I alone to wait for him.

"That thing is not going in me, Charlotte," I warn her as soon as the door closes behind the scrub-clad woman. "You better figure something out before the doctor gets in here, or I will lose my shit all over this exam room!"

Charlotte starts to pace next to the paper-covered table.

"Well, obviously you can't let him give you that ultrasound or he'll figure out right away you're not pregnant," she says. "I don't know why *you're* freaking out. It's not like you've never had a penis in there before, and like the nurse said, it's not much different than that."

My silence immediately gives me away and Charlotte stops pacing to stare at me. "Holy shit, there's no way you're still a virgin. What about prom and Quinn Curtis?"

I growl at her and point an accusing finger her way. "I *knew* you read the texts on my phone that weekend, you lying slutbag!"

The morning after that disastrous prom night I walked into my bedroom after taking a shower and caught Charlotte standing by my dresser with my phone in her hands. She told me she accidentally erased all her contacts and needed Gavin's number.

"How else was I supposed to find out how it went? You refused to answer any of my questions, dick-face vagina-hole!" she fires back.

"Maybe because it wasn't any of your business, you asshole fuck face!"

We stare at each other angrily for a few minutes before we both burst into laughter.

"Oh, my God, we sound like Mom and Aunt Claire," Charlotte giggles.

"Dick-face vagina-hole?" I ask through my laughter.

"Oh, please, like asshole fuck-face was any better," she smiles. "Grandpa George would be so disappointed in our lack of follow through with strings of curse words."

Charlotte hops up on the examine table, the paper cover crinkling noisily under her. When the room is silent again after she gets situated, I sigh heavily and move to lean against the table next to her.

"According to Quinn, it was amazing," I tell her. "According to me, his picture is now in the dictionary next to the words 'just the tip.'"

Charlotte laughs, looking at me questioningly.

"Seriously. He barely got the tip in before he came, screaming to God about how good it felt. Tampons have gone in my body further than that boy's tiny penis," I complain.

"So, technically you're a pregnant virgin," she smiles.

"Just call me the Virgin Mary," I reply sarcastically.

"What are the chances the doctor is really old and senile, and we can switch vaginas without him noticing?" Charlotte asks right as the door opens.

A very handsome, very young man who doesn't look a day over forty walks in wearing a white lab coat and a nametag that reads *Dr. Christenson.*

"Not good at all," I whisper as he looks up from his clipboard and smiles.

"How's your vision, doc?" I ask casually. "Twenty-twenty or blind-as-a-bat?"

He looks puzzled at my question and I don't blame him. I don't even understand half the things coming out of my mouth lately myself.

"Do you have the results from the urine sample?" Charlotte asks.

"I do and congratulations," he tells me with a smile. "You are definitely pregnant. I just need to do an internal ultrasound so we can nail down how far along you are and discuss your next couple of visits."

Charlotte hops down from the table and slides her hand through the crook of my arm. "Actually, doctor, I'm really sorry about this, but my sister isn't feeling very well so we're going to have to reschedule. She's already thrown up twice, so we really need to be going."

I put my hand over my mouth and make some pretend gagging noises as we walk to the door.

"Morning sickness…can't stop puking," I mutter behind my hand in between gags, giving him an apologetic look.

"Yep, so much puking," Charlotte agrees, a loud gag coming out of her own mouth.

"What are you doing?" I whisper as we move through the door.

"I'm the one fake gagging, not you!"

"I."

Gag

"Can't."

Gag

"Help it," she finishes as we rush down the hall towards the bathroom instead of the waiting room.

"Your fake gagging made me real gag!" she complains, dropping her hand from my arm and running the rest of the way to the bathroom and right to the toilet.

Once again, I'm stuck in a small, enclosed space listening to my sister upchuck the contents of her stomach while I hold her hair back.

While I hold my breath and try to ignore the smell and sounds coming out of Charlotte, I feel my phone vibrate in my pocket. Holding Charlotte's hair with one hand, I pull my phone out with the other and smile when I see a text from Marco.

"Marco apologized for not calling," I tell Charlotte.

She lifts one arm from the bowl and gives me a thumb's up while she sits back on her feet and sighs in relief.

"Oh, and good news," I continue, reading the second text he just sent. "He's finally finished throwing up hot dog pieces and feels much better."

Charlotte whimpers, quickly sitting up and sticking her head back over the toilet bowl, another round of gagging overtaking her.

"You hairy-ball-sack-whore-of-a-whale's-dick!" she curses in between gags.

"Oh, pipe down you smelly-ass-giant-vagina-scrotum-licker!" I shout back, quickly shoving my phone back into my pocket and holding her hair back with both hands.

There's nothing quite like the love between two sisters.

Chapter 10

- Titillating Tube Socks -

Marco

"TODAY'S MY DADDY'S birthday. He farts a lot."

I don't even get my mother's front door closed all the way before a squeaky little voice starts rattling off strange, random facts.

"My dog Ralphie pees on all of our pillows. Daddy called it *humping* but mommy said I can't say that word and I'm 'upposed to say he's peeing."

Valerie, my four-year-old niece and the spitting image of my sister Tessa with her long, curly black hair and big blue eyes, starts running around in circles in front of me.

"Hump-hump-hump, I'm gonna pee on you!" she chants loudly as I pat her on the head awkwardly and walk towards the noise I hear coming from the kitchen. I love my niece, especially now that she can walk, talk, and take a dump without assistance, but I'm not really that great with kids. I love kids, don't get me wrong. I'd like to have my own some day, I just don't know what to say or do when I'm around them. At least I got a weekend off from getting yelled at for teaching her new swear words at Sunday dinner last week, since Valerie spent the night at Tessa's husband's parent's house. Hopefully, I can remember to watch my mouth today and avoid my mother's wrath. Tessa should be the one getting in trouble, since she hasn't taught her offspring to stop repeating everything people say.

I find Rosa carefully ladling sauce from a giant pot into mason jars spread all over the island in the middle of the room.

"Canning sauce for the winter?" I ask, walking up to the opposite side of the counter from my sister and dipping my finger into one of the mason jars, bringing it up to my mouth for a taste test.

"Don't put your dirty fingers into the sauce," Rosa scolds, smacking the top of my hand. "God only knows where you've put those fingers lately."

I know where I'd *like* to put my fingers, but after Molly had to watch me throw up in her parent's bushes the other night after proving it was possible to eat an entire bag of dicks, I'm not sure these digits will be going anywhere near the Promised Land any time soon.

"Hump-hump-hump, I'm gonna pee on you!" Valerie shouts happily into the kitchen as she races by to head to one of the spare bedrooms my mother converted into a toy room for her only grandchild.

Rosa gives me a dirty look and I put my hands up. "Hey, don't look at me like that. I did NOT teach her those words. Where is Tessa anyway? Shouldn't she be keeping an eye on her spawn?"

"She asked us to watch Valerie for a few hours so she could get some work done while Danny is out of town at a conference," Rosa explains distractedly as she starts putting lids on the already-filled mason jars.

I've been friends with Tessa's husband Danny since high school, and I don't hold it against him that he broke the cardinal rule of Guy Code by dating my sister. Mostly because when he's in town, he breaks up all the estrogen in this house so I don't feel like I'm starting to grow a pussy being surrounded by women all the time.

"Where's Ma?"

"Grabbing more supplies from the basement," she replies, finishing with the last jar and letting out tired breath.

"Good. Since we're alone, I can kick your ass in peace for the shit you pulled on Facebook," I tell her.

"I have no idea what you're talking about," she says, unable to hide the smirk on her face as she crosses her arms in front of her and stares at me.

"You made me sound like a giant pussy. A smiley face? Really?"

Rosa laughs. "Hey, I did you a favor with that Molly chick. I'm trying to make you look like less of a dick so when she finds out you're Alfanso D., she won't hate you so much. Wait until you see what I posted today."

My jaw drops and I quickly pull my phone out of my back pocket, immediately going to Facebook. The Alfanso D. page has over two-hundred notifications and I hold my breath as I click on the post pinned at the top.

"What did you do?! Oh, sweet Jesus on a jelly bean…you asked her on a date?!" I screech.

I read the post out loud because clearly reading it in my head wasn't torture enough.

"Dear Molly Gilmore," I pause and give my sister a little growl of annoyance. "Gee, thanks so much for tagging her in this post."

She takes a bow and I remind myself that hitting a girl, even if she's your annoying older sister is frowned upon, and turn my attention back to the post that is sure to ruin my life. "In case you didn't see my previous apology, I'd like to take this opportunity to publicly apologize to you in front of all my readers. I would also like to officially ask you to have dinner with me so I can prove to you that the D. in my name does not stand for *dick, douchebag, dummy or dipshit.*"

Rosa quietly mouths the words along with me, smiling happily when I get to the end.

"Poetry. Pure poetry," she murmurs. "Now you can profess your love to her and tell her you want to make babies with her."

A hysterical laugh flies out of my mouth, but it's quickly cut off and exchanged for screams of pain when something hard starts smacking repeatedly against the back of my shoulder. I'd know that stinging pain anywhere, and when I whirl around with my hands up to block my face, sure enough, my mother is standing there with a wooden spoon in her hand, hitting every part of me she can reach.

"HOW COULD YOU DO THIS TO ME, ALFANSO? I HAD TO HEAR ABOUT IT FROM THE WOMEN AT THE BEAUTY PARLOR!" she screams, the wooden spoon slapping against the side of my arm.

"Ma! Cut it out!" I yell back, dodging her flailing arm wielding the spoon of torture, the same spoon she's been using on my sisters and I since we were mouthy little asshole kids.

"I could have had a heart attack!" she screeches, chasing me around the island with the spoon above her head. "I could have died and you don't even CARE!"

Luckily, Rosa snatches the spoon from mom's hand when she races by her, so at least I can stop running away from my mother and her wooden spoon like a wuss. Unfortunately, when I stop and stand next to my sister, my mother doesn't even notice the spoon is missing and her hands start wind-milling against my arm like she's in a catfight with a chick.

"It's like you don't even love me!" she wails, her little hands reigning hellfire against my forearms while I shield my face. "I went through thirty-seven hours of labor with you, and I had to find out from a stranger!"

Not knowing what else to do, I start whipping my own hands against hers until we're having the world's most pathetic slap fight in the middle of her kitchen.

"It was two hours of labor and you got an epidural after the first contraction!" I remind her, our hands still smacking rapidly together.

"Well, it FELT like thirty-seven hours!" she argues. "How could you not tell your own mother that you're going to be a father?!"

"WHAT THE FUCK?!" Rosa and I yell at the same time.

My mother manages to end our slap fight and whack both of us upside the back of our heads at the same time.

"YOU GOT SOMEONE PREGNANT?"

"WHO TOLD YOU THIS?"

Once again, Rosa and I shout at the same time, her at me and me at our mother. We turn to face each other and both point a finger in each other's faces.

"WHO THE HELL DID YOU KNOCK UP?!"

"STAY THE HELL OUT OF THIS!"

I groan in frustration when we do it again, and before I can try once more to speak on my own, our mother grabs both of our earlobes and yanks our heads close to her face.

"Ow, ow, ow, ow, ow!" Rosa and I whine, neither one of us caring when our words overlap this time because it fucking hurts!

"Ho intenzione di spingere il cucchiaio finora nel culo verrà fuori dalla tua bocca!" Our mother shouts in rapid-fire Italian.

Rosa and I immediately clamp out mouths shut. We only truly fear our mother when she does two things: Screams our full names or speaks in Italian. I can't speak fluently, but I know enough to get by and I'm pretty sure she just said something about shoving her spoon up our asses until it comes out of our mouths.

When Rosa and I remain silent for a few seconds, mom finally releases our ears and we back away from her, rubbing our earlobes while shooting each other accusatory looks.

"How could you do this to me, Alfanso?" Mom starts in again, stomping away from me and out of the kitchen before I have a chance to explain.

I have no choice but to race after her as she storms across the hall into living room, muttering in Italian under her breath while she begins grabbing giant plastic shopping bags from the couch and starts placing them at my feet.

"Mom, I didn't do anything. Will you just let me explain?" I ask as she makes five trips back and forth between the couch and me until there are at least ten bags lying at my feet.

"I distinctly remember your father showing you how a prophylactic works when you were thirteen and I started finding crusty socks under your bed," she starts.

"Jesus, mom!" I yell.

"Eeeeeeew, you did it into socks?" Rosa says in disgust as she comes up next to me.

"I was thirteen!" I shout, wishing Molly was here to see that my family could give hers a run for their money in the crazy department. Then I realize I'm talking to my mom and my sister about my mastur-bation habits when I was a teenager, and I immediately erase that thought.

"You should have done it in the shower like a normal teenager!" Rosa argues.

"Yes, because I got so much bathroom time living with three women!" I fire back. "It's not like the sock thing happened all the time, only when it was more convenient."

"I bought you a twenty-pack of tube socks every other week when you were in eighth grade," Mom adds. "I thought you had a foot fungus problem until I found sixty-two pairs stuck to the floor under your bed."

Just a few minutes ago, I thought my mom finding out about this thing with Molly would be the worst thing that could possibly happen to me. Clearly, I was wrong.

"Uuugghhh, I will never be able to look at another pair of tube socks without throwing up in my mouth," Rosa complains.

"Can we please get back on track here?" I ask with an annoyed shake of my head.

Mom reaches into the front pocket of her apron and pulls out a banana and a condom, holding them out to me.

"Fine. You're going to demonstrate the proper way to use protection, and you're going to keep doing it until you get it right," she informs me. "Take the banana and the prophylactic. I had to ask the pharmacist to show me where to locate these things, and then he had to explain all the different kinds. It's no wonder you screwed this up. Ribbed and magnum and tingling sensation...I do not understand today's youth and why they make things so difficult. Your father and I managed just fine with the 'pull-out-and-pray' method."

Rosa starts laughing and I start wondering what the possibilities are that I'm adopted.

"I'm not going to demonstrate anything and stop saying *prophylactic*; it's freaking me out!" I complain, crossing my arms like a child and refusing to take the things in her hand.

Picturing my mother going to the pharmacy and asking where the condoms are is bad enough. Having to hear her continue to say that word over and over will make me never want to have sex again.

"We're not leaving this room until you put this on the banana!" she argues. "I got glow-in-the-dark so we can be here all night!"

Grabbing the items from her hands so she stops shaking them in my face, I toss them over my shoulder and the banana thumps on the floor out in the hallway.

"I know how to use a condom, we are never speaking of my childhood masturbatory habits ever again, and I did NOT get anyone pregnant!" I yell at the top of my voice.

"I'm confused," Rosa states.

I sigh, realizing I've reached a new low when I'd rather go back to talking about jerking off into gym socks than trying and explain this to them.

"It's a long story," I mutter.

Both of us stare at our mother as she bends down and starts pulling things out of the bags by my feet.

"There's no sense in lying about it now, Alfanso. I had a nice long chat with that Molly girl's aunt at the beauty parlor, and then we went shopping together," she tells me happily, her mood doing a complete one-eighty as she digs through one of the bags and the sound of crinkling plastic fills the room.

Rosa's head whips up from watching Mom dig through the bags and she stares at me in shock. "Wait, Molly as in *'Cut the cord from mommy'* Facebook Molly? The Molly you just publicly asked out on a date on social media? That's who you knocked up?"

"YOU asked her out on a date, not me! And yes, *that* Molly," I reply, quickly backpedalling when Rosa opens her mouth to most likely call me a bunch of names. "But I did NOT get her pregnant!"

Mom stands up and begins shoving things at me, one after another until my arms are full of....

"Are these bibs? And bottles and baby socks and...what the hell is THIS?" I ask, staring at the box she just put on top of the pile I'm trying not to drop.

"It's a breast pump," Mom says with a huff, like I'm a moron for not knowing. "I also got ten packs of diapers, three receiving blankets, four different styles of pacifiers because you never know what the baby will like, diaper rash cream, and a baby monitor."

Her face scrunches up in concentration for a minute and while she thinks, I try to force my brain to process what is happening.

"Oh!" she announces excitedly, clapping her hands together. "I knew I forgot something. Rosa, go out to my trunk and get the Diaper Genie."

"What the hell is a Diaper Genie? Is that like, a guy who changes all the diapers? Why didn't Tessa have one of those?" I ask, my brain clearly not catching up as fast as I'd like.

"I think now would be a good time for that long story you mentioned before Mom starts building an addition on the house for a nursery," Rosa whispers, as my mom hands her a tiny little baby shirt.

"Awwww, look," Rosa says, holding it up in front of her. "It says *World's Greatest Aunt!*"

I finally get my head out of my ass, opening my arms and letting everything my mom shoved at me fall to the floor, snatching the shirt from Rosa's hands that she's cooing over.

"Heeeey! Give me my aunt shirt back!" she complains.

"You don't need a damn aunt shirt because you aren't going to be an aunt again!" I argue, holding it out of her reach as she tries to grab it back. "And I don't need a magic genie to change diapers, or any of this other stuff, because I'm not going to be a father! I didn't get anyone pregnant."

Bending down to avoid the evil-eye both of the women in the room are now giving me, I start shoveling all the items I dropped back into the bags.

"Molly is doing a favor for her sister, and I'm not kidding when I say it's a long story," I explain, wondering if I could have Molly give all this stuff to Charlotte and earn me a few more brownie points so she'll forget about the whole puking in the bushes thing the other night. "She's pretending to be pregnant and I'm pretending to be the father because her sister wants to wait until after her wedding in a few weeks to break the news to everyone. I'm sorry I didn't tell you, but I honestly never thought you'd run into one of Molly's relatives and find out. It's not that big of a deal, but you guys absolutely CANNOT tell anyone about this."

Rosa pats me on the back when I stand back up. "Damn, I guess you don't need my help clearing Alfanso D.'s name. You could tell her you're Satan at this point and she'd probably shrug it off since you're going through so much trouble for her family. You actually *do* have a brain."

I ignore the brain comment instead of saying something sarcastic because I don't like how quiet our mother is, and if Rosa and I start firing insults at each other, she might make good on that threat of shoving a spoon up our asses.

"Look, Auntie Rosa! I put a dress on the 'nanana!"

Rosa and I turn around and find Valerie sitting in the middle of the hallway behind us, proudly holding up the banana I threw, now covered in a florescent green condom.

Our mother pushes her way between us, walking over to Valerie, squatting down in front of her and taking the condom-covered banana from her hand.

"What a pretty dress for the banana!" Mom exclaims. "I have thirty-nine other dresses, in all the colors of the rainbow. Why don't you teach Uncle how to put a dress on the banana, since he doesn't seem to care about me at all?"

I roll my eyes at her dramatics as she stands back up and helps Valerie up from the floor as well.

"How could you do this to me?" she whispers as my niece starts making airplane noises and flying the condom banana around the hallway. "Is it too much to ask that my son give me another grandchild? What am I supposed to tell the women at the beauty parlor now?"

One minute she's beating me with a spoon when she thinks I got someone pregnant, and now she's bitching at me for NOT getting someone pregnant. I need a drink.

"If you'll excuse me," she says with a haughty lift of her chin. "I'm going to rearrange my bookshelf to make room for your next porn cookbook, now that I know I won't need the space for pictures of my new grandchild."

I think I'd prefer having the spoon shoved up my ass right about now...

"I believe this would be a good time to get drunk and tell me the rest of the story," Rosa informs me as Valerie races up to us and starts smacking me in the leg with the banana.

"Hump-hump-hump! Banana's gonna pee on you!"

Rosa laughs, walking away from me as I try to get the phallic-shaped fruit away from our niece.

"Hey! A little help here!" I shout to her as she keeps going.

"Hump-hump-hump!" Valerie shouts. "Uncle, why is the green dress all slippery? It's making my hands yucky!"

Rosa's laugh echoes down the hallway as she gives me a wave over her shoulder.

"I'll have the wine ready when the four-year-old finishes teaching you how to dress a banana!" she shouts, disappearing into the kitchen.

I finally manage to wrangle the banana out of Valerie's hand, hearing the front door open and shut while I try to keep it out of her reach.

"GIVE ME BACK MY HUMPY!" she screams.

Tessa walks up behind her daughter, staring at the banana I'm now holding above my head.

"I think Uncle needs Humpy more than you, Val," Tessa tells her daughter, running her hand over the top of her head. "Grandma sent mommy a text and said Uncle doesn't know how to properly dress a banana so he needs to practice."

Yep, I'd definitely prefer being locked in a trunk and covered in pee.

Two hours and four bottles of wine later, I find myself lying on my mother's kitchen floor next to Rosa, while my mom and Tessa sit at the kitchen table talking about me like I'm not even here.

"It's like he doesn't even care, Tessa," my mother says with a sigh.

"Hey, give me your phone, I've got the best idea EVER!" Rosa tells me, holding her hand out above my face.

"Okay," I tell her, letting my wine buzz speak for me as I slap my phone into her hand.

She's had just as much wine to drink as I have, it's not like she's sober enough to do anything *that* bad.

Chapter 11

— Handy —
Molly

"I CAN'T BELIEVE I took a red-eye flight home for this shit," Ava complains, shaking her head at me in disappointment as she perches on the edge of our mother's desk at Seduction and Snacks.

"Hey, I told you on the phone last night what was going on. It's not my fault you felt the need to get the first flight out," I argue.

Today was my first official day at the headquarters of our family business in the test kitchen. I had a glorious day working alone in the huge industrial kitchen while I got busy tweaking some of the old recipes, and then Ava had to come in and ruin my good mood by dragging me away from my happy place and into mom's empty office on the other side of the building while she was out running errands.

"Charlotte tore me a new asshole for spilling the beans to Mom and Dad so I figured coming home early in your time of need was the least I could do," she informs me. "I still can't believe she's making you do this shit for her, and I can't believe you actually agreed to it."

I was so busy trying to decipher a bunch of weird, random text messages Marco sent last night that when my cell phone rang, I quickly answered it without checking caller I.D., hoping it was him. Ava screamed at me for fifteen minutes about getting pregnant and how she had to find out from Tyler instead of me. When I finally managed to shut her up and tell her the truth, she said she was coming home and hung up before I could say anything else.

"It seemed like a good idea at the time, and did you not hear me when I told you everything she agreed to give me?" I ask.

"Who cares about that shit? Tell me more about this hot teacher of yours that's standing in as the baby daddy," she says with a wicked smile. "Charlotte said his name is Mo or something."

Rolling my eyes, I push myself up from the chair in the middle of the room and start to pace. "His name is Marco, not Mo, and he's not my teacher. Not anymore at least, you know, since I *graduated*."

I pause, wondering if she'll acknowledge my big accomplishment since no one else seems to have remembered now that they have my fake baby on the brain. I'm trying not to let it get to me that no one in my family has said a word about how all of my hard work for the last two years has successfully come to an end. Even today, my first official day of work, which was temporarily scheduled six months ago barring I passed my final, went unnoticed. When I announced I was going to work this morning and waited for it to click in with my mother, all she did was hand me a prenatal vitamin and told me not to take it on an empty stomach.

"Mmmmmm, Marco," she purrs. "Me likey. He already sounds hot, tell me more."

Feeling stupid for thinking Ava of all people would be the one to congratulate me, I continue pacing.

"All guys name their penis, so don't be embarrassed about that. Although Humpy the Wonder Penis is a little much," she muses, causing me to stop pacing.

"Where the hell did you get my cell phone?!" I yell, trying to take it from her, but she moves quickly and smacks my hand away.

"I grabbed it from the kitchen counter before I dragged you in here," she laughs, continuing to read the string of weird texts I got from Marco last night. "You should know better than to leave your phone lying around for just anyone to take."

I haven't even had a chance to try and decipher those texts, and now Ava is going to make it worse.

"Humpy likes to wear green dresses and bananas are delicious," she reads one of the texts out loud. "Yikes, how much time did you say he spent alone with Uncle Drew?"

I finally manage to overpower her and snatch my phone out of her hands. "Your boyfriend dresses up like a horse, your opinion is invalid!"

She hops off of her desk and puts her hands on her hips. "It's not a horse, it's as PONY, show some respect!"

There are so many things I could say right now, but I decide to keep them to myself because spending any amount of time thinking about what Ava and her Brony boyfriend do when they're alone makes me was to dunk my head in a tub full of bleach.

"I see what you're doing by trying to turn this around on me," she says casually, dropping her hands from her hips to lean back against the edge of the desk. "You're avoiding the real issue."

I scoff. "Really? I'm pretending to be pregnant because our sister is too afraid to tell her fiancé the truth. I'm fucking up my life, so she can live happily ever after. How is that avoiding ANY subject?"

She waves me off with a flap of her hand.

"Pshaw, b-o-r-i-n-g," she says in a sing-song voice. "I'm much more interested on you being a pregnant virgin. Let's discuss *that*."

"Oh, my GOD, is nothing sacred in this family?!" I shout in irritation.

And here I thought Charlotte and I finally had a moment in the doctor's office. She probably called Ava five seconds after we left.

"Sacred? You're kidding, right?" she laughs. "Uncle Drew puts a picture of his balls on their Christmas card every year, and forever ruined Taco Tuesday night at mom and dad's when he told us Aunt Jenny's vagina can hold two taco shells without spilling the contents. The *sacred* ship sailed long before we were born."

I cringe, remembering there are much worse things to have floating around in my brain aside from Ava and her pony-loving boyfriend.

"I think we need to discuss when you plan on telling this Marco guy that you haven't lost your virginity," she smirks.

I feel my face heat with embarrassment as she stares at me. Forget the whole fake pregnancy thing. That is a piece of cake compared to *this* torture.

"And don't bother trying to make up some lie about how he's just a guy and it's no big deal," she warns me. "Charlotte already told me how cute you two are together and how you've been all girly and emo that he hasn't called since he met the family."

My mouth drops open in indignation. "I have NOT been girly and emo!"

"So you haven't been checking your phone every two minutes and kept yourself locked in your bedroom playing the soundtrack from *The Virgin Suicides* on repeat?" she asks with a knowing smile.

First Charlotte and now my mother. Forget moving across town, I'm moving to Mexico.

"It's a good soundtrack!" I argue lamely.

"From a movie about five sisters who commit suicide!" she replies. "I repeat, girly and emo."

I groan, throwing my hands up in the air.

"Fine! I really like the guy, and he said he really likes me too which I guess is obvious considering that he agreed to do something so crazy to help me out, but then all the idiots we're related to got ahold of him and he traded in his macho sports car for a mom van, came home smelling like pee and threw up hotdogs for the next two days where I only heard from him twice until last night when he kept sending me texts about bananas wearing dresses, and I'm pretty sure our family ruined him permanently and I'll never see him again," I ramble so fast I barely comprehend what is coming out of my mouth.

Fortunately, Ava speaks fluent rambling nonsense and nods her head in understanding.

"Yeah, Charlotte told me about the bag of dicks thing, too. Bravo to Marco for finally putting an end to *that* argument so we don't have to listen to it at yet another Thanksgiving dinner," she says. "He's not completely ignoring you, so obviously they didn't scare him away for good. The poor guy had to deal with a lot in one day, so cut him some slack. He took his own life in his hands, and you didn't even put out when it was over. That guy is a saint."

Even though my life is on the verge of imploding all because of Charlotte, I can't deny that it was sort of nice when we did have that little moment in the doctor's office, and she's called and texted me nonstop since then checking to see if I've heard anything more from Marco, like she actually *cares*. And I'm more than a little surprised that I actually *like* it.

If Charlotte is the sister I can talk about stupid girl stuff with like my feelings, and it doesn't make me break out in hives, I suppose I can suck it up and give Ava a chance to give me *her* expertise—sex.

"There's no way he expected to get sex after that..." I mutter, biting my bottom lip as I think it over. "Right? I mean, sure we've known each other for two years, but that was the first time we ever hung out and said more than a handful of words to each other."

She laughs and shakes her head at me. "Oh, little sister, you have so much to learn. Tyler expects sex if he remember to put the toilet seat down. Marco met your family on the first date AND had to put up with everyone looking at him the entire time while they pictured him sticking his penis in their little girl. He had to deal with the fact that our parent's brains gave his dick more action than his dick actually got. You're right, sex might have been a bit much, but you could have thrown the guy a bone and given him a handy or something."

I'm pretty sure studying Urban Dictionary would be more beneficial than asking for Ava's advice on sex.

"Can you be serious for one minute?" I ask in irritation. "I don't need you making fun of me for not jerking him off at the end of the night. I'm sure touching a guy's penis when he's throwing up six pounds of hotdogs is no big deal for you, but it's just a little bit out of my comfort zone."

She crosses her arms and speaks to me matter-of-factly. "I am always serious when it comes to sex. While it's true that I happen to have some experience with the aforementioned during a recent bout of the stomach flu and Tyler insisting it was the only way he could stop throwing up, I assure you it wasn't the easiest thing I've ever done."

I never thought I'd see the day when I'd rather talk about Bronies...

"I'm not making fun of you, Molly," she continues. "To avoid any confusion, my advice would be to tell Marco the truth. If he knows you're a virgin, his expectations won't be as high and you won't constantly be worrying that he's waiting for you to do something."

I shake my head at her and roll my eyes. "I can't just come right out and tell him something like that, it's embarrassing."

"Really?" she scoffs. "More embarrassing than our father picturing Marco spraying his seed all up in your business whenever he looks at you?"

"Eeeeeew!" I groan in disgust. "Come on!"

"It's not like you have to give him all the details about Quinn Curtis in the back of his dad's Honda Civic and explain that you sort of had sex, but you're still a virgin because they guy has a micro penis," she informs me.

"Jesus, is there anything Charlotte DIDN'T tell you?" I complain.

"Oh, Charlotte didn't tell me that. I read your texts two days after prom," she informs me with a shrug. "Don't feel bad. I dated his older brother for a week in high school and gave him a blowjob after a football game. I open my mouth wider when I whistle. It runs in the family."

I close my eyes and start rubbing the tips of my fingers against my temples, wondering if it's possible for a brain to literally explode.

"Here, let's practice," she announces. "Repeat after me. Marco, I haven't lost my virginity yet."

I drop my hands from the side of my head and glare at her.

"I'm not just going to blurt out that I haven't lost my virginity. I didn't lose it, I know exactly where it is. It's in my vagina where it will remain until the right time comes along," I tell her indignantly.

"This guy has seen Uncle Drew's balls!" she argues. "In a Walmart parking lot, for God's sakes! There is no such thing as the right time when Uncle Drew's balls have already made an appearance. Do you want to have sex with this guy?"

I roll my eyes and sigh. "Yes."

"Then be loud and be proud!" she shouts, throwing her fist in the air. "I haven't lost it yet, but I want to lose it with you!"

Since I made the mistake of staying in the room and letting Ava give me her stupid expertise instead of plugging my ears and running away as fast as I could, I might as well get this over with so I can pretend like it never happened.

"I haven't lost it yet, but I want to lose it with you," I mumble under my breath.

"I'm sorry, I can't hear you," she says, holding her hand to her ear.

"I HAVEN'T LOST IT YET, BUT I WANT TO LOSE IT WITH YOU!" I yell at the top of my lungs.

"Lost what? Do you need help finding something?"

I scream and whirl around, wishing immediately that the whole brain explosion thing would have happened a few minutes ago. I'd kind of like to be dead right about now.

"Sorry for interrupting, but the woman at the front desk told me you were in here." Marco smiles at me before glancing over my shoulder. "Hi, I'm Marco Desoto. You must be Molly's other sister, Ava."

"Ooooh, an Italian Stallion," she whispers. "You won't have to worry about an inchworm penis with this one."

"I heard you yelling about losing something, need some help?" Marco asks, his eyes roaming around the office.

Ava snorts unladylike and I'm too busy waiting for the floor to open up and swallow me to care.

"I'm pretty good at finding things," Marco announces. "Did you lose your keys? Wallet? Cell phone?"

I'm unable to make my mouth work or form words, and all I can do is watch in mortification as he starts digging through the couch cushions of the love seat against the wall.

"Am I hot or cold?" Marco asks as he moves to a side table and pulls open the drawer.

"I don't know, what do you think, Molly?" Ava laughs.

"I know it's stupid, but did you try your pants?" Marco asks, oblivious to how much enjoyment Ava is getting out this. "I think I lose things all the time and then find them in the most obvious places."

He walks right up to me and starts patting my hips while my sister tries to stifle her giggles behind me.

"I think you're getting warmer, Marco. I'm sure you'll find what you're looking for in her pants," Ava informs him.

Even though the combination of wanting to die and the feel of Marco's warm hands running up and down my hips has turned me stupid, I finally manage to recover enough bodily function to turn my head and glare over my shoulder at Ava.

"I will murder you in your sleep," I whisper through clenched teeth.

She ignores me, grabbing an old-fashioned calligraphy dip pen from the top of mom's desk that she found at an antique store a few months ago, holding it up in the air.

"Oh, look! I found it!" she announces with a big smile. "It's a gift for you, Marco. Molly tried to give it to someone else a few years ago, but he didn't know what to do with it."

I snarl at her as Marco drops his hands from my hips and reaches around me to take the pen from her outstretched hand.

"Wow, this is pretty cool," he muses. "I actually know how to use one of these, too. I took a calligraphy class as an elective in college."

"Awwww, did you hear that, Molly? He knows what to do with this gift you're giving him," she says happily.

"You just have to be careful. It can get really messy if you go too fast or don't know what you're doing," Marco adds.

"Very messy, especially the first time. Never use it on a bed with white sheets," Ava says with a nod.

"A bed?" Marco laughs. "On top of a table is a better idea."

Her eyes light up. "Ooooh, kinky. I like you already, Marco."

Grabbing Marco's hand before this gets even more out of hand, I drag him to the door, staring at Ava as I go, making sure my eyes convey that she should sleep with one eye open for the rest of her life.

"It was nice meeting you, Ava!" Marco shouts as I pull him out the door.

"See you soon, Humpy banana penis!" she yells back.

Marco groans as I hustle him down the hall and as far away from my sister as possible.

"Oh, God, she saw the texts I sent you? This is mortifying," he complains as I push open the front doors of the building and pull him outside.

"Don't talk to me about mortifying until your sister tells you about giving her boyfriend a hand-job to make him stop puking," I mutter.

"Wait, that's a thing? I can't believe I've wasted all these years asking for 7-up when there was a much better alternative," he says in awe.

I can't believe the things that come out of your mouth remind me of something my family would say, and it makes me like you even more.

I need therapy.

Chapter 12

- Dammit, Ian -

Marco

KNOW IT would be wrong to ask Molly to say "hand-job" again just so I can stare at her lips as they form the words, but that doesn't stop me from silently wishing upon a star.

Spending two days away from her was the worst decision I've ever made. She didn't look as happy to see me as I'd hoped when I walked in on her and Ava a few minutes ago. I don't know if it's because she's pissed at me for my disappearing act, pissed at me for the God awful drunk texts Rosa sent to her after I'd passed out on our mother's kitchen floor, or pissed at me that I didn't find what she'd lost back in the office. Right when I opened my mouth to apologize for all three just to cover all the bases, she had to go and say "hand-job," and now my dick and my brain are doing shots and partying it up in the gutter instead of paying attention.

"So, what brings you to Seduction and Snacks today?" Molly asks, stopping next to my van I left parked at the curb in front of the building.

"You look really pretty today," I tell her with a smile, knowing all women appreciate compliments. It should be a piece of cake to soften Molly up and make it easier for her to look beyond my avoidance of her the last couple of days.

"Sucking up to me will get you nowhere," she deadpans.

Or not.

"It's okay if my family was a bit too much for you," she continues, without giving me a chance to say anything. "I get it. Not everyone can handle their unique brand of hazing someone new. If you want out, just be honest with me. I'll tell them you changed your mind or something. Ava is pretty good with computers, I'm sure she can make sure your home address isn't easily accessible anywhere on the internet until everything blows over."

Shit, Rosa was right with all that advice she gave me before I passed out. By staying away from her in the hopes that the image of me hurling in her parent's shrubs would disappear from her mind, all I did by avoiding her was make her second-guess me. I'm just going to pretend I didn't hear the home address thing. Knowing the men in her family would hunt me down and shank me like a thug in the prison yard if they thought I left a pregnant Molly all alone is enough to give me nightmares.

I step right up in front of her until our toes are touching, hoping she notices I smell like Cool Water cologne instead of Cold Water and Piss.

She has a dusting of flour on her right cheek that my hands have been itching to brush off ever since I first walked into that office a few minutes ago. I silently bring my hand up to the side of her face and graze the tips of my fingers against her skin. I keep touching her long after the flour is gone because she feels like velvet—warm and soft and smooth.

"They weren't too much for me, I promise," I insist quietly as she lifts her chin and searches my eyes to see if I'm telling the truth.

"I'll admit, the thirty-eighth hot dog was too much, and I should have tapped out somewhere around thirty-four, but I haven't changed my mind and I'm sorry for being a dick the last few days," I apologize.

"You don't have to say you're sorry," she says with a shake of her head. "I'm the one who's sorry for bringing you into this mess. I know it's crazy, and you probably think I'm the biggest idiot in the entire world for faking a pregnancy for my sister…"

Her voice tapers off and she sighs heavily, looking away from me to stare out towards the street.

"I've spent my whole life feeling like an outsider with my entire family, but mostly with my two sisters," she explains softly. "Growing up, they were always boy-crazy and fashion-crazy and just plain fucking crazy, and I couldn't relate to them. The only thing I've ever been crazy about is baking. Until now. Now, we have something in common and something to talk about and I actually *like* it. It's girly and it's dumb and I'm sure they're going to want to get pedicures and do my hair and watch reality TV together now, but I don't care."

Molly laughs softly before turning her face back to mine, and I can tell by the way she had to force the laugh out that she hates sharing her feelings and acting, like she said, *girly.*

"Can you be a little more specific on the thing you guys have in common now?" I ask with a raise of my eyebrow.

Her cheeks flush in embarrassment and that gives me my answer, but I still want to hear her say it.

"It's the fashion-crazy thing, isn't it?" I tease. "I bet you're going to start demanding everyone in the kitchen at work has to wear designer chef jackets. You're such a fashion whore."

She smacks my chest and laughs.

"You know that's not the crazy I'm talking about and if you make me say it, I will help my mother turn your balls into cream puffs," she warns.

"As long as you like to *eat* cream puffs, I'm okay with my balls *being* cream puffs," I tell her with a wink and a smirk. "Come on, just say it. There's no shame in admitting you're boy-crazy. But you should probably amend it to *man*-crazy because, I mean, look at me."

I put my hands on my hips, puff out my chest and give her my best smoldering look.

"What are you doing with your eyes?" she questions.

I try harder, narrowing my eyes and imagining I'm that Ian Somerhalder guy from *Vampire Diaries.* He has a good smolder. I mean, from what I've heard. From people who actually watch that dumb show because I clearly never would, especially since he had to go and get married and now Team Delena is dead forever.

"I'm smoldering you. It's totally working," I murmur.

"It looks like you have one of those eye-twitch things happening."

Dammit, Ian. You ruin everything.

I relax, softening my face and placing my hands on her shoulders.

"I get why you're doing this and you're right, it's completely insane, but I get it." I knead her shoulders gently. "Doing something like this makes you feel close to your sisters for the first time in your life and you want to hold onto that. I think that makes you brave and amazing, not stupid or crazy."

Silence stretches between us as we stand on the sidewalk staring at each other. I can smell her cinnamon apple skin and there's a glossy sheen on her lips that makes me wonder if she's wearing lip gloss and if it will taste as good as she smells. My dick takes a time-out from the gutter party to rise up and toast me, threatening to bust right through the zipper of my jeans when Molly licks those damn shiny lips.

I want to kiss her more than I want to breathe, but I don't want to do it in front of her place of work while employees come and go all around us. I want to be alone, in a quiet place where maybe I can fake an illness and the kiss can lead to her showing me how to cure nausea by putting her hand down my pants.

"I'm sorry I didn't call or make plans to see you that last few days," I apologize again. "I was a little embarrassed that the first day we spent together ended with me regurgitating hotdogs."

She laughs and rolls her eyes at me, something that has suddenly become one of my favorite things to see.

"I accept your apology, but you owe me," she threatens, jabbing her finger into my chest. "I had to get my fake pregnancy confirmed at the doctor."

My eyes widen in shock, wondering how in the hell she pulled *that* off.

"So I'm guessing somewhere in town there's a roofied doctor waking up with a really bad headache?" I ask with a laugh.

"I wish. Luckily, they confirmed the pregnancy with pee. I had to carry a cup of Charlotte's pee." She scrunches her cute little nose up in disgust, her body shuddering under my hands that are still resting on her shoulders.

She waves her arm in the air and changes the subject.

"If you see me wash my right hand until the skin starts falling off, don't ask any questions," she informs me.

I try not to let it bother me that she takes a step back so I have no choice but to let my hands drop from her shoulders. One of these days I'm going to get this girl to let me touch her and not freak out about it.

"Enough of this mushy crap. Let's move on to Humpy and why your penis likes to wear green dresses," she says with a smirk. "I really don't know if green is a good color for you."

Remind me to never get drunk with Rosa again. Even if she did give me good advice before I passed out in a puddle of my own drool on our mother's linoleum.

"My sister sent those texts, not me. She pumped me full of wine and then stole my phone. Like I'd really name my penis Humpy," I scoff.

His name is Thor, obviously. He's strong and slams it like a hammer. BOOM!

"I'll explain the whole green dress banana thing in the car," I promise, glancing down at my watch. "Right now, we have somewhere to be."

Molly looks at me questioningly as I push her aside and open the passenger door to the van, holding it open for her.

"Get in, don't ask any questions, and don't give me that look for holding your door open like a *decent* gentleman," I warn her. "It's a surprise."

I'm not kidding when I said Rosa gave me some good instructions, after she punched me repeatedly in the arm for staying away from Molly. She called me every curse word she could think of before she told me I was an idiot for being introduced as the baby daddy to her family and then leaving her alone to deal with that shit by herself. It never even occurred to me that her family would probably wonder where I'd been or ask her a million questions about why I hadn't been around, and I knew I had to do something to make up for being such an idiot.

"I don't like surprises," she mutters as she gets into the passenger seat and pulls the seat belt around her.

"Suck it up, buttercup. You'll like this one, I promise," I assure her before shutting the door and walking around the front of the van to get behind the wheel. After spilling my guts to Rosa and telling her everything I knew about Molly and asking her for ideas on how to make myself look like a good guy and other romantic shit I could do to win her over, Rosa pointed out something so obvious that I wanted to punch *myself* in the arm that I didn't come up with it first.

When I called a few people this morning, they were really excited about my idea and even let me make them feel guilty as shit for not doing it themselves. Listening to them kick themselves in the ass over the phone made me forgive them for the car wash ride and bag of dicks contest.

"You're not going to get in trouble for leaving work early, are you?" I ask, even though I already know the answer.

"Nope, as a matter of fact, my mom sent me a text a half hour ago and told me to go home and put my feet up," Molly explains. "My poor fake baby had a rough day."

As I pull out of the parking lot and onto the street, I sneak a glance at Molly as she looks away from me to stare out the window. I really hope this doesn't turn out to be a bad idea. I'll never be able to console Thor if he doesn't get to meet her.

Chapter 13

– Shocker Honor –
Molly

"**S**URPRISE!"

I freeze in the middle of my parent's backyard when Marco and I round the side of the house and twenty-five people jump up from chairs and tables set up all around the yard.

Everyone starts clapping, hooting, whistling and chanting my name. Marco squeezes my hand and I tear my eyes away from the chaos to look up at him.

"If this is a pregnancy party or a stupid baby shower, I'm baking your balls at 500 degrees instead of the required 350," I growl.

He laughs, letting go of my hand to wrap his arm around my shoulder and pull me against his side. I'm in too much shock to move away from him, and he smells so delicious and his body feels so good pressed against mine that I forget about my family wondering if I've lost my mind by letting a guy get all grabby-hands in public.

"No, silly girl. This is a graduation party."

Looking around the yard again, I see what I missed during my initial shock from the shouting and seeing the yard filled with my entire extended family. A giant *Happy Graduation* sign hangs between two trees, a couple dozen cardboard graduation hats hang from all the branches, and the centerpieces on all the paper-covered tables are bouquets of sugar cookies cut out and frosted to look like pastry hats, wooden spoons, whisks and other baking items.

"You threw me a graduation party?" I whisper in awe as a few members of my family start walking across the yard towards us.

"I felt bad that this fake pregnancy thing overshadowed the biggest accomplishment of your life. Just so you know, they all felt really horrible they forgot," he tells me.

It's the sweetest thing anyone has ever done for me, and I have to bite down on my bottom lip to stop myself from crying like a baby.

"I was starting to feel like Molly Ringwald in *Sixteen Candles* when her family forgot her birthday," I whisper.

"Well then, you'll be happy to know I did not sell a pair of your panties in the boy's bathroom," Marco announces proudly.

"Never, ever say the word *panties* again," I warn him as my mom gets up to us and pulls me in for a hug.

"We are the worst people ever and I'm so sorry Molly," she apologizes, raining kisses all over both my cheeks. "You should have smacked us in the face when we forgot to ask you about finals."

She pulls away and holds me at arm's length and I can see tears welling up in her eyes. Mom hates to cry in front of people just as much as I do, so I go easy on her before she starts snotting all over the place and embarrassing herself.

"Brace yourself, Mother. I'm joining Fight Club," I announce, making two fists and bringing them up between us.

"I was being facetious. Don't even think about punching me. I brought you into this world and I can—"

"Ooooh, bad call quoting Bill Cosby," Dad interrupts. "Unless you plan on slipping a roofie in your daughter's drink to make it more authentic."

He pats Mom on the back and then moves her out of the way so he can give me his own hug. "Congratulations, baby girl. You worked your ass off, and I couldn't be more proud."

Uncle Carter, Aunt Claire, Uncle Drew, and Aunt Jenny each take their turns congratulating me, giving me hugs and apologizing for being assholes.

"It's good to see you came back, M.O.," Uncle Carter tells him, giving him a pat on the shoulder. "I thought for sure those hot dogs killed you, or at the very least you got a brain aneurism from the brushes at the car wash. You're like a fucking cat!"

Aunt Claire looks at her husband in confusion. "Because he's selfish and licks his own ass?"

"I meant because he has nine lives, but sure, you're way is good too," he tells her with a shrug.

"Why did you call him Mo?" Aunt Jenny asks Uncle Carter.

"Minivan Operator," Uncle Carter replies. "You know, minivan? From Urban Dictionary."

Aunt Jenny smiles and nods her head in understanding. "Oh, I get it! Because you can fit four people in the front and nine people in the back!"

Uncle Carter shakes his head. "I don't think it means what you think it means."

Aunt Jenny rolls her eyes. "Yes I do. Drew and I have done the minivan and he can definitely fit nine in the back."

Everyone groans and Marco leans down close to my ear.

"I'm ashamed to say I really thought you were kidding about them," he whispers.

"Since we're all here, we need to discuss something important," Mom announces as Marco moves away from my ear. "Grandpa George is on his way and he doesn't know about the pregnancy."

Grandpa George is actually Aunt Claire's father. Even though he's not blood-related, I've known him all my life, and he's always been Grandpa George to my sisters and I.

Mom turns to Marco. "George is…how should I say this?"

"He's old school and even though he was pretty good about me getting pregnant in college, that was a while ago, and I don't know how he'd take something like this in his old age," Aunt Claire explains. "Plus, I'm pretty sure he was the one who shot a man in Reno, just to watch him die."

Everyone nods silently in agreement.

"So, can everyone promise they will not tell George about the pregnancy until we absolutely have to?" Mom asks.

Everyone raises their hands and mumbles their agreement.

"Shocker honor!" Uncle Drew shouts, holding his hand in the air with his thumb holding down his ring finger, his pointer and middle fingers pressed together, and his pinky sticking out to the side.

"What the fuck is shocker honor?" Uncle Carter asks.

"I was never a Boy Scout, so it would be sacrilegious to say scout's honor," Uncle Drew explains. "Since I'm not only a member, but also the president of Shocker Nation, this makes more sense."

Dad shakes his head. "It makes no sense. Shocker honor isn't a thing and you can't swear on it."

"Shocker honor is too a thing and it's a very important thing," Uncle Drew argues. "There is nothing more serious than two in the pink, one in the stink."

"He's right, there isn't," Aunt Jenny adds with a serious nod. "It's more important than a pinky swear."

Aunt Claire looks over my shoulder and waves. We all turn around to see Grandpa George and his wife Sue coming around the side of the house.

"Another thing you guys should know, Sue had some sort of accident the other day that affected her ear drums," Aunt Claire quickly explains. "I guess she can't hear very well, so you might have to talk a little louder."

She walks around Marco and I to greet them. "Hi, Dad, thanks for coming. Can I get you something to drink, Sue?"

"OH, NO THANK YOU! IT'S TOO HOT FOR SOUP!" Sue shouts with a smile as Aunt Claire leads them over to our group.

Grandpa George, not one for public displays of affection, gives me an awkward one-armed side hug and hands me a card.

"Congratulations, Molly. There's fifty bucks in there. Don't spend it on anything stupid," he warns me as I take the card from his hand.

"There goes your plans of spending your graduation money on booze and sex," Uncle Drew laughs.

"NO, IT'S NOT A ROLEX, BUT THANKS FOR ASKING!" Sue shouts, holding up her wrist and pointing to her gold watch.

"Care to tell me how Sue lost her hearing since you were a little vague on the phone yesterday?" Aunt Claire asks her dad.

"Eh, I let off a couple M-80's in the backyard and she was standing too close," he says with a shrug.

"Why in the hell were you lighting M-80's in your backyard?" Aunt Claire furrows her brow in dismay.

"That's the dumbest question you've ever asked me," Grandpa George mutters, shaking his head. "I found them in a box in the garage. One does not just leave M-80's in a box when they find them. Have I taught you nothing?"

Before Aunt Claire can scold him, Gavin and Charlotte walk over to our group to say hello.

"What's new, Grandpa George?" Charlotte asks, kissing him on the cheek and giving Sue a quick hug.

"PIGEON FORGE? NEVER BEEN, BUT I HEAR IT'S NICE!" Sue yells.

Aunt Claire smacks Grandpa George on the arm when he chuckles.

"I can't believe you're laughing at her!" she whispers. "You should be ashamed of yourself."

He shrugs, sticking his hands in his pockets. "I asked her this morning if we had anything to fix a drain clog and she thought I asked for a blow job. I picked up ten cases of M-80's on the way home from the hardware store."

Aunt Claire makes a gagging noise and covers her ears while Uncle Drew gives grandpa a high five.

"You kids ready for the wedding?" Grandpa asks Gavin and Charlotte. "You gonna wear a fancy tux or get a new suit?"

"I ALREADY TOLD CLAIRE I DIDN'T WANT SOUP, GEORGE," Sue shouts with a frown.

I watch as Charlotte's eyes widen in horror and her face starts to turn green.

Aunt Claire and Uncle Carter both start talking very loudly about how there isn't any soup, making sure to enunciate that word and drag it out each time they say it so Sue can understand them. The more they say it, the more Charlotte starts to look like she's going to puke right here in front of everyone.

"Uuuggghhh," I moan loud enough to make them stop talking. I put my hand on my stomach and grimace. "Please don't say that word, it makes me sick."

Grandpa George looks at me questioningly. "Why in tarnation would that word make you sick? Soup is delicious and good for you. We just had split pea soup with ham last night for dinner."

Charlotte's hand flies up to cover her mouth and Grandpa George notices out of the corner of his eye, turning his head in her direction.

"And what the hell is wrong with you? Don't tell me soup makes you sick too? Has everyone in this family turned stupid?" he asks.

"WHY WOULD CUPID BE HERE? I THOUGHT YOU SAID THIS WAS A GRADUATION PARTY, NOT A VALENTINE'S DAY PARTY?" Sue yells to Grandpa George.

"Charlotte thinks she's coming down with the flu," Gavin explains, rubbing his hand soothingly against her back. "But Molly's pregnant and *that word* makes her throw up."

Everyone groans and Aunt Claire smacks Gavin's arm. "Did you not hear me when I told you as soon as you got here that we weren't going to tell grandpa about Molly right now?"

Gavin winces. "Oops, sorry. I totally forgot. Charlotte told me she cancelled the ice sculpture for the wedding and I got distracted."

Uncle Drew throws up his hands and huffs. "No ice sculpture? Are you kidding me with this shit? What the hell am I going to lick at the reception? You guys ruin all the fun."

I give Charlotte a knowing look and she rolls her eyes at me, her face finally returning to a normal color now that all the soup talk is finished.

"I was wondering if any of you girls would follow in your Aunt Claire's footsteps," Grandpa says with a sigh. "I hope you were smarter than her and at least know the guy's name."

"Heeeeeeeeey!" Aunt Claire protests, putting her hands on her hips.

"Oh, I'm sorry, I didn't realize we were able to change history. If that's the case, I can tell all the guys at the VFW my daughter got married and THEN got knocked up, like a good daughter should,"

Grandpa states. "No offense, Molly."

"None taken," I reply, grabbing Marco's arm and pulling him closer to my grandfather. "This is Marco, my boyfriend. Marco, this is Grandpa George."

Marco holds out his hand and gives my grandfather a smile. "It's nice to meet you, sir."

Grandpa stubbornly keeps his hands in his pockets for a few seconds, finally removing one slowly. Instead of grabbing Marco's hand, he sticks a toothpick in his mouth and starts to chew on it. After a few tense moments, he removes the toothpick and holds it up in front of Marco.

"See this here toothpick?"

Marco nods silently.

"If you don't do right by my granddaughter, I will gouge out your eyes with it, then rip off your scalp and skull-fuck you," he says quietly, sticking the toothpick back in his mouth.

"SOMEONE'S MOVING TO SUFFOLK?" Sue asks loudly.

"Well, this has been fun," I mutter, grabbing Marco's hand again before he passes out or runs away in fear. "I need a drink, who wants a drink?"

Everyone raises their hands and we all move towards the coolers my parent's set up by the food tables. Opening the first one, I find it filled with ice and beer. Quickly grabbing two of the bottles, I hand one to Marco and then twist the top of mine, sighing happily when I hear the seal *pop*.

I bring the cold bottle up to my lips, my mouth watering for some much needed alcohol. The beer is an inch from my mouth when it's quickly snatched out of my hands and replaced with a cup of apple juice.

"That baby already has enough problems with our family's DNA flowing through it, don't make it worse by getting it drunk," my mother scolds, chugging the beer she just took from me.

I watch longingly as she downs half the bottle before she saunters off to greet more family members.

"So, hey, thanks again for the graduation party," I tell Marco, trying not to glare at him while he drinks *his* beer. "If we ever do this again, let's do it when I'm not fake pregnant and I can get wasted and pretend like I'm not related to any of these people."

Marco laughs and leans forward, pressing a quick kiss to my lips. Just like with everything he does with me, it's easy and natural and he makes it feel like he's done it a million times before. I love that he organized this party for me, and I love that he made my family feel bad about not acknowledging my graduation, but would really love it if we were alone right now so he could kiss me again. I know that makes me sound all stupid and girly and exactly like my sisters, but I'm so distracted by his lips that I don't care.

"I'll make you a deal. I'll distract everyone so you can sneak a few beers if you promise you won't let your grandfather skull-fuck me," he negotiates alcohol for protection like he's been a part of this family for years.

I hold up my hand, putting my fingers in the same formation as Uncle Drew did earlier.

"Shocker Honor, I promise I will never let my grandfather skull-fuck you with a toothpick."

Chapter 14

- I Have a Vagerie -

Marco

CAN'T BELIEVE I agreed to this. What the hell was I thinking? Oh, I know. I was thinking that I'd do whatever Molly asked of me after she protected me from imminent skull-fuckage at her graduation party the other day. I was so happy to have my brain non-fucked with a toothpick that I told her I wanted to take her on a date. As much as I like her family now that they've decided not to kill me, I wanted to do something with her away from their prying eyes where we didn't have to watch what we say about this whole pregnancy business. I made the mistake of telling her we could go wherever she wanted.

"Your mom likes this brand of wine, right?" Molly asks as we walk up the steps of my mother's front porch.

Yep, Sunday dinner. Molly decided our first official date should be Sunday dinner with my family. I am so screwed.

"My mom likes anything with the name wine in it," I joke. "Don't worry about the wine. You should really be more concerned with my mother hitting you with a wooden spoon because I didn't knock you up, while at the same time complaining I almost killed her when she thought I *did* knock you up."

After the graduation party ended, I drove Molly back to Seduction and Snacks so she could get her car, and I told her all about how I had to come clean with my mom and sisters about what's going on.

"I still can't believe she goes to the same salon as my Aunt Claire," Molly mutters. "And that the two of them went baby shopping and my aunt never said a word to me about it."

Opening the door and motioning for her to go in ahead of me, I call for my mom as soon as we get inside.

Three sets of feet pound against the floor like a herd of elephants as my mom, Tessa, and Rosa all come racing out of the kitchen and down the hall.

Mom goes right up to Molly and pulls her in for a tight hug, kissing both of her cheeks before pulling back to look her up and down.

"You're prettier than your pictures on The Facebook," she exclaims with an approving smile.

"It's just Facebook, Mom," Rosa tells her. "Hi, I'm Rosa."

Mom moves out of the way so Rosa and Molly can meet.

"You know I don't understand that interwebs thing," Mom complains. "And you still haven't fixed the remote so I can send those text message things and—"

"Molly, this is my other sister, Tessa!" I interrupt, hoping Molly doesn't remember what I said in the car on the way to meet her family when I mentioned how Alfanso D.'s mother probably tries to send text messages from the television remote.

My sisters take turns giving Molly hugs as well and my mother ushers all of us into the living room.

"I thought we could have a nice little chat while the lasagna is baking," she says, taking a seat on the couch.

"Wow, you have so many books," Molly exclaims, walking over to the bookshelf and glancing at all the titles.

"I usually prefer autobiographies, but my daughters keep buying me romance novels," Mom tells her as Molly walks the length of the built-in bookshelf along the back wall. "I really enjoyed that *Fifty Hues of Black*. It was quite spicy."

My sisters laugh and I try not to let this information ruin my appetite.

"Mom, it's called…you know what? Never mind, I'm just glad you enjoy them," Tessa laughs.

"Oh, my God. I can't believe you have a copy of this," Molly states.

I watch in horror as she pulls *Seduction and Sugar* off the shelf and turns around, holding it up.

Oh, fuck. Please let these crazy women remember that Molly doesn't know I'm the author yet. Please, for the love of God. I promise I'll go to church more than just on Christmas and Easter. I promise not to masturbate more than two...make that four, times a week. I will let Grandpa George skull-fuck me AND give me a minivan and I'll say ten Hail Mary's for saying the word 'skull-fuck' in this prayer.

"Wow, you even have a signed copy," Molly muses as she flips open the front cover.

Thank fuck I wrote that dedication in Italian because I knew it would make my mother forgive me for writing a dirty cookbook.

"What does it say?" she asks.

"It says, 'Thank you for loving this cookbook and for your kind email telling me I'm the most decent, dedicated and delightful man you've ever known.'" I quickly tell her before my mother can open her mouth.

My sisters both cover their mouths to hide their laughter and my mother gives me the stink eye. She was not happy when I told her she needed to keep quiet about this until I had a chance to tell her myself.

"Well, that's...nice. And unexpected," Molly mutters, turning around to slide the cookbook back on the shelf. "I've had a few exchanges with the author on Facebook and he's a real piece of work."

She turns back around and my mother pats the spot on the couch. Molly sits down and when I move to take the spot next to her, my mother quickly slides up against Molly, forcing me to sit on the other side of my mother. I plop down with a sigh as my sisters both sit down across from us on the love seat.

"Marco, did I tell you that guy asked me out on a date on Facebook?" Molly asks with a laugh.

"You don't say?" I reply, glaring over at Rosa while she beams at me.

"I happened to be on the author's page the other day and saw your comment to him," Rosa tells her. "He really does sound like a momma's boy. Nice job on the cutting the cord comment."

If I glare at my sister any harder, I'm going to pop a blood vessel in my forehead.

Molly laughs and rests her elbow on the arm of the couch. "Thanks, I was pretty proud of that one. Of course the guy had to go and apologize and be all nice. I'm sure it was just a publicity stunt. Now I don't know what to think about the whole date thing."

"I think you should go," Tessa pipes up.

"Um, hello?" I mutter in irritation, waving my hand in the air. "Person she's already dating, sitting right here."

Sure, we haven't been on an official date yet and we haven't had a chance to talk about being exclusive, but I think fake knocking her up and being a fake baby daddy gives me the right to call this thing between us whatever I want.

"You and that Alfanso D. sound a lot alike," Rosa muses. "I bet if Molly agrees to go out with him, she'd probably find out you're almost like the same person."

Why couldn't I have been an only child?

"I think I have enough on my plate right now, so I think I'll stick to just dating your brother," Molly laughs, looking behind my mother's head to give me a wink.

"Marco tells me you just graduated from the school where he teaches," my mother states, pulling Molly's eyes from mine. "I hope my son was a good teacher."

Mom gives me a dirty look, a nice little warning that she will kick my ass if she hears anything bad about me, quickly turning and smiling at Molly like she didn't just silently threaten to end my life.

"He was a very good teacher, one of the best," Molly tells her.

I'm too busy patting myself on the back to predict the next words out of my mother's mouth.

"I wish he'd spend more time focusing on teaching instead of writing that porn," she complains.

If we were in a bar, I'm pretty sure you'd be able to hear the screech of a needle sliding across a record as the entire place goes silent.

Molly chuckles. "I'm sorry, I thought you just said writing porn."

It's like we've all started playing a game of freeze tag and the person who's "it" is being a major asshole and refusing to unfreeze everyone. My sisters aren't moving or blinking, my mouth is stuck in a blow-up doll "Oh" face, and I'm wondering how long a person can hold their own breath before passing out.

I'm pretty certain that *I'm* the asshole and I know I should say something—*anything*—to change the subject, but words are potatoes and four is a purple cat.

Molly realizes she's the only one laughing and looks around the room at everyone's shocked expressions.

"Um, Marco?" she asks softly.

"Ha ha, so, funny story," Rosa pipes up and I finally breathe, taking back my wish to be an only child as long as she does something to fix this fucking situation.

"Marco here writes porn!" she announces. "Well, he likes to call them *erotic stories*, but whatever."

So, I'll just go ahead and die right about now.

"He's quite good at it too," Tessa adds, playing along with Rosa. "He writes fanfiction. *Vampire Diaries* fanfiction to be more specific. You should let her read the m/m one you did with Damon and Stefan."

Tessa winks at me and I vow to make sure Valerie goes to her first day of preschool with a backpack filled with condom-covered bananas for show-and-tell.

I can see by the confused look on Molly's face as she looks back and forth between my sisters, and I that she's not sure if she should believe what they're saying. I hope to God she doesn't think I'd write a story like that. I mean, come on. Damon and Stefan are brothers, that's just disgusting.

"Let's talk about something else," my mother suggests, folding her hands in her lap.

At least my mother loves me enough to stop this insanity before my sisters make it worse.

"Molly, has Marco ever told you about when he was thirteen and I found all of his socks stuck to the floor under his bed?" she asks Molly sweetly.

"I think we should talk about Molly and the awesome thing she's doing for her sister," I proclaim, stopping my mother before she goes off on a masturbation tangent.

Seriously, it's like they get a sick thrill out of making me look like an asshole. A porn-writing, tube-sock-masturbating asshole.

"You must really love your sister," Mom states. "Your Aunt Claire told me over lunch the other day that your family is very close."

Molly nods. "I do, and we are. They drive me crazy, but I'd do anything for them. Clearly, since I'm lying to all of them just to make sure my sister gets to marry the man she's been in love with since she was a little girl."

The pounding of little feet echoes out in the hallway and a dark-haired ball of energy flies into the room and dives onto Tessa's lap.

"Aren't you supposed to be taking a nap, little girl?" Tessa asks Valerie as she wraps her arms around her daughter's waist and pulls her back against her chest.

"Naps are dumb," Valerie announces. "Who are you?"

She points at Molly and then squirms out of Tessa's hold to march over and stand in front of her.

"I'm Molly," she greets her with a smile.

"My name's Vagerie."

Everyone laughs when she says her name wrong and mom shoots Tessa a questioning look.

"Why is my granddaughter calling herself *Vagerie?*"

We hear a laugh from the doorway and I let out a sigh of relief when I see my brother-in-law standing there.

"Sorry, that's my fault," Danny explains. "Tessa told me we need to start using proper words for body parts whenever Val asks about them, and her new favorite word is vagina."

Valerie nods excitedly, moving right up to Molly until she's pressing her little body against Molly's knees.

"I have a vagerie and are you the Molly that Mommy says Uncle wants to hump?"

I immediately cough and choke at the same time and my mother reaches over and pats me on the back.

"It's okay, hump means pee, but I don't think people are 'opposed to pee on each other," Valerie informs her before turning her head towards me. "Uncle, you aren't gonna pee on her, are you?"

Jumping up from the couch, I grab Valerie's hand and pull her towards the doorway.

"Come on, Val, let's go run with scissors and light some matches." I ignore the laughter coming from all four women in the room. "When we're done, I'll pour you a bowl of sugar and give you some Red Bull to wash it down."

"YAAAAAAY I love sugar!" Valerie cheers as we walk passed Danny and I call him a traitor for laughing with everyone else.

"Make sure she gives you another lesson on how to properly dress a banana," my mother calls after me. "You wouldn't even know how to take care of a pretend baby, let alone a real one."

I walk faster with Valerie, knowing it's probably not wise to leave Molly alone with those people for any length of time, but I have to get out of that room before I lose my shit.

"My cat licks his butt hole. Can you lick your butt hole, Uncle? Mommy says everyone has nipples, but I think she's lying. My Barbie's don't have nipples. Do you have nipples?" Valerie rambles as we make our way to the spare bedroom.

Kids are so weird.

Chapter 15

— Ganja Grandma —
Molly

LEANING AGAINST THE door frame of my parent's living room, I watch my uncles and Marco all huddled together, deep in conversation. It's so crazy how well he fits in with my family that it's hard to believe he hasn't been around them more than a handful of times. I'm trying to not let it get to me that we haven't had more than a few minutes alone since this insanity started, but I only have myself to blame. Marco asked me out on a date and I chose dinner with his family instead of going somewhere alone. It was nice to witness someone else's family be embarrassing instead of my own, but I should have consulted one of my sisters before immediately deciding on a family dinner for our first real date.

"How you feeling, honey? You up for tonight?" my mom asks, coming up next to me.

"Feeling great and I can't wait for tonight," I tell her, even though I'd rather have a root canal than participate in the activities my mother and aunts have planned.

Tonight is Charlotte's bachelorette party, and while I'll be busy watching everyone get white-girl-wasted and make bad choices as I sip on fucking apple juice, the guys are going to hang out here. Gavin decided he'd rather have a more relaxed bachelor party, much to Uncle

125

Drew's dismay, especially since mom made the whole "No Strippers in the House" rule after my dad's bachelor party. Obviously I wasn't born yet, but I've heard the stories. Aunt Claire warned all of us kids years ago to never mention my mom's favorite couch and how she dragged it out into the front yard and lit it on fire, screaming about "stripper juice stains" for the whole neighborhood to hear.

"What if we put plastic on the furniture?" Uncle Drew asks, leaning out of the huddle to shout to my mother.

"What if I light your balls on fire?" she replies.

"Wouldn't be the first time," he mutters, going back to the guys.

"So, what's this big announcement you have for us?" I ask my mom.

We were originally all supposed to meet at Charlotte and Gavin's place and go from there, but my mom called everyone this morning and said she had something to tell us and wanted everyone to come here first.

"It's a surprise. Something needs to be set up first so it shouldn't be too much longer," she tells me. "Oh, Grandma Madelyn decided to join us tonight, so prepare yourself."

I let out a surprised laugh. My Grandma Madelyn is my mom's mom and she's a tad uptight, a tiny bit snobby, and a control freak when it comes to any kind of big event. She's been driving mom and Charlotte insane lately, calling ten times a day to check on the wedding plans. I don't really see her letting loose or boozing it up with everyone else in the hotel suite we booked downtown Cleveland for tonight. At least I'll have one sober person to keep me company though. Well, besides Charlotte, but she has to act drunk and that's going to be just as bad. She's been freaking out all week about how she's going to make it look like she's drinking in front of everyone, so I filled up five flasks with water and stuck them in my purse. Ava packed three of her own filled with orange juice, and we plan on shoving them at her any time someone else tries to give her a real drink.

"I DON'T WANT YOUR HUSH MONEY!"

The front door slams shut and my mom and I turn our heads to see what the hell is going on.

Tyler, Ava's boyfriend, stands in the entryway with Grandma Madelyn, holding out a wad of bills to her.

"It's not hush money, Madelyn, it's gas money," Tyler explains. "You already offered to take the stuff to my dad's house and I want to pay for your gas."

Grandma looks at the money in his hand with disgust while mom and I make our way towards them.

"That's drug money! I don't want your drug money!" Grandma shouts, crossing her arms over her chest.

"Drug money spends just as well as regular money!" Tyler argues. "What do you think I used to pay for that new TV Ava and I got you for your birthday last year?"

Tyler told me a few months ago that he started growing pot to sell to his friends so he could make some extra cash to buy Ava an engagement ring. I'm not a prude and I've smoked it a time or two, but I told him he was an idiot and nothing good could come from that endeavor since the stuff still isn't legal in Ohio.

"What the hell is going on?" Mom asks.

"Um, well, you see, one of my friends overheard our landlord talking to someone about there being pot in a some of the apartments," Tyler explains. "I got a little freaked out there would be a raid or something, so I packed everything up in my trunk and got it out of there just in case."

Mom sighs and shakes her head.

"I was pulling it out of my trunk to put in Dad's car when Madelyn came up and asked if she could help," he says with a shrug. "When she asked what was going on, I told her I was just moving some of my stuff back to Mom and Dad's, and she offered to help so they wouldn't have to."

Mom sighs again and I wonder if she's lost the ability to speak or if she's just letting out all the pissed off air so she doesn't start screaming obscenities in front of her mother.

"Is your father aware you planned on putting illegal narcotics in his car?" Mom asks.

"You've met my father, right? He offered to smoke it all so the cops wouldn't find it," Tyler replies.

Tyler found out not too long ago that his biological father is my Uncle Drew. It's a long story that involved a drunken one-night stand in college, but there you have it. This information, while a tad shocking, at least gave all of us a reason for why Uncle Drew and Tyler are so strangely similar.

"I thought it was just clothes and nick-knacks until I smelled skunk. I know that smell. I've smoked the ganja a few times in my day, but I've never seen so many pounds of the ganja in one place," Grandma tells us, whispering the word "ganja" each time she uses it.

"Please tell me you did not bring a trunk load of marijuana to my house," Mom finally speaks.

"Of course not," Tyler replies. "I'm not an idiot. It's just two totes of marijuana, not an entire trunk load."

Mom and I both shake our heads and I wonder if I should start restraining her now or wait until she makes a lunge for his throat.

"The dried buds are all carefully sealed in zip lock bags, don't worry."

Grandma drops her arms to her sides and studies Tyler for a few seconds.

"Buds as in flower buds? Like house plants?" she asks.

"Sure, just like house plants," Tyler nods, deciding it's best to humor her so she stops screaming about hush money.

"Well, in that case, put them in my trunk and I'll take them to my house," she informs him.

"Mom!" my mother yells.

"Oh, Liz, it's fine. You know Drew and Jenny don't have green thumbs and they'll just kill the plants. I can water the ganja on Thursday when I water my ferns and lilies," she informs her.

"Excuse me, could you say that one more time, a little louder? Stan, get a mic on her, would ya?"

We all turn and see a guy standing behind us in the hallway with a huge camera on his shoulder, while another guy stands next to him holding a long metal pole with a giant microphone attached to the end.

"Surprise!" Mom says with fake enthusiasm. "The big announcement is that Claire and I were asked to do a documentary about our daily lives and running a business."

Grandma quickly smooths her hair back and straightens her clothes, smiling brightly for the camera.

"I don't know if I'm comfortable being on television, Liz," she whispers through her smile.

"It's a little late for that, Ganja Grandma," Mom mutters.

The front door opens and Tyler jumps out of the way as Ava pokes her head inside.

"The limo is here, bitches!" she shouts. "Any female who plans on being a drunk whore tonight should immediately report to the driveway!"

Mom groans, closing her eyes and dropping her head.

"What's with the camera?" Ava asks, staring at the two strangers in the hallway, happily recording the shit show in front of them.

"Oh, no big deal. They're just filming a documentary on our family," I inform her. "You're just in time for the episode about Grandma becoming a drug dealer."

The camera and sound guy quickly turn away from us when the guys walk out of the living room in the middle of a heated argument.

"I jerked-off into socks when I was a teenager, for Christ's sake. It's not like I still do it now!" Marco yells loudly, coming to a quick stop when he sees the camera and microphone.

Dad, Uncle Drew, and Uncle Carter all slam into the back of him when he stops so suddenly.

"What the hell, M.O.? Did your crusty socks stick to the floor or something?" Uncle Drew asks with a laugh. "Hey, are we on TV?!"

I quickly skirt around the camera crew and up to Marco, going up on my tiptoes to give him a kiss on the cheek and a sympathetic pat against his chest.

"It's fine, I'm sure this thing isn't going to air on any major networks or anything," I whisper.

"Actually, it's probably going to be syndicated on the Discovery Channel in all fifty states," the guy holding the microphone informs us.

"So, I just told a few million people I used to masturbate into my socks," Marco mutters.

"But you looked good doing it!" I say cheerfully.

"Can we please get moving? All this standing around is killing my buzz," Ava complains.

Charlotte comes bounding down the stairs just then, stopping at the bottom and looking around at everyone. "Sorry I took so long getting ready. What did I miss?"

"Jizz socks!" Uncle Drew shouts.

"Anyone have a preference on where we go tonight to film?" the camera guy asks. "Stay with the guys or go with the ladies?"

Drew walks around the guys and throws his arm over the cameraman's shoulder. "Might as well stay with us, man. I can't promise you strippers, but I *can* promise a turtle porn snuff film, and I have a guy from the zoo stopping by in an hour to let us play with a meerkat. Should make for good television entertainment, especially if we can get the meerkat to watch the turtle porn."

Charlotte grabs my arm and drags me away from Marco while everyone else says their good-byes. Once again, poor Marco is suffering at the hands of my family and I can't help but wonder how much more he's going to able to take before he heads for the hills. Not to mention the fact that I just kissed him in front of everyone, including a camera crew.

While the women pile into the stretch limo parked in the driveway, my sisters and I stand outside the vehicle for a few private minutes. Ava pulls one of the flasks out of her purse and hands it to Charlotte.

"Start chugging it in the limo," Ava tells her. "Make sure to giggle and yell a lot."

Charlotte takes the flask and rolls her eyes. "I've been drunk before, Ava. I think I know what I'm doing."

"And I've seen you drunk before. It's not pretty," Ava replies. "You go from telling everyone you love them to sobbing in two-point-three seconds. As a fake drunk, I expect better of you."

Aunt Claire leans her head out of the limo and looks at the three of us.

"Let's go, assholes. There's a bottle of vodka on ice at the hotel with my name on it and it's not gonna drink itself," she announces before pulling her head back inside.

"You people better not get on my nerves tonight," I mutter as I wait for Ava and Charlotte to get in the limo. "Drunk people are complete idiots when you're sober."

I hold onto the door and listen to Ava start up a chant with the rest of the women until the sounds of ten females screaming "Drunk bitches" repeatedly fills the quiet night. As I bend down to get in the limo and seal my fate, I hear my name shouted from the house. Quickly pulling back from the open door, I turn around to see Marco jogging down the front porch and across the yard.

All these years of making fun of my sisters for losing their heads over guys…is this what it was like for them? The nerves, the sweaty palms, and racing heart whenever you're in the same vicinity as him? The constant anxiety that you aren't smart enough, good enough or pretty enough to keep the interest of someone like him? I spent so much of my life making fun of how Charlotte and Ava behaved and I thought they were sad and pathetic. I get it now, and I'm ashamed of myself for being so hard on them. I watch Marco's face light up as he rushes towards me and I want to crawl under a rock because I don't feel worthy of that look in his eyes. The one that says he likes me, in spite of my family, and that I make him happy. The pressure of this is so much worse than anything I did in culinary school.

I move towards him in a trance, meeting him in the middle of the front yard. It's not fair for someone to be so good-looking without even trying. Even in a tight, long-sleeved grey t-shirt and worn jeans he looks just as good as he would if he were wearing a tux.

"I'm glad I caught you before you left," he smiles, the dimples in his cheeks making my knees weak.

"What's wrong?" I whisper, hoping he didn't race out here to ask for advice on how to make Uncle Drew stop dropping his pants and showing everyone his balls.

"Nothing's wrong, I just forgot something."

I open my mouth to ask if he forgot to write down the number to Poison Control in case Tyler gets into the nail polish remover again, but before I can take a breath, his hands are cupping my face and his lips are on mine. With my lips still parted to speak, his tongue slides easily into my mouth. All the blood in my body rushes to my nether regions and with every brush of his tongue against mine, I feel myself getting lightheaded. My hands fly to his chest and I grab onto handfuls of his shirt to hold myself steady as he kisses me soft and slow and the world around me disappears. He tastes like peppermint and smells like cookies, and I want to jump into his arms and wrap my legs around his waist. My heart thumps rapidly in my chest as our tongues swirl together until I'm not sure where he begins and I end. Our mouths have become one and have replaced everything in my brain with cheesy romantic poetry and dreamy Jane Austen quotes.

I need to stop this kiss before I turn completely stupid.

I never want this kiss to end and I don't care if it turns me into Uncle Drew.

Marco slowly ends the kiss, gently biting my bottom lip as he pulls his mouth from mine. With my face still cradled in his hands, he presses his forehead to mine and sighs.

"Sorry, I tried to wait until we were alone to do that, but I think hell might freeze over before then," he laughs softly.

"GET A ROOM, YOU WHORES!"

The lust-filled excitement in my body quickly vanishes when I hear Ava yell to us from the limo.

"Wrap it up before you knock her up on the front lawn! Oh, wait…" Ava adds with a loud giggle.

"I should probably go. The drunks are getting restless," I tell him softly, wishing I never had to move and his warm, soft hands never had to drop from my face.

"Be careful," Marco says as his hands slide from my face and down the sides of my neck to rest on my shoulders. "Never take a drink you didn't pour yourself, and if you're being attacked, always scream 'fire' instead of 'help'."

I snicker, unclenching the death grip on his shirt to rest my hands on top of his on my shoulder.

"I'm hanging out with my aunts, sisters, and cousins all night," I remind him.

"You're forgetting I've met those women. You should be more afraid of *them* giving you a roofie and trying to rape you," he responds with a serious expression on his face.

"I'll call you later to make sure you're still alive," I tell him, regrettably taking a step back from him.

He laughs and sticks his hands into the front pocket of his jeans. "Don't worry about me, I'll be fine."

"Hey, Minivan Fuck Nugget! Do me a favor and grab the blow torch, edible underwear, Christmas tree tinsel, and the bag of goldfish from my trunk on your way in," Uncle Drew shouts from the open front door.

"Goldfish, as in goldfish crackers?" Marco yells back.

"Uh, no. Twenty-four *live* goldfish. Why in the world would I have goldfish *crackers* in my trunk? I thought you said he was smart, Molly?" Drew complains before going back inside.

Marco shakes his head and starts backing away from me as I do the same, refusing to take my eyes off of him as I move towards the limo.

"My mom keeps a cookie jar on top of the fridge with bail money in it, just in case," I inform him as my butt bumps against the side of the limo.

"Good to know," he replies with a wave, turning to jog to Drew's car parked in the driveway.

I take my time climbing backwards into the limo, staring at Marco's ass as he leans into the trunk of Uncle Drew's car. After that kiss, there is no way I'm waiting another second when this night is over to be alone with that man. Maybe I can sneak a few shots of liquid courage when no one is looking and have Ava and Charlotte give me some more advice. I don't know the first thing about flirting or seducing a guy, and judging by that stellar kiss, I'm going to need all the skills I can get. It's time for me to consult the experts.

"Don't knock it until you try it; pony play is very erotic," Ava informs the group as I sit on the comfortable leather bench next to Charlotte, closing the door behind me. "The plastic hooves are a little hard to get used to at first, but once you add the tail and the unicorn horn, you really get into it."

Did I say experts? I meant mental patients.

Chapter 16

- Fuck Betty White -

Marco

⟶

"SORRY, NO TAKE backs. You already said you'd kill Demi Moore, marry Taylor Swift, and fuck Betty White," Drew reminds me.

"I blurted it out without thinking!"

"Hide yo wives, hide yo grannies!" Drew cheers.

"My wife is going to be your child's grandmother. Do you want to fuck her too? Or are you more selective with your grandmother fucking?" Jim asks.

Oh, for the love of all that is holy...playing Fuck, Marry, Kill seemed like a much better idea than being forced to watch that weird as shit turtle porn video again. Who knew turtles were so vocal during orgasm?

"I do not want to sleep with any grandmothers!" I protest.

Thankfully, the camera crew decided to pack it up and go home after Drew tried to get the meerkat to eat live goldfish out of the edible underwear he put on, and none of this is being recorded for the world to see.

"Alright, I've got *Friendship Rocks*, *Call of the Cutie*, and *Dog and Pony Show*. Which one will it be, boys?" Tyler asks, walking into the room with three DVDs in his hands.

"Ooooh, definitely *Dog and Pony Show*," Drew says with smile and a nod.

"We are not watching that stupid My Little Pony shit," Jim tells Tyler, grabbing the DVDs from his hands and chucking them across the room.

"Wait, MLP movies? Wow, that is NOT what I thought *Dog and Pony Show* was," Drew mutters.

"What the hell else are we going to do, then? Thanks to Drew we don't have a meerkat to play with anymore," Tyler complains.

"How the hell was I supposed to know? Jesus, you give a meerkat one sip of beer and you'd think I tried to poison him with the way that stick-up-his-ass zookeeper acted," Drew mutters.

"I'm pretty sure beer IS poisonous to an animal like that," Carter tells him.

"Excuse me for not being up-to-date on my meerkat knowledge," Drew grumbles. "It's not my fault the little guy liked it and wanted more. He was thirsty after all of that underwear candy. Fucking Tom Brady…"

Drew notices all of us staring at him in confusion and he shrugs. "I didn't feel like Sunshine Wiener Schnitzel was a good name for him, so I changed it to Tom Brady. It's always Tom Brady's fault."

We sit here for a few quiet minutes, staring into our bottles of beer.

"This is pathetic. Are we really this old that we don't know how to throw a good bachelor party anymore?" Carter asks.

"It's all Liz's fault for not letting me have strippers," Drew complains. "Stupid strippers and their stupid snail trails…"

"I think we should watch some student/teacher porn in honor of Marco and Molly," Tyler suggests with a wag of his eyebrows. "I bet you could tell us a few stories about bending that one over your desk and spanking her with a ruler, am I right?"

He nudges Jim with his elbow and gives him a smirk.

"I bet I could tell a story about how I shoved my entire arm up your ass, how about that?" Jim replies.

"Awww, no fair!" Drew complains. "I was going to tell that story later. No matter what anyone tells you, KY Tingling Jelly shouldn't go in your ass. I was shitting fire for three days, let me tell you."

I quickly chug the rest of my beer, hoping the alcohol kicks in soon and erases everything from my mind that happened tonight. Well, except the kiss. Damn, that fucking kiss almost made me come in my pants. As soon as Molly walked out the door all I could think about was kissing her. Shit, from the moment I open my eyes every morning until I fall asleep, that's all I think about. I couldn't stand going one more second without knowing what kissing her would be like instead of just dreaming about it. I ran outside as fast as I could and I couldn't wipe the goofy grin from my face seeing her still standing next to the limo.

God, those lips. That tongue. That fucking mouth that tasted like sweet, crisp apples, just like I wondered. I think I might've been better off not knowing. Now that my suspicions are confirmed, I'm never going to be able to get rid of my hard-on. I want to strip her naked and taste every inch of her skin. I want to bury myself inside of her until we both lose our minds. I want to hear her scream my name and claw at my back until...

"What are your immediate future plans with my daughter?" Jim asks, pulling me out of my horny thoughts and hoping I didn't mutter any of them out loud.

"Um...to spend time with her, and...uh, yeah. Hang out and stuff," I tell him uncomfortably. I don't really think he'd appreciate me telling him all the ways I want to fuck his daughter.

"I mean, are you planning on making an honest woman out of her and proposing?" he questions. "It's the least you could do after you defiled her and ruined her for any other man."

Wow, really? And here I thought Jim was starting to take a liking to me. What the hell is wrong with my dick and sperm that he thinks it would defile Molly? I'll have you know my sperm is very nice, and I've gotten quite a few compliments on how appealing to the eye my penis is.

"She's not defiled," I grumble. "The Desoto sperm is filled with all sorts of good stuff."

"My sperm is filled with pineapple. I eat two pineapples a day leading up to blow job day," Drew comments.

"She's twenty years old and just finished college. What man is going to want a woman tied down with another man's child?" Jim asks, folding his arms and glaring at me.

"Um, how about me, the father of the child?"

The fake child, but whatever. I know I freaked out in the beginning and couldn't imagine being with her if she were having someone else's kid, but things have changed since then. If Molly really were pregnant by someone else, it wouldn't matter. I'd find a way to deal with the knowledge that she had someone else's gross spooge all up in her, and I'd deal with everything that comes along with helping her raise that child, because in the end, she's still the same girl I've wanted for two years. She's still Molly and even if we don't know each other well, even if tonight was the first time I kissed her and there's still so much I need to learn about her, she's gotten into my heart and under my skin, and I'm not going to let anything ruin that.

"At least Gavin has the good sense to wrap his dick up to prevent shit like this, because he and Charlotte are smart and they don't want kids," Jim informs me.

"That's what you think," I laugh, realizing immediately I should have kept my mouth shut.

Everyone looks at me funny and I quickly blurt out the first thing I can think of.

"I mean, I wrap my shit up too, but accidents still happen. I even double-bag it. That's right, I wear two condoms so suck it!" I tell them. "But you know what, sperm is conniving and vindictive, and if they want to chew their way through two layers of latex, they will sure as shit gnaw through that stuff and give you the finger while their little spermy tails are moving them right along. Fucking sperm and their spermy tails…"

Realizing I sound like a complete moron, I slam my empty bottle on top of the coffee table and grab another beer from the ice bucket in the middle. I down the entire thing, wiping my hand across my mouth when I finish.

Tyler decides to break the tension in the room by walking over to Jim and getting down on one knee in front of him.

"Jim, give me your hand," he states, holding his palm out.

"What the fuck are you doing?" Jim complains.

"Just give me your hand, I need to ask you something."

Jim looks at him in disgust, and then smacks Tyler's hand away.

"Fine," Tyler huffs. "We'll do it your way."

He clears his throat and lifts his chin, resting his hands on top of Jim's knees.

"Jim, I'd like to officially ask for your daughter's hand in marriage," Tyler tells him confidently.

"Fuck, I think I'm going to cry," Drew mumbles with a sniffle, rubbing his fists against his eyes.

"Get the fuck off your knee and remove your hands from my legs," Jim growls.

"I'm sorry, Jim, but I need to do this the right way. I want you to see that I will spend as much time on my knees as it takes to please you."

Drew laughs and holds out his fist for Carter to bump. "Ha ha, that's what she said!"

Jim glares at him and Drew gives him the finger.

"Oh, fuck your face. Like I was the only one thinking it."

"I can't believe you're going to get married," Gavin says quietly. "What happened to bros before hos?"

Tyler snorts. "Really, dude? You're getting married in like, a few weeks. You already made the decision to quit me for a ho so it's time for me to get my own life and my own ho."

Jim snaps his fingers in front of Tyler's face. "Hey, asshole. The hos you're referring to are my daughters."

Gavin and Tyler ignore him and continue with their own weird conversation.

"I didn't quit you, I just asked the love of my life to marry me. I'm sorry if that gets your panties in a twist," Gavin complains.

"I wore Ava's panties ONCE and you were supposed to keep that a secret, fucker!" Tyler yells angrily. "You're my best friend, and in some circumstances you will come first, but not when it has to do with marriage, which you should understand. I'm sorry, but I'm picking the ho this time."

Jim punches Tyler in the arm and pulls back his fist to do it again when Tyler holds up his hands in surrender. "I'm sorry, I'm sorry! Ho is a term of endearment, I swear!"

"Whatever," Gavin grumbles. "It's not like I'd marry you anyway. It just would have been nice to be asked."

Tyler gives him a smile, pounds his fist against his heart and points at Gavin. "You're my boy, Blue Balls."

Gavin does the same with his fist and Tyler turns back around on his knees to face Jim.

"So, do I have your permission to marry Ava? I've already made the calculations and I only need to sell two more ounces of weed to be able to buy her the ring she wants, and since I have roughly thirty ounces heading to Madelyn's house—"

"Twenty-five," Drew interrupts. "Sorry, that shit is full of sorcery. It kept calling my name and I couldn't resist. Speaking of that, you're out of Cheetos and Fruity Pebbles."

Jim sighs, shoving Tyler's hands off his knees. "You didn't knock her up, did you? Do I have to get my shotgun?"

Tyler quickly shakes his head. "No, sir. We are extremely careful. I always wear a condom, and when I don't, I pull out faster than a roadrunner speeding away from dynamite. No sperm has touched your daughter's ovaries, I can promise you that."

Tyler looks over his shoulder and gives me a smirk. If he wasn't so much like a girl and hitting girls is frowned upon, I'd punch him right in the face.

"Get off your damn knees, dumbass. I'll let you marry Ava as long as you never use the words *sperm* and *your daughter's ovaries* in a sentence again. Ever. If you even think those words in my presence, I will kill you and make it look like an accident," Jim threatens.

Tyler pushes himself up from the floor and leans in to hug Jim, who immediately holds his hand up and presses it against Tyler's face to hold him off.

"Stop trying to hug me."

"Can I call you dad, then?" Tyler asks, his words muffled behind Jim's palm.

"Not if you want to keep your dick from being shoved down your throat."

My phone vibrates in my back pocket and I quickly pull it out and step out of the room while Drew runs over to Jim and Tyler and tries to make a group hug happen.

When I get out the hallway, I look down and smile when I see a text from Molly.

Send me a penis of yur picture :)

I laugh when I see she screwed up her words and must have managed to sneak some alcohol at the party, and then my laughter dies when I realize what it is she's trying to ask. She wants me to send her a picture of my penis. My heart starts racing and my palms start sweating as I run down the hallway to the closest bathroom.

Flipping on the light switch and locking the door behind me, I turn in circles trying to figure out where I can stand that will give me the best lighting. It's not very bright in here and there are too many dark shadows. This is not going to make my penis look the best that he can be, dammit! I need a spotlight or a bulb with a minimum of seventy-five watts for optimum photographic beauty.

Realizing I'm not going to get what I need in here, I see another door by the shower. Walking across the large bathroom, I open the door and see that it leads into a bedroom. Poking my head into the room, I see exactly what I need in the far corner. I move quickly across the carpeted floor, unbuttoning my jeans as I go. I don't have a lot of time to do this before the guys will wonder where I am.

I close my eyes and play back the kiss out in the yard, remembering the feel of Molly's tongue against mine and the soft little moans she made into my mouth. I need a chubby for this photo to really impress Molly and a chubby is what I'm now holding in my hands thanks to that quick little trip down memory lane.

It would be great if I could say that my girlfriend's father didn't walk in on me two minutes later sitting at his wife's make-up table with the bright lights lining the mirror highlighting my dick in one hand while I held my cell phone pointed down at it in another, staring at a framed photo of his wife which I swear was a total accident, but that would be a lie.

While I apply pressure to my bloody, split lip and wonder if I still have the ability to eat solid foods, Drew sits down next to me on the floor of the bedroom. He hands me a bag of frozen peas to hold against my eye, giving me a sympathetic look.

"Don't feel bad, dude, we've all spanked it a few times to a picture of Liz, she's hot."

Fucking Betty White. I blame her for all of this.

Chapter 17

— Lips, Tongue, Penis, Suck —
Molly

"OH, MY GOD! Are you drunk?!" Charlotte whispers hysterically.

I sway a little bit as the room spins, grabbing onto the edge of the bar in the kitchen of the ginormous suite we've been celebrating in.

"Bugger off, you daft cow!"

"Why are you speaking with a British accent? What the hell is happening right now?" Charlotte complains, grabbing my arms and giving me a little shake.

"I'm practicing for when I travel the world. I want to fit in with the locals in London. Top o' the mornin' to ya, eh?!"

Charlotte shakes her head at me, all three of them. "That was Irish and I think Canadian. How much alcohol have you snuck?"

I hold up one hand and spread out all five fingers.

"Seven many," I mumble, trying to focus on my fingers and wondering why we have so many. Why five and not four? Do we really need a ring finger? It holds no purpose aside from giving us a place to put rings.

"You're lucky mom and Aunt Claire haven't come back yet from apologizing to the strippers and aren't witnessing this right now," she mutters.

"Why aren't *you* out there with them?" Ava asks, coming up beside us. "You're the one who puked all over the poor guy's stomach."

Charlotte rolls her eyes and puts her hands on her hips. "I already apologized to him and offered to pay for a new thong. He was just so greasy and he kept slapping his flaccid junk against my knee, and it reminded me of bologna and I couldn't help it."

Luckily Charlotte was able to play off her stripper-inducing puke by batting her eyelashes and giggling about being soooooo drunk. I had already snuck into the bathroom for the tenth time to take a shot by the time the three hip-thrusting, dick-dangling men showed up so watching her vomit made me run right to the bathroom and purge the demons. Everyone had a good laugh about how my "baby" didn't like strippers.

"WOOOHOOO bring back the naked men! Charlotte, why aren't you drinking?!" Grandma Madelyn yells, dancing her way past us and sloshing her drink all over the floor.

Charlotte holds up her flask of water and takes a sip, which makes Grandma throw her arms up in the air and shout again, throwing the contents of her drink all over the wall in front of her.

"Jesus, who knew Grandma was like a Gremlin? You feed her booze after midnight and she turns into crazy drunk monster," Charlotte mutters.

"So, did you text Marco? What did you say?" Ava asks, looking away from grandma as she gets up on the coffee table and starts thrusting her hips to the loud music blaring through the sound system in the living room.

"I said I'd like a spot of tea while I get snookered," I giggle.

"Why do you have a British accent? Charlotte, why does she have a British accent?" Ava asks, looking away from me to question our sober sister.

Charlotte shrugs. "It appears our sister turns British when she gets drunk."

"Oh, are you guys talking about foreign languages?" Aunt Jenny asks as she stumbles over to us, drinking the last bit of martini from her glass before smacking it down on the bar behind me.

"I don't get why we can't just all speak American," She complains.

"You've got British and Alaskan and Canadian and Texan…why do we need all these different languages mucking everything up?"

Charlotte puts her arm around Aunt Jenny and gives her a squeeze. "Oh, Aunt Jenny. You always know how to make me feel like the smartest person in the room."

Aunt Jenny beams at Charlotte and gives her a sloppy kiss on the cheek. "I love you too, Charlotte!"

The three of us watch her stumble over to Grandma and get on top of the coffee table with her.

"Alright, back to the important matter at hand," Ava says, turning back to face me. "What did you say to Marco? Did you text him what I told you to?"

I pull my phone out of my back pocket and hand it to her without a word. She presses a few buttons and her eyes widen in shock.

"You asked him for a picture of his penis?!" she shouts.

"I tried to do what you said and tell him to come up here because I got us a hotel room, but I couldn't figure out how to type all those words," I tell her with a shrug.

"Did he send the picture? Let me see!"

Charlotte leans over Ava's shoulder and we both stare at her.

"What? I'm getting married, I'm not dead. Marco is hot and I'm sure he has an equally hot penis," Charlotte explains.

"Sorry, no Italian sausage for you tonight, Char. But he did send a close-up picture of a bloody lip, which is a little confusing," Ava tells us, turning the phone around for me to see.

"Shit. Did dad beat up his face?!" I yell, trying not to sway so I can get a better look at the photo. "Oh, no. His poor, pretty face. I really like that face."

Ava turns the phone back around and starts rapidly punching buttons.

"What are you doing? Are you telling him to send the picture penis again?" I ask, leaning forward to see what she's typing.

"Forget about the penis picture, you drunk slut. I'm doing what you were supposed to do and telling him to come up to the hotel."

My phone makes a *whooshing* sound, signaling that she sent it. She sets it down on the counter and walks around the bar, grabbing a glass from one of the cupboards and filling it up with water. She slides it across the counter to me and points at it.

"Chug it. Time to sober up, bitch."

I grab the glass and drink, half of it dribbling down my chin.

"I don't think this is a good idea. Should she really try and seduce him when she's drunk?" Charlotte asks as I slam the empty glass down and ask for a refill.

"She needs to be a little drunk or she'll chicken out. Some liquid courage is always good the first time you touch a penis," Ava announces, sliding another full glass of water towards me.

"Hey, I've touched a penis before. It was the size of a piece of Pez candy, but it was still a living, breathing penis," I inform them, bringing the glass up to my mouth.

"That doesn't count. Quinn yanked your hand away as soon as you touched it. Haven't I always told you guys that it's never a good idea to have sex with a virgin?" Ava sighs. "They're so wound up with years of pent-up sperm they'll blow their load if the wind changes direction. Always go with someone who has experience."

The water starts churning in my stomach and I quickly put the glass down.

"Marco has experience," I whisper nervously. "And he's older. He knows what he's doing, and I've only touched a Pez Penis. What the fuck am I doing?!"

Charlotte smacks my cheek, grabs both of my arms, and turns me to face her. "Snap out of it, woman! There is no instruction manual for this shit. No one knows what they're doing. You just go with the flow and do what feels right."

I nod even though everything she's saying just makes me more nervous. Why isn't there an instruction manual? Sex For Partial Virgins 101.

The ding of my cell phone sounds from the counter, and I watch as Ava picks it up and smiles.

"Buckle up, slut. There's a penis with your name on it headed this way. He was already headed down here to see if you needed rescuing so he's right around the corner. There's also a partially melted bag of frozen peas and a raw steak coming as well, whatever that means," Ava states. "I really hope Uncle Drew hasn't been teaching him anything weird tonight."

My eyes widen and I whip my head back to face Charlotte.

"What if he wants to have sex with the steak? What if he wants to use the peas on me? Is that a thing? Like some sort of tiny Ben Wa balls or something?" I ask her in a panic. "I knew I never should have left him alone with Uncle Drew! Now he's got ideas. Weird, kinky ideas that involve frozen food and I don't know how to have regular sex, let alone frozen food sex!"

My scalp starts to get itchy and sweaty and I can't remember if I put on deodorant before I left the house. At least I put on good underwear.

"Speaking of Ben Wa balls, did you hear Aunt Jenny had to go to the emergency room AGAIN last week because she got them stuck up in her?" Ava laughs. "Uncle Drew asked if they could have their own parking space. I guess after the nurses spent so much time watching Aunt Jenny waddle across the parking lot while doing lunges, the doctor submitted the request to the hospital board for safety reasons."

I whimper and my lip starts to quiver.

"I don't want to go to the emergency room because frozen peas get stuck in my vagina!" I wail.

"Oh, for the love of God," Charlotte mutters. "Ava, stop freaking her out. Molly, no one's putting frozen peas up your who-ha. No one says you have to have sex with him tonight. You two need to be alone. Maybe start with something simple. Get to know his penis. See what he likes and take it slow."

I look at Ava to see if she agrees and find her nodding in approval.

"Slow is good. Try a blowjob. It's pretty impossible to screw those up. As long as your mouth is on his dick, he's not going to care about anything else."

Okay, I can do this. I can put my mouth on a penis. I've seen porn and I know how it's done. In theory.

"Why is it called a blowjob? Don't you just suck on it? There's no blowing involved, right?" I ask.

"Since you're a beginner, just stick with the sucking for now. When you graduate to the advanced class, we'll discuss the use of popsicles and lube that heats up when you blow on it. For now, just focus on the basics. Lips, tongue, penis, suck. The end," Ava explains.

"Lips, tongue, penis, suck," I repeat.

"I thought it was lick, slam, suck?" Grandma asks, dancing by us again and overhearing what I said. "Have I been doing tequila shots wrong tonight?"

She turns away from us when the hotel door opens and my mom and Aunt Claire walk back inside.

"Girls, you didn't send those strippers away, did you?" Grandma shouts across the room. "I need to borrow one of those boy's wieners to lips, tongue, penis and suck with my next tequila shot. I guess that's what the kids are doing these days."

There's a loud knock at the door, saving mom and Aunt Claire from trying to respond to Grandma. Aunt Claire moves to the side while my mom opens the door, holding it wide so Marco can come in.

"Oooooh, forget the stripper! I'll use *his* penis!" Grandma announces.

"You better get over there and get him to your room before Grandma ruins him," Charlotte whispers. "There is no coming back from false teeth falling out on your dick during a blow-job."

She pats me on the back and Ava gives me a thumb's up. "You got this. Embrace your inner slut."

I can do this. I can totally do this.

"Did someone order a hot piece of man-meat?" Aunt Claire shouts, sliding her hand around Marco's elbow and leading him into the room.

Mustering up as much confidence as I can, I raise my hand and smile.

"That would be me. Looks like my delivery came in thirty minutes or less."

Aunt Claire deposits Marco in front of me, grabbing Charlotte's arm and waving Ava over to join them as they head into the living room area.

I look up into Marco's face and I gasp.

"Holy shit! You have a black eye!"

Reaching my hand up, I gently touch the purple area on his upper cheekbone, jerking my hand away when he winces and gasps.

"Oh, no, your lip," I mutter, my fingers tracing over the crusted blood on his bottom lip.

The picture Ava showed me on my phone didn't come close to how bad it looks in person. His poor, perfect lip that rocked my world with that kiss earlier is now out of commission.

"It's okay. It looks worse than it is," he tells me, placing his hands on my hips and pulling me closer. "Just promise me if your dad asks you to search my place for pictures of your mom that you'll ignore him and not ask any questions."

I have no idea what he's talking about and I don't care. I'm sad I won't be getting any more kisses from him tonight, but that just makes what I'm about to do easier. No kisses means I won't be distracted and I won't attempt to waste time or try to chicken out before getting to the good stuff.

I'm putting Marco's penis in my mouth tonight and nothing is going to stop me.

Chapter 18

- Hairball -

Marco

THE DOOR CLOSES behind Molly and I watch her stalk towards me, looking so confident and beautiful that I almost can't breathe. It's deathly quiet in this room, especially compared to the one we just left filled with drunk women screaming and dancing on tables and loud, techno music that made my ears bleed. It's too quiet and I can hear my heart pounding in my chest. I don't want Molly to know I'm nervous to be alone with her. I want her to see me as strong and confident, not a pussy with sweaty palms. I was already on my way down here to see if she needed saved from bachelorette party hell, and as soon as I got her text telling me she got us a hotel room, I knew it was time for me to come clean about Alfanso D. Even if nothing happens in this room tonight, I can't keep this from her any longer. It makes me sick to my stomach to keep lying to her whenever she talks about him. Me, him, me…what the fuck ever. I've never felt this way about anyone before and I don't want to fuck things up before they even really begin. She deserves better and on top of that, Rosa liked Molly so much after dinner the other night that she told me if I didn't tell her soon, she'd do it herself and it wouldn't be pretty.

"It's so quiet in here," I mumble lamely, trying to fill the silence and build up the courage to come clean.

Molly doesn't say a word, just walks right up to me and shoves her hands against my chest, sending me flying backwards. I bounce on top of the king-sized bed, and she jumps on top of me and straddles my thighs. I reach up to grab her hips and she quickly stops me, wrapping her hands around my wrists and pulling my arms above my head as she leans forward. Her tits press against my chest and her hair forms a curtain around our faces as she looks down at me.

"Keep your hands up here and don't move them until I say so," she demands, letting go of my wrists and sliding down my body.

"Holy shit this is hot," I whisper as she trails her hands down my chest and stomach, stopping when she gets to the button of my jeans. Maybe I'll wait until after she finishes whatever she's planning to do to me to tell her the truth. I mean, what's another couple of minutes in the grand scheme of things?

"Just so there's no confusion, we don't have to do anything tonight. We can talk or watch TV or do whatever you want," I tell her.

I will legit cry like a baby if she stops, but it's impossible for me to be an asshole with her. I didn't come over here with any expectations aside from finally being alone with her. Sure, I'm a dude and I always want sex, but I don't expect it, especially with Molly.

"Watch TV or let me put my mouth on your penis, your choice," she replies.

Her fingers pause on the zipper of my jeans and my jaw drops open as I stare at her while she waits for me to remember how to speak.

"Penis mouth," I mumble. "Definitely penis mouth."

She nods, her hands going back to work as she unzips my pants. "Wise decision."

I watch in awe as she sits up on her knees, swiftly yanking my jeans over my hips and to the middle of my thighs. She scoots her body down my legs until she gets to my knees, bending forward over my legs until her face is right above the crotch of my boxer briefs. I can feel her warm breath puff against the thin cotton material and it's like a mating call to my dick. He jerks and twitches and struts his stuff like a peacock showing its feathers.

"I'm serious, Molly. We really don't have to do anything. I know you've been...uuuhhhh...drinking and I don't want to take...holy fuck…advantage of you," I tell her, tripping over my words, moaning and cursing when she slips her fingers in the waistband of my briefs and tugs them down until my penis is on full display.

"I think you're confused," she says softly, her breath warming my dick, making it jerk with excitement again. "I'm taking advantage of *you*. Just close your eyes and don't move."

I do as she says, afraid she'll change her mind if I don't follow her orders. My head flops back onto the bed and I close my eyes and hold my breath, waiting for the heavenly feel of her lips on my cock.

Waiting.

Waiting.

Still waiting.

I open one eye and lift my head to see her staring down at my penis with a look of concentration on her face. Maybe the women I've been with lied. Maybe I don't have a pleasing penis. What if it's ugly? What if Molly is repulsed by it? I knew I should have just taken the damn picture in the bathroom and sent it immediately. At least then she would have been prepared and had time to get used to it. Damn my need for good lighting!

"Everything okay?" I ask, chuckling nervously.

She nods without looking up. "Just getting to know your penis. Charlotte suggested it so I'm giving it a try."

I should be embarrassed that she was talking about my penis with her sister, but I spent the evening telling her father how good my sperm was and then had to explain to him I wasn't masturbating to a picture of his wife in their bedroom while he beat the shit out of me. She can discuss my penis with whomever she likes.

"Take your time. Whatever you need," I tell her, dropping my head back to the bed and relaxing now that I know she isn't disappointed that I have an ugly penis.

"Feel free to…holy mother of God," I mutter with a groan when I feel her hand wrap around the base of my cock.

I try to come up with something more to say, something hot and sexy like, *Yeah, that's it baby, harder,* but as soon as I open my mouth, her warm, wet lips are sliding over the head of my cock and all I can manage is, "Fuuuuuuuuck-shit-damn-good-God-almighty-mouth-penis."

I've had plenty of blowjobs over the years. Some good ones and some bad ones, but I can't for the life of me remember anything about them once I feel Molly's mouth on me. I can't even remember my name or what day it is when she starts bobbing her head up and down, sucking on me and swirling her tongue around the head of my dick each time she gets to the tip.

Grabbing handfuls of the blanket above my head, I hold on for dear life when her hand tightens around the base of my cock and she moves it up and down the length along with her mouth. Each time she goes down, she takes me in her mouth a little further until I see stars behind my closed eyes and I'm a little embarrassed at how fast my orgasm starts to approach. I'm pretty proud of the fact that I can last as long as a woman needs and I've never been a two-pump-chump, even as a teenager, but I've never had a woman's mouth on my dick that I fantasized about for two years and it's overwhelming. Pushing aside the shame of my weakness, I realize I should warn her I'm dangerously close to coming. I learned my lesson back in high school with Michelle Johnson, but I was a rookie then, figuring if she was going to put her mouth of my dick, she should know the only possible outcome would be me having an orgasm, and therefore she should expect it to happen at any moment, moving away if needed. I kept my lips sealed and started coming in her mouth with a smile on my face. She jerked away from my dick mid-orgasm and the mistake of not warning her resulted in screaming, crying, and jizz in the eye. Michelle wasn't too happy either.

As soon as I feel the head of my dick touch the back of Molly's throat, my balls tighten, my legs start to tingle and I open my mouth to give her the required warning in case she's not a swallower.

Before I can say anything, I hear her gag and the words die on my tongue. One might think the sound of a chick gagging on your dick would be a turn-off, but one would be wrong. Feeling bad that I'm disobeying one of her rules, I open my eyes and lift my head to watch. There's nothing hotter than watching a girl go to town on your dick.

Unfortunately, her long hair is hanging down over her face and I can't get a good view of her mouth, but at least I can imagine what it looks like as I feel her take me deeper, another small gagging sound coming from her.

I smile and give myself a mental pat on the back for having such a monster dick that it makes her gag. I'm so busy giving myself a high five and enjoying the way her tongue feels sliding up and down my cock that it takes me a second to realize she's still gagging. There's a musical rhythm to it now—*slurp, gag, slurp, gag, slurp, gag.* I admire her determination and her refusal to quit, and it almost makes me wish I wasn't seconds away from coming so I could make it last all night.

Then, something horrific happens. It's so horrific that I should look away, but it's like driving up on a car accident and slowing down to see if there are any bodies lying in the road. It's wrong and you feel dirty for doing it, but it's impossible not to stare. My eyes are glued to Molly's body and I can't force myself to look at something else. Anything else, for fuck's sake.

She gags harder and louder and her back bows while she continues trying to swallow my dick. The sounds coming from her mouth immediately stop being hot and move right into something out of a scary movie. She's choking and gagging so violently that her back keeps arching with every sound she makes until she starts to resemble a cat trying to cough up a fur ball. I've had a few pet cats over the years. I've watched them stop what they're doing to choke and heave and bob their head until they manage to yak up whatever was stuck in their throat. That's what is happening right at this moment and there's nothing I can do to stop it.

I'm so conflicted. Molly's giving me a blow-job.

My dick is making her choke like a cat trying to bring up a wet, slimy ball of hair.

But Molly's giving me a blow-job!

"Hey, are you okay? It's fine, you can stop," I mutter, my ears ringing with the sounds of her retching and my eyes glued to her back as it continues to spasm.

She shakes her head *no* as much as she can with my dick still stuffed in her mouth and works through the pain like a trooper. I'm ashamed to say that even with how horrified I am right now, my dick is still hard as a rock and my orgasm continues teetering close the edge.

She tries to speak, but her voice comes out garbled and muffled. It sounds like she's saying "I'm not a quitter," but it's impossible to know for sure since she refuses to remove her mouth from my dick and tries to say the words again.

The vibrations from her voice are like a bolt of electricity shooting right to my balls and while she does her best impression of a hairball yacking cat straddling my thighs, I come so hard and so quickly it takes the breath from my lungs and I lose the ability to think. My hips jerk and my mouth opens wide with a pathetic, high-pitch squeak instead of a manly shout as I experience the best, and possibly weirdest, orgasm of my life.

My happiness at learning the girl of my dreams is in fact a swallower is short-lived. With the pleasure of my orgasm still floating through my dick and balls, Molly's back arches one last time and she finally gets that pesky hairball up. Or the gallon of vodka she must have downed before I got here. For the first time in my life, and hopefully the only time, a girl pukes on my dick.

Oh, Jesus Christ! Not only is there puke on my dick, there is puke filled with jizz on my dick. I don't give a fuck if it's my own jizz, it's jizz-puke and it's ON MY FUCKING DICK!

She finally removes her mouth from me as the last of the puke trickles out onto my penis and I prepare myself to give her as many words of comfort as I can so she isn't embarrassed because Jesus fucking Christ she just puked on my cock!

Don't worry about me and my dick covered in vomit mixed with mucusy spooge. It's fine; it's totally fine that I can feel it dripping down my balls and into my ass crack. I need to play it cool or she'll never want to put her mouth on my penis again.

Molly quickly sits up on my legs and drags the back of her hand across her mouth. I give her a second to compose herself and pretend like the puke sliding down my hips and between my legs is just warm water. Slimy, jizzy water. It's fine, puke washes off of balls, no biggie.

As long as Molly is okay, I can handle pukey balls.

She finally lifts her head to look at me and I give her a small smile.

"It's okay, no big deal," I reassure her.

Without a word, she slides off my lap and crawls up to the top of the bed, flopping face-first into the pile of pillows.

I watch her quietly for a few minutes and she doesn't move.

"Molly? Are you okay?"

Instead of getting an answer, I hear a tiny little snore and then the deep sounds of her breathing.

As carefully as I can, I scoot myself to the edge of the bed, trying to keep the puke contained to my lap as I contort my body and quickly shuffle to the bathroom to shower. Once I'm cleaned off, I wrap a towel around my waist and strip the covers out from under Molly's passed out body. I toss them in the corner of the room and grab the extra blanket from the top shelf of the closet, crawling into bed next to her. Turning off the lamp on the bedside table, I unfold the blanket to cover us both. Gently turning her body to the side so I can press myself against her back, I wrap my arms around her waist and pull her snugly against me.

Closing my eyes, I nuzzle my nose into her hair and breathe her in. Partially because I love the way she smells, but mostly because it masks the smell of vomit lurking in the air. Maybe I should be freaked out that my first sexual encounter with Molly ended with her puking on my dick, with said dick still in her mouth. I'm sure any other guy would have left her alone in this hotel room and gotten the fuck out of dodge, but I'm not just any guy. I'm a sick fuck and I don't care if my balls smell like puke for the next couple of days. I don't even care if my jizz going down her throat was the cause of her upchuck instead of the booze she drank. I'll let her cough up a hairball on my dick any time, as long as she still wants to put her mouth on it again after tonight.

I drift off to sleep with a smile on my face that my night ended better than I thought it would after Molly's dad introduced me to his fists.

Who knew vomit balls would trump a black eye and a bloody lip?

Chapter 19

— Poop Sex —
Molly

"**A**RE YOU EVEN listening to me?" I whisper angrily, peeling back the curtain just enough to make sure mom is still busy talking to the seamstress.

"Molly, I don't have time to hear the dick puking story again. I have bigger problems right now," Charlotte complains, huffing and grunting as she tries to suck everything in as hard as she can as I go back to trying to zip her into her wedding dress.

"I threw up all over the first penis I ever put in my mouth!" I whisper-shout angrily, planting my feet wider and tugging on the zipper as hard as I can. "Does that not sound like a huge fucking problem to you?"

It's been two weeks since the night I became the Incredible Dick Puking Molly, and I've tried to get Charlotte to help me since then and she's brushed me off every time. It's bad enough I passed out right after it happened and Marco had to clean up my puke by himself. It's even worse that I woke up the next morning feeling like I'd been run over by a truck with only a vague memory of what had occurred the previous night. Even the feel of Marco's arms holding me and how good it felt to have him curled up around me couldn't stop the feeling of dread in the pit of my stomach, knowing something horrible happened even if I couldn't remember everything. Marco tried to pretend like everything was fine, but not even his hot body wrapped in just a towel could distract me from the overwhelming smell of puke in the room. After twenty minutes of me arguing with him to tell me what happened, he finally did and I immediately wished I'd ignored the puke smell and let my brain keep what I did a nice little secret locked away forever.

"Maybe the zipper is broken. That's probably what it is, just a broken zipper," Charlotte mumbles.

"The zipper isn't broken, tubby. How is this possible when you're only like five minutes pregnant? How does this dress not fit when you've been puking every day since the stick turned pink?" I complain, immediately regretting my use of the puking word since it just makes me remember what I did the first time I had a penis in my mouth.

"Shut the fuck up, dick-bag!" she yells through clenched teeth. "You call me tubby one more time and I will punch you in the throat!"

The curtain slides open and Ava sticks her head in the dressing room. "Everything okay in here? Why is it taking so long for you to put on a fucking dress?"

I drop my hands from the zipper and back away from Charlotte. There is no way that zipper is going to budge.

"Fatty here doesn't fit into her wedding dress anymore," I tell Ava.

Charlotte's arm flies back and her forearm smacks against my throat. I start choking and wrap my hands around my neck, giving Charlotte a dirty look.

"I warned you," Charlotte growls, returning my dirty look as she stares at me over her shoulder.

"You told me not to call you tubby, you didn't say anything about fatty, you fatty-fat-ass-dick-head," I growl back in between coughs.

"You seriously can't zip the dress?" Ava questions, stepping inside the small room and pulling the curtain closed behind her.

She steps forward and tries to zip it herself, giving up after a few hard tugs.

"Nope, not gonna happen. This size two no longer fits your size eight ass," Ava informs our sister. "Maybe you should have eased up on that entire box of Twinkies you inhaled for breakfast this morning."

Charlotte stomps her foot and whirls around, the dress billowing out around her as she turns. It really is a beautiful dress and she looks stunning. From the front.

"They're the only things that I can keep down so shut the fuck up!"

The curtain slides back again and this time, Aunt Claire pokes her head in. "They're getting a little stingy with the free champagne out here, can we speed things along?"

Charlotte quickly moves in front of me so the huge gap in the back of her dress can't be seen in the full-length mirror behind her.

"This isn't a bar, Aunt Claire. I think five glasses is enough," Charlotte tells her.

"I had cancer! Have you no shame?" she argues.

"There is a statute of limitations on how long you can keep using that to make us feel bad," Ava says. "It's not going to work because you want more booze."

Aunt Claire gives her the finger. "You're mean and I don't like you very much right now."

"Why am I the only adult in this room?" Ava complains with a roll of her eyes.

"I *am* acting like an adult, you're just being a meanie doo-doo head," Aunt Claire states, sticking out her tongue as she pulls her head back and yanks the curtain closed.

"We'll just tell them you've been stress-eating," Ava says with a shrug. "Weddings are stressful, it's easily believable. It's not like they didn't witness you inhaling that box of snack cakes in the car. Oh, wait. They didn't because you hunkered down in the back seat and made Molly hold the box and pretend like she was the one eating them."

I nod in agreement. Not my finest hour pretending to chew every time our mother looked in the rearview mirror or Aunt Claire turned around to look at the three of us.

"Oh, just so you know, Marco hasn't said a word to Tyler about the night of the great penis purge," Ava tells me while Charlotte reaches behind her to try and zip up her dress on her own. "Don't worry, I didn't tell him, I just nonchalantly asked what they talked about when he got home from grabbing a beer with Marco last night. If Tyler knew, it would have been the first thing out of his mouth since that man cannot keep a secret. Not only can your man handle a little vomit on his junk, he doesn't gossip about it. You've got yourself a keeper."

I close my eyes in mortification as she laughs, refusing to give her a high-five when she holds her hand up in the air.

Even though I wanted to lock myself in my room and never face Marco again after the night in the hotel room, he made that impossible to do. He wouldn't let one day go by without seeing me, and as much as I wanted to hide from him so I never had to think about what I did, I wanted to be around him even more. He came up to work every day and took me to lunch, he planned dates and things for us to do almost every night and he never let more than a few hours go by without calling to tell me he just wanted to hear the sound of my voice. My two year crush and only a handful of weeks with him has shot me right up the hill of *falling* in love with him to tumbling over the edge and head over heels, madly, passionately *in* love with him.

"What am I going to do if I can never give him another blowjob? What kind of a relationship can we possibly have if I can't put his penis in my mouth without throwing up?" I ask, trying to keep my panic at a minimum before I curl up in the fetal position and cry.

"Stop being a drama queen, for fuck's sake. So you threw up on his dick? Come back to me when you've had accidental anal," Ava says with a sigh. "At least you had the luxury of passing out after you threw up. I couldn't sit down for a week and I was afraid to take a shit for four days."

I grimace and throw my hands up.

"Seriously, you have *got* to stop with the over-sharing," I complain.

"Maybe I should give Gavin anal and then tell him about the baby," Charlotte thinks aloud. "Anal can make anything better, right?"

Ava nods. "Sure. Anal is pretty much the sexual duct tape of the world—it fixes everything. I should put that on a t-shirt."

While Ava ponders her idea, I turn my focus to Charlotte.

"Have you even tried talking to Gavin about kids yet or are you just planning on dropping this huge bomb on him as soon as he says *I do*?" I ask, trying not to sound annoyed.

"You can't rush something like this, Molly. It's a very delicate situation."

Her annoyance comes through loud and clear and it pisses me off.

"Oh, by all means, take your time. In fact, why don't you wait until you go into labor to break the news? I'm having so much fun fucking up my life and having mom and dad upset and disappointed in me instead of enjoying what should be the best time of my life. As long as you're happy, Charlotte, that's all that matters," I bite out sarcastically.

Ava pats me on the back in sympathy and Charlotte immediately bursts into tears.

"I'm so fat and Gavin is going to leave me, and now you hate me and I'm going to be pregnant and alone and this baby is going to hate me for ruining it's life!" she wails.

"Oh, give me a fucking break!" Ava complains. "Turn off the fake waterworks. I am not afraid to punch a pregnant chick so cut that shit out."

Charlotte huffs in annoyance, the tears in her eyes immediately disappearing, proving that Ava was correct and she was faking it. She almost had me feeling sorry for her pathetic ass.

"Jesus, are you even human?" I mumble.

"It's a gift," she shrugs, resuming her struggle to try and zip her dress. "I just imagine someone I love dying in a really horrible way."

"You need to be medicated. If Gavin doesn't dump your ass when you tell him about the baby, he sure as shit will when he figures out you're psychotic," Ava states.

"Your boyfriend can't get it up unless you dress up like Mister Ed so fuck off," Charlotte replies. "I think I've almost got it."

Charlotte pants as she twists and turns with her arms still behind her back. Her face is red and glistening with sweat as she struggles for a few more seconds before dropping her arms and sighing in relief. "I did it!"

She turns to show us, Ava and I sharing a quick look behind her back.

"Yep, you did it!" Ava cheers as Charlotte turns back around with a smile. "You moved the zipper a whole centimeter. Well done, fatty."

Charlotte lunges at Ava and I quickly jump forward, wrapping my arms around her and holding her back while she pulls and struggles and curses.

"You dick-bag-whore-fuck-ass-licking-twat!" Charlotte screams, not even bothering to keep her voice down.

"Fuck right off, you selfish cunt!" Ava yells back.

Charlotte stops struggling and I let out a low whistle.

"Damn, going right for the C U Next Tuesday, huh? That's harsh," I tell her.

Ava shrugs. "It couldn't be helped. Can we call a truce for now and get this shit show over with? Aunt Claire is going to start throwing punches if she goes much longer without champagne."

I drop my arms from around Charlotte and she takes a deep breath for courage. I decide to keep my mouth shut for now and suck this crap up a little longer. I'm pissed and I'm frustrated and I just want this whole thing to be over with, but I know it's just as bad for Charlotte. She's nervous about everything running smoothly with the wedding she's been planning since she was a little girl, she's pregnant and scared and now her dream dress that she loved the minute she first tried it on six months ago doesn't fit. And least I have one good thing in my life that makes all of this bullshit better, even if I'm now afraid of his penis.

Ava and I leave the dressing room first and I hold the curtain open for Charlotte to walk through. Mom, Aunt Claire and Aunt Jenny stop talking and stare at Charlotte as she walks out of the room.

Mom immediately bursts into tears and Aunt Claire silently grabs a box of Kleenex from the table next to her, shoving it into mom's stomach.

"Oh, honey, you look so beautiful," Mom gushes as Charlotte smiles at the praise, lifting up the skirt of her dress and doing a little twirl.

"Why isn't your dress zipped?" Aunt Claire asks when Charlotte stops twirling.

"I'm stressed. I've been stress-eating and gained a little weight, and it's no big deal and it happens to every bride," Charlotte rambles.

"Oh, my gosh, you too?" Aunt Jenny asks. "I'm so nervous and excited about the wedding I've been eating in my sleep. I'm sleep-walk eating."

Mom blows her nose and Aunt Claire holds up her empty champagne glass, signaling to the owner of the shop. "Something tells me I'm going to need a refill."

Aunt Jenny continues as Mom tosses her tissue and box of Kleenex to an empty chair. She walks behind Charlotte to try and zip the dress, glancing at the camera man and sound guy standing next to Aunt Claire with their equipment pointed right at Aunt Jenny.

"Do you guys ever take a lunch break or anything? Now might be a great time for that," Mom informs them.

Daren the camera guy, or Dicky Daren as Uncle Drew likes to call him, who has been recording our family's every move for the last two weeks, tilts his head to the side of the camera and shrugs.

"Sorry, folks. Producer says I have to get everything. Don't worry, they'll edit out anything they don't think is interesting."

At this point, the documentary their filming will be approximately 85,000 hours long instead of a two-hour special. Our family doesn't know how to do anything uninteresting.

"Does that mean you'll include the footage of you letting Drew fondle your wanker? Because that was pretty interesting, Dicky Daren," Aunt Claire says with a wink.

"He didn't fondle it; he grazed it on accident when he tripped over the microphone chord! I have never let a dude fondle my penis!" Daren argues. "I mean, not that it's wrong or anything. I'm down with the gays and they're cool and everything, but I prefer chicks on my dick."

Stan, the sound guy, elbows him in the side and nods to the camera.

"Fuck! Of COURSE I didn't stop recording," Daren mutters, shifting the camera more securely on his shoulder and moving his face back behind the eye piece.

"You should be loud and proud about that shit, Dicky Daren," Aunt Claire says with a laugh. "You got at least an hour of footage of Drew going on and on about how big your penis is and how he's pretty sure it's the size of his forearm. Do you know how many women you could bang if that airs? Seriously. You'd have to beat them off with a stick."

Mom laughs, her fingers still trying to pull up the zipper that won't budge. "Forget the stick, he could just beat them off with his python penis."

Daren starts muttering to himself behind the camera, something about crazy women and how he doesn't get paid enough for this shit, and we go back to pretending like he's not there.

"Okay, back to what I was saying," Aunt Jenny continues. "I couldn't understand why I gained like ten pounds in two weeks until I woke up one morning with an empty box of Ho Hos on my pillow and chocolate smushed on the sheets. Drew assumed it was poop and thought I wanted to try some skate play. I tried for over an hour to convince him it was just chocolate, but he didn't believe me. Now he won't shut up about it and keeps telling me there's no shame in admitting I like poopy sex."

The shop owner who was on her way to Aunt Claire with a freshly opened bottle of champagne immediately turns on her heels and runs away.

"I believe you mean *skat* play, not skate play, Jenny," Aunt Claire mutters. "And can we please get out of here so I can find the closest drug dealer? I'm gonna need to shoot up some meth or something to erase that information from my mind."

Mom gives up on trying to zip Charlotte's dress, telling her not to worry and that she'll just have the seamstress sew a piece of fabric in to hide the problem.

Ava and I help Charlotte out of her dress and we all head out to the car to leave the poor owner in peace so she can cry alone after what she just witnessed, while Daren and Stan load the equipment in their van to follow behind us. Aunt Claire tried to lose them last week just for fun and it ended in a high-speed chase, three annihilated mailboxes, one flat tire, two dead squirrels, and my mom never letting Aunt Claire behind the wheel of a car again.

My phone beeps as Mom pulls out of the parking lot while Aunt Claire complains there's a guy with a walker moving faster than we are. I smile when I see a text from Marco and block out the sounds of my mom and my aunt arguing from the front seat.

Clear your calendar tonight and plan on getting naked. Puking permitted, but not required.

He always knows just the right thing to say to make me feel better.

164

Chapter 20

- Pez Penis -
Marco

"IT'S FINE. IT happens to a lot of guys."

Molly rubs the palm of her hand in slow circles against my back and gives me a sympathetic smile.

"It's not *fine* and it doesn't happen to me!" I yell, immediately feeling bad for raising my voice when she's being so nice and understanding. She shouldn't be nice. She should be laughing and making fun of me and storming out of here in disgust. It's what I deserve.

"Seriously, it's no big deal. Stop beating yourself up about it."

She leans in closer and kisses the top of my shoulder.

"This is embarrassing. I swear to God this has never happened to me before, ask anyone," I mutter.

All I wanted was to give Molly a perfect, romantic, wonderful night. Was that too much to ask? Am I being punished because I still haven't told her about Alfanso D.? It's not like I can just blurt it out. I thought if I turned on the charm and left her feeling satisfied, she'd have no choice but to forgive me. I can't do anything right.

"Marco, it's nothing to be embarrassed about. We can try again later," she encourages, running her fingers through my hair.

Her touch makes my dick stir, and I'm honestly a little surprised I can still get it up at this point.

"It won't be the same," I mumble. "The first time is always special and now I've ruined it."

She sighs and wraps her arms around my waist, squeezing me tight.

"It's because of me, isn't it? You're off your game because every time you look at me you remember the worst blowjob you've ever received," she whispers sadly.

Quickly turning towards her, I cradle her face in my hands and stare into her eyes.

"Stop it. This has nothing to do with you, I swear," I reassure her. "You turn me on just by breathing. I promise you, that blowjob was stellar, and regardless of the puke, your determination and won't-quit attitude scored you a lot of blowjob points in my book."

She smiles at me, and I drop my hands from her face to wrap them around her back and pull her closer.

"It really does happen to everyone, it's not that big of a deal."

I scoff and raise one eyebrow at her. "Has this ever happened to *you* before?"

She bites her bottom lip, but doesn't say anything.

"See?! It's just me! I'M the problem!"

"No you're not," Molly says with a sigh. "I just haven't been doing it as long as you."

She drops her arms from around my waist as I turn towards the kitchen counter, picking up the ruined soufflé with a scowl.

"Exactly my point," I tell her, walking over to the garbage can and dumping the dessert angrily inside. "I'm a pro. I've been baking soufflés since I was in elementary school, and I have NEVER had one collapse. This is mortifying."

I could blame Molly for ruining the dessert, but that's not exactly fair. I'm the one who was holding the oven door open to check on it when she got here twenty minutes ago and I'm the one who let the handle slip from my hands and slam shut when she walked into the kitchen wearing a tiny, blue strapless dress that clung to her tits, hugged her curves and fit her like a second skin. Her long, shiny black hair was curled into soft waves that hung around her shoulders, and don't even get me started on the matching blue fuck-me heels she had on that made her tall enough for her lips to be perfectly aligned with mine when she stood in front of me.

Maybe the soufflé could have survived the slamming of the oven door, but I definitely killed it when I grabbed her hips, turned her around and repeatedly pushed her body against the double oven to kiss her. And then I made sure it would never survive by continuing to hump her against the damn oven while I lost my mind between her legs with my tongue in her mouth.

Not only was she so fucking hot it made me want to drop to my knees and thank God for bringing her into my life, she looked so worried and nervous standing in the middle of my kitchen while she fidgeted with the dress and nervously shifted back and forth on her feet. When she shyly whispered that Ava picked out her clothes and did her hair and that she felt stupid, I knew I had to do something to erase that panicked look from her face like she was waiting for me to laugh at how she looked.

"So, now that my plan of making you fall madly in love with me as soon as you took a bite of my world famous soufflé that I never share with students is ruined, what do you want to do?" I ask, deciding to stop being a baby over a stupid dessert and concentrate on the gorgeous woman standing in my kitchen.

I spent all day cleaning this place up so it didn't look like a pigsty bachelor pad, and I made sure any evidence of Alfanso D. was safely hidden out of sight. I am determined to come clean with her tonight, but I want it to come from *me* and not have her find out by seeing all of my notes for the next book lying around. Since I trade working summers every year with another teacher, this is my summer to be off for three months and every minute I haven't been with Molly, I've been working on the book. My entire apartment was littered with sheets of notebook paper with scribbled ideas on them, post-it notes with recipes stuck to all the walls, and several copies of *Seduction and Sugar* lying all over the place so I could go back and reference whatever I needed. Now that everything has been shoved into the spare bedroom closet, I don't have to worry about her finding something before I can explain it myself. Which WILL happen before this night is over.

"Hmmmm, what should we do?" Molly ponders, tapping a finger against her lips. "I believe you mentioned something about getting naked in your text."

Tell her right now before she gets naked. Molly naked will result in you turning stupid.

"Yes, I believe I did say something to that effect. Why don't we sit down and talk first," I suggest as she walks slowly around me and heads into the living room.

Perfect, she wants to talk. Chicks always want to talk before getting to the good stuff. Just pretend like she never mentioned getting naked and everything will be fine.

I follow behind Molly, unable to move my eyes away from her ass as her hips gently sway while she walks into my living room. When she turns around in front of the couch, I'm still staring and now my eyes are glued to her crotch.

Focus, dammit! Don't think about what her pussy looks like. Don't drool wondering if it's shaved or full-on bush, trimmed or cut into a neat little design like a lightning bolt or arrow pointing down. Move your eyes up, asshole!

"We could talk, sure," Molly says softly, her fingers playing with the hem of her dress that stops at the top of her thighs.

Fuck, her legs are so long and smooth with just a hint of muscle definition that assures me she could wrap them around my shoulders and hold on for dear life.

GAAAAAAAAAH, FOCUS! I'm Alfanso D., I'm Alfanso D. Just get it over with!

"Great! Perfect," I reply with a clap of my hands, entirely too excited to sit down and talk instead of sitting down and burying my face in her vagina. "How about we sit on the couch and talk."

And then I'll bury my face in your vagina.

"How about you start talking and I'll get comfortable."

Mentally screaming at my dick to take a nap for a few minutes instead of trying to claw his way through my zipper, I smile and take a step towards the couch, figuring Molly is going to take her shoes off and put her feet up on the coffee table to get comfortable or something.

I barely take one step towards the couch before my feet refuse to move and I freeze like a deer caught in headlights.

When Molly said she'd get comfortable, she really meant it. In one smooth, quick motion, she grabs the hem of her dress and quickly slides the material up and off her body, tossing it to the side where it lands in a puddle on the carpet.

"Sweet baby back ribs," I whisper.

Molly crosses one leg in front of the other and casually clasps her hands together behind her ass, the motion pushing her tits out until I'm pretty sure I feel a little drool dripping down my chin.

She's wearing a black lace thong and a matching black lace strapless bra, the material so sheer I can see her nipples. And Land O'Lakes what wonderful nipples they are.

"Do you still want to talk or is there something else you'd rather do?" she asks innocently.

Talk? What's talk? Who said talk? Do I know the word talk?

"I might have a few ideas, but I think I need a little more inspiration," I tell her quietly, surprised I'm able to unglue my tongue from the top of my mouth and remember how to string words together.

Her hands move up behind her back and she expertly unclasps the hook of her bra, the sheer black lace dropping from her body to land at her feet.

"Damn, you're like a ninja with that thing," I whisper, unable to remove my eyes from her naked tits. "It takes me at least five tries to unhook a bra. It's like I have giant gorilla fingers whenever I get near those damn things."

Okay, I know I said I wanted to talk, but this is just pathetic. Why am I rambling about gorilla fingers when there's a half-naked woman in my living room with the best pair of tits this side of the Mississippi. And the other side of the Mississippi. And all down the fucking Mississippi.

STOP THINKING ABOUT MISSISSIPPI AND START THINKING ABOUT TITS, YOU PUSSY!

While I'm busy standing in the middle of my living room having an argument in my head, Molly walks towards me until she's right in front of me. She slides her hands around my waist and presses her naked body against me. I can feel her nipples poking into my pecs, and I swear I hear the sound of my zipper ripping to shreds as my dick tries to hulk his way out of my jeans and into the Promised Land.

My head finally catches up with my body and I move my hands to her hips, sliding them around to clutch her smooth, perfect ass.

"I'm just going to apologize ahead of time for ruining this," I whisper.

"Why would you ruin this?" she asks, pressing her hips against mine and gently kissing my chin.

"I mean, *I* wouldn't ruin it, but I'm pretty sure my dick will," I mutter, moaning softly when she kisses a trail across my jaw and to my neck.

"My dick is an asshole and never listens to me. You're so fucking hot and beautiful, and I'm pretty positive he's going to ignore all the baseball stats and college football teams I can name in alphabetical order and come in about five seconds if you keep doing that," I ramble in one long incoherent sentence, moaning again when she wraps her lips around my earlobe and gently tugs on it with her teeth. "Fucking hell, you're so good at this."

Her lips immediately disappear from my ear and she leans back just enough so I can see her face. Gone is the confidence and determination I love so much and in its place is the same nervous and scared look she had when she first walked into my kitchen.

"Hey, what's wrong? Was it the dick thing? I was just kidding. Sort of. I mean, I've always been able to last as long as I need to, but I've never been with someone I fantasized about for two years. I'm having a hard time believing this isn't a dream, but I promise I'll try my best to keep my dick in line," I over-explain.

She laughs softly and shakes her head. "It's stupid, but I need to tell you something. Ava told me to tell you but Charlotte told me to keep my mouth shut because it would ruin everything, but I can't do it. I am really out of my element here and Ava even made me practice this in front of the mirror until I could do it without rolling my eyes or covering myself up but I still feel like a liar and a hypocrite and I don't want to keep this from you because I really like you. I more than like you. I'm just going to spit out and if you want me to leave, I'll understand."

I don't feel so bad anymore about the whole gorilla fingers thing when Molly rambles without taking a breath and it just makes me want to stick her in my pocket and keep her forever. You know, if Harry Potter were a real person and he'd let me borrow his wand to make her tiny. But there would have to be a reverse spell where I could make her big again so she'd have normal-size hands and a normal-size mouth and a normal-size vagina because I might not have a dick the size of a python, but I'm pretty sure it could still kill a teeny tiny Molly that fits in my pocket.

Mental patient, party of me, your padded cell is now available.

Removing one hand from her ass, I bring it between us and under her chin, tipping her face up so she'll stop staring at a spot in the middle of my chest and look at me.

"No matter what you tell me, I would never make you leave, Molly. Don't you get it? Don't you see what you've done to me?" I rasp. "I've never been this crazy or this tied up in knots before and it's all because of you. Because you're just as amazing as I thought you'd be when I first saw you in the school kitchen with powdered sugar on your cheek and more talent in your pinky finger than the entire class put together."

I see tears pooling in her eyes and it makes my heart skip a beat, which I'm pretty sure might be a sign of a stroke or possibly a heart attack but since I still have feeling in my left arm, I'm just going to ignore it.

"I think I've been in love with you since that very first day when the entire class groaned after I said we'd be starting with sugar sculptures and your eyes lit up in excitement," I tell her with a smile. "I know it's crazy, and I know we're in the middle of a shit show situation with your family, and I *know* we've only spent a few weeks together, but I'm falling in love with you Molly Gilmore. I love how much you care about your insane family, even if you try to deny it. I love your talent in the kitchen, and I love that you're a hard ass with everyone but me. I love your smile and your laugh and how you smell like apples and cinnamon and how being with you is as easy as breathing."

She closes her eyes to stop the tears from falling, opening them right back up to roll them at me in that fucking adorable way I love so much.

"You're crazy and wonderful, and I think I'm falling in love with you too, and I'm still a virgin, but technically I've kind of, sort of had sex, so I use the term partial-virgin because it was one time and he only partially got his penis in before he finished, and his penis was literally the size of a piece of Pez candy and my sisters like to call him Pez Penis now and make fun of me because now I'm a pregnant partial-virgin, and I just wanted you to know because I don't want to keep any secrets from you."

She finally stops talking and takes a deep breath, letting it out slowly.

I know I should have paid really close attention to every word she said, but she talked incredibly fast and my brain shut down after the words "falling in love with you too" and "virgin". Then it came right back to life when she said she didn't want to keep any secrets from me. Now is my chance. Now is the perfect opportunity to tell her who I am. It doesn't get any better than this moment, right here.

"Say something so I don't feel like even more of an idiot because I'm half-naked in your living room, talking like a dumb girl about dumb feelings and other dumb girl stuff that gives me hives," she complains.

I open my mouth to spit it out, I swear I do. The words are right there on my tongue and I even take a deep breath, full of confidence now that I know she loves me back. Then Molly has to go and move her hips, doing this incredible little swirling motion that rubs her lace-covered vagina against my dick.

I'm such a cheap whore with a one-track mind.

"So, when you say partial-virgin, it's because you and some fuck-for-brains were naked and something resembling sex occurred, correct?" I ask.

You know, just to clarify and make sure we're on the same page.

"Sure, I guess you could put it that way," she nods, still moving her hips the tiniest bit, just to make sure my dick is paying attention. "His penis, was legit the size of the head of your penis. My fingers have gone deeper than his Pez dispenser."

And that's it, folks. My brain is tapping out and my dick is now in charge. When a chick talks about fingering herself, there's no coming back from that shit.

In one quick motion, I keep one arm behind her back and bend down to slide the other one behind her knees, scooping her up into my arms as I charge through the living room, down the hall and into my bedroom.

"If you're okay with this, I'd like to release you of your partial-virgin status," I tell her as I gently lay her on top of my bed and move on top of her, holding myself up on my arms so I don't crush her.

"I think I'm more than okay with that," she whispers, sliding her fingers through my hair at the back of my head and pulling my face down to hers.

"You should probably start reciting those football teams now," she breathes against my lips. "Don't forget I was raised in a sex shop. I took my first steps in the lesbian porn aisle and my first word was orgasm."

She wraps her legs around my hips, locking her ankles together against my ass and uses her muscles to pull the lower half of my body closer until my denim-covered dick is nestled right against the heat of her soon-to-be no longer a partial-virgin vagina.

Her hips start rocking against mine, and I tell myself it's totally fine if I wait one more day to tell her about Alfanso D. She is in need of my expertise and who am I to let a woman in need down?

"Air Force, Akron, Alabama, Appalachian State, Arizona," I begin chanting softly between kisses as I move down her neck and across her chest before wrapping my lips around one of her perfect nipples.

Molly's back arches and she lets out a low moan that makes my dick twitch and with excitement.

"Arwiwona Fate, Arwansas Fate, Wamy," I recite with a muffled voice, refusing to remove my mouth from her nipple.

"God I love football," Molly says with a sigh.

Chapter 21

- Drunk Babies -

Marco

"BEATED UP THE hooky again, Uncle! Ooooh, steal anodder car and shoot more people!" Valerie shouts with excitement as she bounces up and down on the couch next to me.

"It's pronounced *hooker*, not hooky, and I don't need to steal another car right now, sweetie," I explain, jerking my body to the left as I aim the PlayStation controller at the screen and make my car swerve around a pedestrian.

Letting my four-year-old niece watch me play Grand Theft Auto for the last hour probably wasn't the best decision I've ever made, but at least it kept her in one place instead of screaming and climbing the walls.

No, seriously, she actually climbed the wall in my bedroom like fucking Spiderman. It's Tessa's fault. She told me to give her a piece of chocolate every time Valerie goes to the bathroom on her own. No one gives me a Snicker's when I take a shit without assistance, but whatever. Valerie must have a bladder the size of...I don't know, something really fucking small because she has gone to the bathroom every two minutes for the last three hours. I'll let her swim in the sugar bowl as long as she doesn't piss on the carpet.

"Shoot him in the head! Make his head explode!" Valerie screams, clapping her hands together when I shoot a cop trying to arrest me.

"Do you remember what I told you, Val?" I ask, pausing the game to look down at her.

"Grand Feft Auto isn't real life. It's bad to shoot people, even hookies. I mean hookers," she tells me with a serious face.

"You've learned well, Grasshopper," I reply with a nod and a pat to the top of her head.

Once I finally found something to hold her interest for more than two seconds that wouldn't cause death or dismemberment and a seriously pissed off sister, it actually hasn't been so bad hanging out with my niece. When I asked Tessa if I could babysit her for a few hours today, I thought she was going to choke to death she laughed so hard. After she finally stopped laughing and realized I wasn't laughing with her and I was totally serious, I had to sit there for an hour while she gave me a quick course on Babysitting for Dummies. When she finished and gave me a list of telephone numbers for every person she's ever met in her entire life, including the numbers of ever hospital in a three-hundred mile radius, she made me sign a piece of paper stating she has permission to cut off my balls with a pair of rusty scissors if anything worse than a paper cut happens to her child under my care.

I've had a goofy fucking grin on my face ever since I successfully took care of that pesky partial-virgin status for Molly, but at the same time, I feel like the biggest jerk in the world that she trusted me and gave something so important to me and I still haven't managed to tell her the truth. The more time we spend together and the longer I wait, the worse I feel, yet I keep coming up with one excuse after another to keep putting it off.

Molly's giving me a blowjob—it can wait.

Molly's naked in my living room—what's one more day?

Molly wakes me up with her head under the covers and her mouth on my dick—she needs to rebuild that confidence and overcome the penis puke, I can't ruin that.

Molly takes me on a tour of Seduction and Snacks and asks me to fuck her in the warehouse in the vibrator aisle—I swear I'll do it after her orgasm when she's relaxed but one orgasm turned into four and I needed a nap.

Molly asks me to help her with a troubling recipe, and before I know it, there's chocolate sauce on my penis and dripping off her tits— chocolate on tits is delicious. No explanation needed.

Molly brings home toys from work and asks if I want to watch her use them—I AM JUST A MAN, STANDING IN FRONT OF A WOMAN, ASKING HER TO GET HERSELF OFF!

Before I knew it, the day before the wedding was upon us and I knew I needed to wait until it was over. Charlotte has turned into a bridezilla, and Molly is stressed about her parents finding out the real truth and them being mad at her for lying. She has too much on her mind right now that it wouldn't be right to add one more thing that I know will upset her.

Since there's no use denying how much of an asshole I am and I'm scared to death Molly will never trust me again or let me put my penis inside her which would be a tragedy I'll never recover from, I'm doing whatever I can to show her I'm not that person anymore. I overheard her talking to Ava on the phone last week when she thought I was sleeping and I still can't get her words out of my head. She was on her iPad going back through every damn post I made on the Alfanso D. page for the last six months. Even though I couldn't hear what Ava was saying, it wasn't too hard to figure out whenever Molly would say, "I know, right? He's such a pig" or, "You've got to be a pretty stupid woman to ever sleep with someone like that."

Yes, I was a pig. Yes, I was a bit of a man whore and yes, I exploited my sexcapades in a cookbook. I put up posts about how easy it was to sleep with any woman you wanted as long as you fed her chocolate. I made comments putting women down, putting relationships down and putting people down who had kids. I was *that* guy. The frat boy who refused to grow up.

Well, I'm assuming my behavior was like a frat boy since I was never actually *in* a frat, even though I tried to join one and was asked to never come back when I suggested we all go to a cooking class instead of doing keg stands.

And this leads us to where I am now, the day before Charlotte and Gavin's wedding where Charlotte will finally break the news to her betrothed (after he says I do of course, so he's less likely to leave the country), Molly will finally get to stop pretending she's pregnant, and I'll get to stop flinching every time her father jumps out at me and screams "BOO!". Actually, that will probably always happen even after he finds out I didn't impregnate his daughter since he still thinks I like to beat-off to photos of his wife.

I spent the last few days going back and forth with my publisher about this next cookbook and a new idea I came up with, trying to convince them I can make it just as good as the first one. They finally agreed last night, which brings me to the reason I am currently teaching my niece fun new vocabulary words and how to properly execute a kill shot while in a high-speed chase. Molly changed everything and I want her to know that even if she never trusts me again. What was originally going to be a sequel to *Seduction and Sugar* with even more over-the-top sex stories and matching recipes, is now: *Baking and Babies: How to Spice it Up in the Kitchen AND the Bedroom When You Have Kids.*

I've listened to Molly's aunts and uncles and her mom and dad tell stories over the last few weeks about what it was like after they added kids to the mix and how they managed to keep the romance alive. Some were funny, some were sweet, and some were downright horrifying. Pampers really needs to get their act together if babies can manage to shit so much that it leaks out of their diaper, up their back and sometimes in their hair. I'm a grown ass man and even *I* can't produce that much shit at one time.

All these stories were perfect for this cookbook, but I knew I needed real-life experience. The people who loved my first cookbook loved it because I shared a big piece of myself and my life on every page, even if I did it in a really slutty way and was never afraid to admit it on social media. A few hours with my niece seemed like the perfect way to get some experience as well as spend some time with her and learn how to not be so afraid of kids. They're not so bad once you get the hang of it. They really are like tiny drunk people and I've been around my share of enough drunk people to know the following rules apply to both:

1. Be prepared to make a Taco Bell run for the border. They will scream for Taco Bell (can be substituted for McDonalds) until you have no choice but to give in and go to the drive-thru in your pajamas in the middle of the night if you want them to shut up.

2. Never let them out of your sight, especially around sharp objects, things that are flammable or anything they might trip over and hurt themselves.

3. Smile and nod no matter what they mumble, slur, scream, or cry. Pretending like you understand them will eliminate arguments and or more crying.

4. If they say they're going to puke, do not hesitate to move your ass. Carry them like a football, drag them by the arm or toss them over your shoulder. Do whatever it takes to get them to a toilet, bush, sink or in some cases, the side of the road.

5. Know that accidents *will* happen. They can and will pee their pants, shit their pants and if you ignore number 4, puke on you and themselves. Keep a change of clothes and a container of wipes on hand at all times.

6. Watch what you say. If it's something you don't want repeated very loudly to everyone within shouting distance, don't say it. Everything you say can and will be very hilarious to them and they take enjoyment in your misery.

7. Some of them like to be naked. They have no shame and don't see the problem with taking their clothes off in public. Understand that clothes can sometimes annoy them. The clothes make them hot, make them itch, are too tight, too loose, or too ugly. Calmly tell them they have to put their clothes back on and offer assistance. If that doesn't work, some may become argumentative and may even lash out by kicking, screaming, biting and or hitting. If that happens, throw your coat or the closest blanket around them and drag them away.

8. Always be firm and speak slowly, enunciating each word carefully. They don't always understand the words coming out of your

mouth so try not to lose your temper or get frustrated. Don't be afraid to use a loud voice or threaten punishment, especially if their life could be at risk.

9. Never let them use your cell phone, iPad, iPod, laptop, or any other device that will connect them to your social media. They can and will post very bad things, but just know they aren't doing it on purpose. It's very easy to punch a few random buttons and the next thing you know, there's a dick pick you sent to your girlfriend and forgot to erase on Facebook and your mother has been tagged.

10. Memorize the number for Poison Control.

I really should buy Valerie a pony or something. A few hours with her and this book practically wrote itself.

Valerie suddenly jumps down from the couch and runs out of the room.

"Hey! Where are you going?" I shout.

"I GOTTA PEE!" she replies.

Tessa really needs to get that shit checked. I haven't even given her anything to drink since she's been here just to try and prevent any accidents. While I listen to the sounds of the toilet flushing and the sink running and know Valerie didn't somehow escape from a window, I quickly send a text to Tessa and tell her to call Valerie's pediatrician.

Tessa immediately replies with a comment about how I just might make a good dad someday, and I pat myself on the back until she sends another text immediately after, telling me to just make sure I pick the right woman and not try to fertilize the entire state.

It's annoying, but I deserve it. I'm going to prove to everyone with this cookbook that I've grown up and it's all because of Molly.

Tossing my phone onto the coffee table, I watch Valerie come racing back into the room and hop back up on the couch next to me.

"Did you wash your hands?" I ask.

She reaches up and wipes her wet hands on my cheeks.

"That better be water and not pee," I mutter, wiping the wetness off my face.

"Hump-hump-hump, I just peed on you!" she shouts, falling back into the couch in a fit of giggles.

Her laughter stops abruptly and she quickly sits back up, holding her hand out in front of me.

"I went poop. Gimme chocolate," she states.

I reach for the bag of Hershey Kisses on the table next to the couch and try not to panic when I realize it's empty. Valerie looks at the empty bag in clutched in my hand, her eyes filling with tears and her bottom lip starting to quiver.

"Hey, it's okay! Don't cry," I beg. "How about a box of cereal? Or some grapes. Grapes are really yummy!"

Valerie isn't buying it and she crosses her arms in front of her angrily.

"Chocolate! I poop and I get chocolate, mommy says so!" she yells.

Shit, rule number three, just remember rule number three.

I smile and nod, exaggerating my enthusiasm. "I know! You're such a big girl for shitting all by yourself. I mean, dropped a deuce. No, that's bad too. You pooped! Yaaaay you pooped on the potty!"

Valerie isn't amused even when I wave my hands in the air above my head.

"How about I let you beat up some hookers, rob a bank, and shoot up a strip club?" I ask with a sigh, dropping my hands into my lap.

Her eyes light up and she starts bouncing up and down on the couch again.

"I wanna drive the black car and run people over, and can I stab someone wif a knife? I like it when the blood squirts all over and they fall down!"

Shaking my head, I hand over the controller and un-pause the game.

"Have at it, kid. Just remember—"

"Grand Feft Auto isn't real life," she cuts me off in a robotic voice, her eyes never leaving the TV.

Look how easy it was to teach a four-year-old something new? Maybe I will make a good father someday. Hopefully Molly will agree.

Chapter 22

— Pumpkin Roll Punany —
Molly

"SEE? THAT'S WHERE you went wrong. You have to separate the eggs first and only use the egg whites. You're such an amateur," Uncle Drew complains, shaking his head at Tyler as I walk by them.

"Hey, Molly! You're, like, a cook and shit, right? You can answer this question for us," Tyler says, grabbing my arm to stop me from walking right on by them and pretending like I don't know them.

"I'm actually a classically trained French Pastry Chef," I remind him.

They both stare at me in confusion and I sigh.

"Yes, I cook and shit."

Tyler smiles and Uncle Drew lifts his beer bottle and gives me a wink.

"Egg yolks or egg whites? Which is better?" Uncle Drew asks.

"Um, it depends what you're making," I reply, shocked and a bit happy that these guys recognize and understand my passion and career expertise. "If you're talking about making whip cream, you never used the yolks, but if you're making, say a nice béarnaise you would-"

Uncle Drew puts his hand on my arm and snorts. "Imma let you finish but..."

"But, we're talking about which works better as a substitute for sex latex, obviously," Tyler finishes for him with his own snort and eye roll.

"Please tell my idiot son that only egg whites harden when brushed on the nipples so you can gently peel it off," Uncle Drew states, turning away from me to glare at Tyler. "I even dog-eared that chapter in the porn book for you AND highlighted it."

Tyler throws his hands up in the air in annoyance. "Do you know how long I had to sleep on the couch after mixing up Pumpkin Roll Punany and Baking Bread and Butt Bumps? That book you gave me had half the pages stuck together and I fucked everything up. It turns out, spanking a woman with a pumpkin roll is very messy and mixing fresh bread ingredients in a vagina really DOES cause a yeast infection."

I close my eyes and wonder why I ever thought our family could have a nice, dignified evening out in public for once as Uncle Drew and Tyler continue arguing back and forth. Not even the beautiful, fancy atmosphere of one of the nicest restaurants in town could make these people behave.

My eyes slowly open when I feel a pair of warm lips press to the side of my neck. I smile even though my uncle and Tyler are still arguing, but now it's over who can successfully use the word *nipples* in every sentence in regards to dinner.

"My nipples get hard just thinking about the chicken parm they're serving."

"I can see cousin Rachel's nipples through her white shirt."

"OVERRULED!"

"On what grounds?!"

"Incest is only legal in porn and erotic fiction!"

"Fine. Sustained, but I'll need to see you in my chambers."

I turn away from the idiots in front of me and wrap my arms around the waist of the smart, beautiful man behind me.

"Do I even want to ask?" Marco laughs, running one of his hands up and down my arm.

"Not unless you want to lower your I.Q. by about a hundred points."

Pushing up on my toes, I give him a quick kiss, pulling back to smile. "Thank you for coming to the rehearsal dinner tonight."

His hand continues moving up my bare arm and over my shoulder, wrapping its warmth softly around my neck so he can slide his thumb back and forth over my cheek.

"Free booze and a five course meal? Like I'd say no to that!" He laughs. "Or a chance to see your sexy ass in a hot dress again."

I let Ava dress me again for Gavin and Charlotte's rehearsal dinner since the last time she did, Marco couldn't keep his hands off me. Tonight, she stuffed me into a skin-tight red halter dress that I have to say, makes my boobs look amazing.

"Marco! Just the man I want to see," Tyler yells from behind me as Marco keeps his hand in place on my neck and takes a sip of his drink with the other.

"You look like the type of guy that's used *Seduction and Sugar* on a few women before. What's your take on the Tiramisu and Titty Twister chapter?" Uncle Drew asks.

Marco's drink goes down the wrong pipe and he immediately starts choking and coughing. I quickly move to his side to pat his back, giving my uncle a dirty look.

"Seriously, Uncle Drew? I think Marco has a bit more class than that."

Marco starts coughing harder, and I take the drink from his hand as he bends at the waist and puts his hands on his knees. Uncle Drew and Tyler finally walk away, muttering something about how no one appreciates good porn anymore.

After a few minutes of rubbing my hand soothingly against Marco's back, he finally stands up and takes a deep breath.

"I should have know *those two* would consider that stupid book their bible," I laugh. "Are okay?"

Marco takes his drink glass from my hand and sets it on a nearby empty table, turning back to grab both of my hands.

"I need to tell you something," he whispers.

"My family is full of idiots?" I ask with a laugh. "I'm aware."

"I'm an idiot too. A really, really big idiot. I need to—"

Glancing over Marco's shoulder, I see Charlotte finally alone, standing in the corner of the room on the other side of the restaurant and I hold my hand up distractedly.

"Sorry, can you hold that thought?" I ask, my eyes glued to Charlotte as she checks something on her phone. "Charlotte is finally alone and I need to talk to her really quick."

Marco looks a little frustrated that I interrupted him, and I immediately feel bad. I thought he was going to tell me something stupid my dad and Uncle Carter said to him since he'd been busy talking to them over by the bar before he came over here, but maybe I was wrong.

"Never mind, I'll talk to her later."

He shakes his head and gives me a quick kiss on the cheek. "No, it's fine. It can wait. Does this have anything to do with the private little conversation I saw you and Gavin having a little bit ago?"

It has *everything* to do with that talk my soon-to-be brother-in-law had and if I'm lucky, we can finally be finished with this stupid charade once and for all.

"That it does," I tell him with a smile. "Brace yourself, Marco. If all goes well, I should be un-knocked up by the third course."

He quickly gets down on one knee, grabs my hips, and presses his lips to my stomach.

"What the hell are you doing?" I whisper loudly, looking around in embarrassment when a bunch of people start staring.

"If this whole thing is coming to an end, I feel like I should go out with a bang," he explains. "Really put everything I've got into this role to make it memorable. Besides, I've gotten to know this little fake fetus the last few weeks. We've bonded. I'm going to be sad to see the little bugger go."

I clutch onto the shoulders of his dress shirt and try pulling him up from the ground, but he's not budging.

"No matter what you hear tonight, Cletus the Fetus, Daddy loves you," he speaks softly to my stomach. "We've had some good times, we've had some bad times, and we've had some times where you've needed to cover your little fake fetus ears because your mommy is a screamer."

I smack his arm, shooting a nervous smile to all the people watching us with sappy looks on their faces.

"Oh, my God, get up!" I whisper through my embarrassed smile.

"I know, Cletus the Fetus, Mommy confuses me too. Oh, my God is usually followed by *'Go down!'* when she screams it," Marco tells my stomach.

"If you don't get up right now, I will tell everyone your soufflé couldn't get it up," I growl.

He quickly stands and gives me a shocked look. "You wouldn't? It was ONE time and you said it happens to everyone!"

With a laugh, I grab his tie and yank him down to my lips, pressing my mouth to his. When the people standing closest to us start to clap and cheer, I pull my lips from his before I get too carried away.

"Save me a seat, I'll be back in a few," I tell him, smoothing his tie down before heading in Charlotte's direction.

"I'll miss you Cletus! Remember me fondly," Marco calls after me.

I ignore him and charge through the crowd, standing quietly behind Charlotte while she's still staring at something on her phone. I lean over her shoulder and immediately regret it when I see she's watching some sort of horror movie, the screen filled with what looks like bloody roast beef falling out of a wound in someone's body that has blood and guts and internal organs spilling out of it.

"What the fuck are you watching?"

Charlotte screams, dropping her phone as she whirls around to face me.

"Dammit, Molly! I thought you'd finally gotten tired of sneaking up on people. It's like you get some sort of sick thrill out of making people scream," Charlotte complains with a sigh, bending down to grab her phone.

"It's true, I do. I keep your screams in a jar in my closet next to the severed heads," I explain with a shrug. "Want to tell me why you're watching the world's most disgusting horror movie right before dinner?"

"It wasn't a horror movie, it was a Youtube video of a live birth," she tells me, setting her phone on the table next to her.

"That was a vagina?" I ask in shock. "I knew they were pretty resilient, but how the hell do they come back from something like that? It looked like it went through a meat grinder. Your vagina is going to look like a raw hamburger patty covered in ketchup and thrown at a wall."

She glares at me, her hands on her hips and her foot tapping against the floor. "Thanks a lot. Like I'm not freaked out enough as it is."

I pat her shoulder comfortingly. "Well, you'll be happy to know I have one less thing for you to be worried about. I had a nice little chat with Gavin earlier. He wanted to apologize for being a dick and so angry when he walked in on us in the bathroom that day and also for avoiding me since then."

Charlotte's eyes widen in fear and her hands drop to her sides. "Did you tell him? What the fuck did you say to him?!"

"Calm the fuck down, burger vag," I sigh. "I didn't tell him anything, but you definitely will before this night is over. It turns out, Gavin wasn't angry, he was jealous. Because he's decided he wants kids and he's afraid to tell you since you guys both agreed not to have them. So, now you can tell him tonight and not have anything at all to worry about tomorrow."

I smile happily, waiting for her to tell me how amazing I am and how it's all thanks to me that she can marry the love of her life without having any secrets between them.

"Are you insane?!" She screeches. "I can't tell him now, at our rehearsal dinner! He'll want to tell everyone and then mom and dad will know and it will start a huge argument and this perfect night will be ruined!"

"Did you even hear what I said?" I yell back. "Your fiancé wants kids. You can finally stop telling him you have the flu and that your ass isn't the size of Texas now because of stress-eating. This is a *good* thing, dumbass!"

She huffs, snatching her phone from the table as the owner of the restaurant announces for everyone to take their seats so they can begin serving the first course.

"You bitches want to tone it down a little? People are starting to stare," Ava tells us as she walks up next to us.

"I'll tone it down when meaty vagina here tells Gavin the truth," I announce petulantly.

Charlotte grimaces and Ava sighs.

"I'm just going to pretend I understand the meaty vagina reference before Charlotte pukes on my shoes. I thought we were waiting until after the wedding?" Ava asks.

"We ARE," Charlotte growls. "I don't want anything to ruin tonight or tomorrow. What's the big deal, anyway?"

"The big deal is that I just told you your fiancé wants kids and all you care about is having a perfect wedding!" I argue.

"Wait, Gavin wants kids?" Ava asks in shock.

"Not only does he want kids, he's been jealous of my fake pregnancy this entire time and is freaking out about telling Charlotte he's changed his mind," I inform her.

The pissed off and annoyed look on Charlotte's face immediately disappears and she smiles brightly at something behind me.

"We saw you guys having a little argument. Don't mind us, just carry on," Dicky Daren tells us as he aims the camera in our direction.

Charlotte laughs nervously. "Oh, no, we're not arguing! We're...ummmm, excited. Molly just told us she felt the baby kick!"

The camera flies in my direction and I can hear it clicking and whirring as it zooms in on my stomach.

"Right, Molly? You felt the baby kick because that would be sweet and awesome and wouldn't cause anyone like Mom and Mad to scream and fight and ruin this entire night, right?" Charlotte asks, her eyes wide and pleading with me as she presses her hands to my stomach.

"You are such an asshole," Ava mutters to Charlotte, as the camera pans to Ava's face. "I mean, an asshole for getting to feel that little spawn kicking before me!"

Ava's hands also fly to my stomach and all three of us look into the camera with fake smiles while I silently curse Charlotte.

"Yaaaaay, it kicked," I cheer in a monotone voice with fake enthusiasm.

Someone clangs their silverware against a glass across the room and Dicky Daren finally finds something more interesting to record as he walks away from us.

All three of us let out a sigh when we're alone again.

"I'm sorry," Charlotte whispers. "I just don't want anything to mess this up. Please, Molly, just until after the wedding. I know I'm being selfish and I know you hate me, but this is the only wedding I'll ever have and I want it to be perfect."

With an annoyed growl, I point my finger at Charlotte's face. "You better hope this is your only wedding because if there's a second one, I will fuck that shit up."

Charlotte squeals, throwing her arms around me to squeeze me so tight I can't breathe. "You are the best sister in the whole world!"

Ava clears her throat. "Um, hello? What about me?"

Charlotte finally releases me and scowls at her. "You sent me that birthing video and told me it was a cute kitten compilation."

"Well, it *was* about pussies, so technically I didn't lie. I just forgot to mention it was about pussies that look like a serial killer got ahold of them," Ava shrugs.

Leaving them to bicker, I turn and make my way to the table where Marco is sitting. He sees me coming and pulls my chair out for me, resting his arm on the back when I sit down.

"Everything go okay?" he asks softly as the servers come out of the kitchen and start putting plates in front of everyone.

"Super," I tell him with a bright smile. "You'll be happy to know Cletus kicked for the first time. It was a joyous event."

Marco slides a glass of orange juice across the table to me and gives me a sympathetic smile.

"Yum, more mommy juice," I grumble, bringing the glass to my lips and taking a huge swallow.

My throat burns and my eyes water as soon as the liquid slides down my throat and I slam my fist against my chest as I cough.

"I guess I shouldn't have asked the bartender to put enough vodka in there to choke a horse," Marco whispers in my ear as he pats my back. "Fetal Alcohol Syndrome for our baby it is!"

I get my coughing under control and manage a small laugh. "Thanks for sneaking me a drink. I'm going to need about ten more to get through this night."

Clinking my glass against Marco's beer bottle, I hold it up for a toast.

"Here's to one more night with our little bundle of joy. May our baby have your good looks and my charming personality, minus the swearing and underage drinking."

A server's arm that was sliding between us suddenly drops the plate of food right into Marco's lap.

"YOU'RE having a baby?!"

Marco's chair flies backwards as he pushes his feet against the floor to quickly remove the boiling hot shrimp scampi appetizer from his crotch, and I turn around to look at the woman who just yelled and dropped the plate.

I practically motorboat the woman standing between us since her giant fake boobs that are popping out of her shirt are right at my eye level.

"Megan, I didn't know you worked here," Marco says with an uncomfortable laugh while he swipes away the food with his cloth napkin. "It's been a while. How've you been?"

I look back and forth between Tits McGee and Marco, wondering how they know each other, hoping they're neighbors or cousins. Please, God, let them be related.

"Did I really hear you say you're having a baby? I think I'm going to be sick," Bimbo Barbie says with a grimace, tossing her perfect blonde hair over one shoulder.

"Um, Molly, this is Megan Levine. Megan, this is my girlfriend, Molly," Marco says without looking up, suddenly very interested in getting the stains out of the crotch of his pants.

She doesn't even glance in my direction, and if I didn't already hate her because of her fake tits, big hair, tiny waist and all around perfect body, I sure as shit would now. She looks right over my head like I'm not even sitting here.

"It must take a lot of skill to say the word *girlfriend* without laughing," she says with a smile that is definitely not friendly. "Looks like nothing has changed and you're still sleeping your way through another stupid porn cookbook. If you decide to include another story about me in this one, at least get the facts straight. The Chocolate Sauce Suckfest was *my* idea, and I'm the one who told you to use milk chocolate instead of semi sweet. The least you could do is put my name in the acknowledgements."

So, not a cousin, unless it's recently become acceptable to blow your relative.

I try really hard to say something awesome and sarcastic to make her feel like an asshole, but I'm too busy wondering why Marco would ever want someone like me when he had someone like *her*. Also, what in the holy fuck is she talking about? Porn cookbook? Acknowledgements? Is everyone a fan of that stupid *Seduction and Sugar* book but me?

"Oh, how cute," Megan purrs. "I think your *girlfriend* is in shock. You might want to do something about that, Alfanso. Or is it Marco? I can never remember which is the right one."

What in the actual fuck of all fucks is happening right now? Am I on drugs? Is *she* on drugs? Is the documentary they've been filming really some kind of hidden camera show where they play jokes on people? Maybe it's an episode of *Intervention* and mom was right. Vodka really is a gateway drug to meth and I became an addict without even knowing it.

I need to say something since it appears as if Marco has become mute. Tell her to go fuck herself. Tell her to take her porn star tits and go back to the stripper pole where she belongs. Tell her she's a liar and snotty bitch.

Wait, did she say Alfanso?

"I puked when I gave him a blowjob," I mutter.

"Blowjob puking?" Uncle Drew pipes up from across the table. "There's porn for that. It's a little disturbing, but surprisingly good quality. Hold on, I have it bookmarked."

Uncle Drew pulls out his phone, and I stare at Marco, waiting for him to explain what the hell is going on before I lose my mind.

"Ava almost did that once, but she made it to the toilet right after she swallowed," Tyler muses. "That's why my pet name for her is Cum-Bubble. She had this adorable little bubble of snot and jizz in one nostril. I think I still have the picture somewhere on my phone."

Why isn't Marco saying anything?

"Holy shit! Are *you* Alfanso D.?!" Tyler suddenly shouts across the table in excitement, staring wide-eyed at Marco. "Dude, Chocolate Sauce Suckfest changed my life!"

He elbows Uncle Drew.

"Hold on, I almost found it. I saved it after the link for grandma banging and before the one for midget anal," Uncle Drew mutters, finally looking up from his phone when Tyler keeps nudging him.

"Dad, we've been in the company of porn royalty this entire time and didn't even know it," Tyler says in awe.

"I'm not a partial-virgin anymore," I mumble stupidly.

"Oh, I KNOW I've got virgin porn on here. You're gonna need to be more specific about the partial thing, though," Uncle Drew says, going back to his phone.

"Molly, I can explain," Marco whispers, finally deciding to speak.

"Oh, this should be good," Blondie mutters with a sarcastic laugh.

I finally clear my head enough to notice the guilty look on Marco's face, and I realize he hasn't said one word about how this bitch is lying or confused or a homeless meth addict posing as a server.

"How about you just fuck right off, Giant Jugs?" I growl, my eyes narrowing at the slut who refuses to walk away.

She gasps and then huffs, looking at Marco like she expects him to come to her defense. When he wisely keeps his mouth shut and his eyes stay glued to mine, she finally storms away, leaving a cloud of fruity perfume in her wake that makes me nauseous.

"Molly, please—"

"Was she telling the truth?" I ask, cutting him off.

I don't know why I'm even asking since I can see it written all over his miserable face. I can't decide if I want to cry or smack him.

Calmly pushing my chair back, I stand and toss my napkin on top of the table.

"I lied. It IS a big deal and it doesn't happen to every guy!" I yell, channeling Rachel from *Friends*.

Marco gasps, but I'm too upset and heart broken and pissed to let the hurt look on his face get to me.

"Ooooh, got yourself a wilting wiener problem, huh?" Uncle Drew asks him with a sympathetic smile. "Don't worry, I've got just the porn for that. Shit, where did I put the link to the toe fucking website…"

On that note, I turn and walk away from the table. I keep my head down as the tears start to fall when I realize Marco isn't going to chase after me, a shout from Uncle Drew making this night even more sad and pathetic.

"Shit! I can't believe someone erased my toe-fucking link. Dammit, Tom Brady!"

Chapter 23

- Smell the Meat -

Marco

L IKE THE FUCKING coward I am, I left the rehearsal dinner last night with my tail tucked between my legs as soon as Molly walked away from me with tears in her eyes. Well, as soon as Drew made me watch twenty minutes of foot fetish porn and Tyler told me he knew a guy who knew a guy who could get me Viagra, but it would involve me stripping at something called BronyCon that I was afraid to ask about.

I knew this would happen and I knew it would fuck up everything, but like an idiot, I just kept putting it off until it all blew up in my face. And blow up it did when a blast from my man-whore past showed up and ruined my life.

Fucking Megan Levine…that chocolate sauce chapter wasn't even about her, but the one with the recipe for a strawberry sauce to add to your bath water for a fresh smelling vagina was. That chick had a nice rack, but her pussy smelled like ham, and not delicious, Easter Sunday ham either. Like ten-day-old rancid lunchmeat ham.

Stupid Megan Levine and her stupid ham vagina.

"Did you call my guy's guy about the dick drugs?"

Tyler comes up next to me and hands me a beer while I stare across the room at Molly. I tried to talk to her earlier at the wedding ceremony, but she pretended like I didn't exist and refused to even look at me. I'm not leaving this reception until she lets me apologize and explain.

"I don't need dick drugs, Tyler, we were talking about a soufflé," I clarify, watching Molly duck down under the head table again for probably the tenth time in the last few minutes.

What the hell is she doing?

"Is that like, French or something? I kind of like it. It sounds more dignified to say *I fucked a soufflé*," he muses. "Is that gonna be in the next book? Can I get an advanced copy?"

I chug my beer for some liquid courage and prepare to head over to Molly, dragging her out of here if I need to.

"The next book is called *Baking and Babies* and has nothing to do with the fucking of desserts," I tell him with a sigh.

"Baking babies? Dude, that's hard-core. I mean, I know kids are annoying and shit, but cooking them? Can you even do that?" he asks.

I watch Molly pop back up from under the table and stand, wobbling a little as she clutches onto the back of her chair. She's so fucking beautiful it makes me want to cry. I've heard women complain about being forced to wear ugly bridesmaid dresses, but there is nothing ugly about the short purple, satin strapless dress clinging to Molly's body. Her hair is up in some fancy do with a few pieces hanging down around her face and my hands have been itching all day to pull out the pins holding it in place so I could watch the silky dark locks spill around her naked shoulders.

"I guess you can slather BBQ sauce on just about anything and it will taste good, but I just don't know if I could stomach eating an actual baby, no matter what you baste it in."

While Tyler continues to talk to himself, I shove my empty bottle at him start walking towards the head table.

"What about Ranch?" Tyler shouts after me. "I might eat a baby if you put Ranch on it."

A few people try to stop and talk to me, but I ignore them and keep my eye on the prize. When I'm a few feet away from the head table, the DJ comes up behind Gavin and Charlotte and speaks into his microphone.

"If everyone could have a seat, we're going to get started with the toasts before dinner is served," he announces to the room.

The reception hall is filled with the sounds of chairs scraping across the floor as everyone sits down. With a quick glance around me, I realize I'm the only one still standing so I quickly grab an empty seat at the nearest table as the DJ hands the microphone to Molly.

She grabs it and moves to stand behind Gavin and Charlotte, swaying a little when she stops and I immediately realize what she was doing each time she disappeared out of sight under the table.

"This is going to be amazing. She's so wasted," Ava whispers with a laugh as she pulls up a chair next to me and flops down.

"Shouldn't you be up there with the rest of the bridal party? And why the hell did you let her drink so much?" I ask in a quiet, angry voice.

Molly blows loudly into the microphone, the speakers screeching with feedback as everyone in the room winces from the ear piercing noise.

"I didn't realize until five minutes ago that she's been inhaling a bottle of vodka under the table since she got here," Ava tells me while Molly giggles into the microphone and apologizes to everyone. "I went to get her some black coffee from the kitchen, but they haven't brewed any yet."

"I'd like to thank everyone for coming out tonight to celebrate the joyous union of my perfect sister and her perfect Gavin," Molly starts, holding her champagne glass in the air.

"I hope someone is filming this," Ava laughs.

"Aren't they just sooooooooo perfect?" Molly asks sarcastically.

"We need to do something. This is not good," I mutter.

"Are you kidding me? This is amazing. Charlotte has been a raging bitch to us all day, reminding us to keep our mouth's shut every five minutes so we wouldn't ruin her *perfect* day," Ava explains while Molly starts to pace behind a nervous-looking Charlotte and a confused-looking Gavin. "I love Charlotte, but I fully support whatever Molly is about to do. Charlotte has been so concerned with having the perfect wedding that she doesn't even realize none of this shit matters in the long run."

I definitely agree with Ava, but I really don't want Molly doing something she's going to regret. Giving a drunk speech in front of two-hundred friends and family when half of them think she's pregnant might be a bad idea.

"Also, you're lucky I'm wearing a dress and not kicking your ass right now," Ava tells me with a glare while Molly instructs everyone to hold up their glasses for her toast. "I don't know what you did to my sister last night, but it must have been pretty bad for her to cry. I've never seen that bitch cry. She collects jars of *other* people's tears under her bed, she never sheds them herself. What did you do?"

I open my mouth to tell her it's a long story and I plan on doing whatever I can to fix it when the sound of loud, heavy breathing echoes through the room.

"Hold on a second. I need to take these fucking heels off, my feet are killing me," Molly says, the words sounding even more garbled since she has her mouth pressed right up against the microphone while she leans against the wall and quickly removes her shoes.

She chucks them right over Charlotte and Gavin's head and they land in the middle of the front table where her parents and aunt and uncles are seated.

"WOOOHOOOOO TAKE IT OFF!" Drew shouts, grabbing one of her shoes and waving it around above his head.

Claire punches him in the arm and I hear her yell at him about Molly being his niece, Drew quickly lowering his arm and his lips form the words, "Oh, yeah. I forgot."

Molly starts walking behind the bridal party, stopping when she gets to a small table at the end that holds trays of appetizers.

"So, I guess you guys all heard that I'm knocked up," she speaks into the microphone, setting her glass down on the table.

"Did she say she's getting locked up? I didn't know Molly was going to prison," someone whispers loudly.

I turn my head and realize I sat down at Molly's grandfather's table and he's currently giving me the stink eye while Sue shakes her head sadly and he chews on a toothpick.

"Skull-fucker," Molly's grandpa mouths silently, pulling the toothpick out of his mouth and pointing it at me.

I swallow nervously and turn back around to watch the train wreck in front of me, wondering if I should go up there and take the microphone away from Molly or if that would just make things worse.

One of the groomsmen leans to the side and holds his hand out for the microphone and Molly smacks him on the hand with it.

"Fuck off! I'm in the middle of something here," Molly shouts when she brings the mic back up to her mouth. "Where was I?"

Yep, going up there would probably be worse.

She grabs one of the trays from the appetizer table and unsteadily carries it back to her original spot behind the bride and groom.

"Oh, yeah," she continues, dropping the tray onto the table next to Charlotte. "So, this one day I was minding my own business, and then BAM, I was suddenly knocked up. And here's the funny thing, I hadn't even had sex! I know, right?"

Charlotte drops her head to the table and Molly laughs.

"Well, I mean, there was this one time with Pez Penis but that doesn't count, and then like, fifteen times with a guy I thought loved me and those TOTALLY count and they were awesome because he doesn't have a Pez Penis, but he's a liar and he lied and I threw up on his penis and everything and he still lied," Molly says with a sniffle.

"Did she say she threw up on a penis?" Sue whispers.

"God dammit, you heard that? There goes my Wednesday blow jobs," Molly's grandfather grumbles.

"DAMN YOU, TOM BRADY!"

I don't even need to turn my head to see who yelled *that*, especially when I hear Jenny tell him to shut the hell up because Molly is trying to confess her sins to cleanse Aurora.

"I'm so happy my sister married the love of her life and had the most perfect wedding ever," Molly continues. "I'm so glad she gets to live happily ever after when my life sucks and it never would have sucked in the first place if I didn't have Cletus the Fetus and a liar liar-pants baby daddy who can't get it up!"

This half of the room all whip their heads in my direction with shocked expressions on their face and I throw my hands up in the air.

"It was a soufflé, dammit! I collapsed a soufflé," I tell them.

"Say it with a French accent, dude! It doesn't sound as pervy that way!" Tyler shouts from the back of the room.

"Is Molly drunk? Isn't that bad for the baby?" Uncle Carter asks his wife.

"Oh yeah, she's trashed. Just wait for it," Claire tells him with a smile.

"Is there something I need to know?" Jim questions Liz.

"You just sit there and look pretty, honey," Liz says with a smile, patting the top of his hand.

"I'd like everyone to raise their glasses and toast the happy, perfect couple sitting right here looking all happy and perfect," Molly tells the room.

While everyone awkwardly lifts their glasses, Molly grabs a huge handful of something from the tray she dropped to the table and then taps Charlotte on the head with the microphone.

Charlotte slowly lifts her head as Molly sticks her hand right up to her face.

"What the hell are you doing? Get that away from me," Charlotte whines, the microphone just barely picking up her words.

"What's wrong, Charlotte? It's just some cured meats from your antipasto appetizer. Mmmmmmm, meat. Don't they smell good? Like meat. Mmmmmmm lunchmeat," Molly says into the microphone, waving a fist full of cold cuts in front of Charlotte's nose.

Charlotte covers her mouth with one hand and shakes her head back and forth frantically.

"Smell the meat, Charlotte, SMELL IT!" Molly yells.

"This is a very strange wedding toast," one of the guests whispers loudly from another table.

Charlotte tries to back away from Molly's meat holding hand, but Molly moves right along with her and smacks her hand full of cold cuts against Charlotte's chest. They stick to her skin as Molly pulls her hand away and laughs into the microphone.

Charlotte takes one horrified look down at the meat stuck to her chest and her cheeks puff out as she leans forward and throws up all over the table.

The room explodes in a chorus of groans and a couple of gags, but Gavin's voice can still be heard above the noise.

"Shit! I thought you said your flu was finally gone?" he asks his new bride, grabbing a napkin to help her wipe her mouth.

"She doesn't have the flu, you dumbass!" Molly informs him. "She's got the meat sweats, isn't that right, Charlotte?"

Charlotte's hand flies back to her mouth, and she turns her head to glare at Molly.

"Stop talking about meat!" she screams behind her hand.

"Fine. SOUP, SOUP, SOUP! CREAMY SOUP, CHUNKY SOUP, GREASY, LUMPY, SOUP, SOUP, SOUP!" Molly yells into the microphone.

Charlotte's eyes get so wide I'm surprised they don't pop out of her head. Sweat drips down from her forehead and she quickly presses her other hand on top of the first one, holding them both as hard as she can against her mouth.

"Honestly, Molly, if you want soup that bad just ask the caterer, there's no need to yell," Gavin complains while he continues consoling his wife.

As soon as Gavin says the word *soup*, Charlotte's body jerks with a heave and she presses her hands harder against her face to keep the vomit in.

"I know I should go up there and do something, but it's like I'm watching a bus full of people slam into a brick wall," Ava mumbles. "It's horrifying and mesmerizing at the same time."

Molly holds the microphone against her mouth and leans in close to Charlotte.

"Say it, out loud," Molly growls.

"Who is Edward, from Twilight?!" Drew shouts excitedly.

"Oh, I get it now. This is like a wedding version of Jeopardy. Soup and meat, soup and meat..." Jenny says, scratching her head as she thinks. "Oh, I know! What are astrophysicists?!"

Drew looks at her in confusion and she rolls her eyes.

"You know, like chocolate and oysters and other stuff that makes people horny," Jenny explains.

"Say it, or I will!" Molly yells at Charlotte.

"Fine!" Charlotte shouts back, dropping her hands from her face and turning to look at Gavin.

"Molly was never pregnant. It was me the whole time, and I'm sorry for lying to you, but I was afraid you wouldn't want to marry me and I love you so much, and I didn't want to lose you and I just wanted us to have the perfect wedding, and I know you probably hate me now and Molly hates me and my parents hate me, and I just threw up in front of everyone I know and I'm sorry I made Molly do this for me, but it's not my fault your boyfriend lied to you about writing porn and WHY THE FUCK DOES THIS SALAMI SMELL LIKE ROTTEN ASS?!" Charlotte screams at the end of her rambling explanation.

"Pumpkin Roll Punany, bro!" Tyler shouts, pounding his fist against his heart and then pointing at me with a wink and a big smile.

"Cheers, mother fuckers!" Molly yells as she leans back from Charlotte. "Gilmore, OUT!"

With that, Molly throws her arm out in front of her and drops the microphone as it screeches with more feedback, thumping loudly through the speakers when it hits the floor.

Everyone mumbles a confused "cheers" in response, but they don't get a chance to drink when all of a sudden a loud, banshee-like scream comes out of Charlotte's mouth as she jumps up from her chair and lunges at Molly.

Ava and I fly up from our chairs as Charlotte quickly grabs the tray of antipasto salad, jerking it in Molly's direction as she charges her. Huge piles of salami and thinly sliced ham soar through the air and smack against the front of Molly's dress.

"Let's see how YOU like the meat sweats!" Charlotte screams as Molly reaches down the front of her dress and pulls out a fist-full of ham.

"I happen to LOVE the meat sweats! Too bad we don't have any ground meat so I could shove it in your fat ass granny panties and you can see what it will be like to have a slimy, meaty vagina in a few months!" Molly screams back.

"I think *I'm* going to puke now," Gavin mutters, pressing his hands to his stomach.

The parents and aunts and uncles all jump up from their table and join Ava and I in a race around the bridal table as Molly and Charlotte scream in unison and start whipping lunch meat at each other's faces.

"EAT THE SLIMY HAM, YOU SLUTTY PREGNANT DICK!" Molly yells, snatching a clump of meat from the table and shoving it against Charlotte's mouth with one hand while she grabs a handful of Charlotte's veil and holds her head still with the other.

"*YOU EAT IT, YOU PENIS-PUKING-PORN-WRITER-FUCKER-WHORE-FACE!*" Charlotte screams back, jerking her face from side to side as Molly keeps trying to shove ham in her mouth.

Ava and I get to Molly first and we both wrap our arms around her, pulling her away from Charlotte as she kicks and screams and curses. Liz and Jim do the same to Charlotte, and we all manage to separate the girls as they continue to fling cold cuts at each other while we drag them apart.

Tyler quickly grabs the microphone from the floor where Molly dropped it, tapping on it a few times before addressing the crowd.

"And that concludes the dinner theater portion of the reception! How about we give these guys a hand for their amazing and artistic portrayal of a white trash family?!" Tyler says, clapping his hand against the microphone as the room slowly joins in. "Help yourself to the open bar and stay tuned for the next show in forty-five minutes. The famous author, Alfanso D. will be cooking up some tasty babies as a special treat for everyone!"

He sets down the microphone and the confused guests start getting up from their tables to head to the bar where hopefully there's enough booze to make all of them black-out.

"You take care of this one, I'm going to help Mom and Dad," Ava tells me, shoving Molly into my arms. "Fix her, or I will use the box of toothpicks in my grandfather's pocket to filet your dick like a trout and shove it down your throat."

My dick tries to claw its way up inside my body in fear when Ava gives me the two-finger warning, point at her eyes and then my crotch area before walking away.

Taking a deep breath, I turn Molly around to face me and quietly begin pulling pieces of ham and salami out of her hair.

"I ruined my sister's wedding and you ruined my heart," she whispers sadly.

Glancing behind her, I see Gavin down on his knees talking to Charlotte's stomach with a huge smile on his face while the rest of her family laughs and jokes with each other around them.

"Only one of those things is true," I tell her quietly as I peal off a slice of ham stuck to her shoulder and toss it to the floor. Gently turning her body around, I point to her family a few feet away.

"I can't believe I'm going to be a dad!" Gavin says happily, placing another kiss to Charlotte's stomach before jumping to his feet and pulling her in for a hug.

Charlotte nestles her face into the side of his neck and mumbles an apology.

"I'm sorry I lied to you. I should have told you the truth, I was just so scared of losing you. I'm such an idiot…" she trails off.

"You're both idiots," Claire tells them, glaring at Gavin. "How in the hell did you not realize your fiancé was pregnant when you live together?"

Gavin shrugs. "I mean, I knew she was acting different, but you always told me if I didn't have anything nice to say that I shouldn't say anything at all. What kind of a man would I be if I told the woman I love that I thought her ass was getting a little big?"

Charlotte starts crying and Gavin quickly backpedals. "I didn't mean it like that! You have a GREAT ass!"

Drew steps forward and nods enthusiastically. "It's true, you do. Tom Brady always grabs the gherkin when he looks at your ass."

Molly turns away from them and I press my hands to her cheeks, tilting her face up to me.

"You have no idea how sorry I am."

She sniffles, swiping angrily at a tear on her cheek. I hate myself for making her cry, but at least she's not running away, refusing to listen. Judging by what just happened, I'm pretty sure she polished off more vodka than everyone in this room combined and who knows if she'll even understand or remember what I'm about to say, but I know it's the only chance I have to explain and I'm taking it whether she passes out or throws up.

Giving up on the meat since there seems to be a hell of a lot stuck to her and down the front of her dress, I grab her face and tilt it up so I can see her eyes.

"I'm sorry for lying to you," I whisper. "It killed me to keep it from you, and I swear on my mother and sister's lives that I've tried to tell you so many times the last few weeks. I'm sorry I'm such an asshole and kept putting it off because I was so afraid of losing you."

She sighs loudly and I start talking faster before she walks away.

"I was a jerk before we got together, and yes, I said and did a lot of stupid shit online just to get people to laugh and buy that stupid cookbook. You changed everything, Molly. You and your crazy family made me want things I never thought I did before. I've never been so tied up in knots or so scared or crazy. You make me crazy, and it's the best thing that's every happened to me," I tell her softly.

"I was so scared to tell you the truth because I know how much you hate that guy. I hate him too but you have to know I'm not him anymore, and it's because of *you*. It kills me knowing I hurt you and it breaks my heart that I'm the reason for your tears. Please, forgive me, Molly. If you give me one more chance, I promise I'll never make you cry again. I'll spend every day showing you I'm not that same jerk who exploited women for a stupid cookbook. Give me a chance to earn your trust again. I love you. I've waited my whole life for someone like you. Stay with me, say you'll forgive me, and I will do anything. Whatever it takes."

I stop talking and hold my breath until she finally speaks.

"You'll do anything?" she asks.

My heart beats faster with excitement even though I shouldn't get my hopes up. There is no way she'll forgive me this easily and I don't blame her.

I nod my head quickly in response.

"Whatever I ask?" she questions.

I nod again and she pushes up on her tiptoes and whispers softly in my ear. When she's finished, she pulls away and I drop my hands from her face with a soft groan.

"Really? Right now?"

She takes a few steps back and grabs the microphone from the table where Tyler left it, her eyes never leaving mine as she comes back to me and holds it out in front of her.

"I'm covered in meat grease and announced to everyone I know that I puked on a dick because I drank half a bottle of vodka to try and stop my heart from hurting," she tells me, pointing towards the room full of people. "Right here, right now."

With a sigh, I bring the microphone up to my mouth.

"Excuse me, could I have everyone's attention, please?"

The low hum of conversation in the room immediately quiets down and all eyes turn to me. I glance at Molly to see if she might change her mind, but she just crosses her arm and waits for me to do what she asked.

I look back out at the crowd and smile nervously.

"So, um, hello everyone. My name is Marco and I just want to thank you all for coming and tell you I masturbate into my socks. Like, a lot."

I laugh uncomfortably at the silence in the room, looking over at Molly again to see her pull a piece of salami out of the front of her dress and take a bite. She motions to me with the half-eaten slice to continue, the meat flopping around in her hand as I look back out at the crowded room.

"I like how the soft, fuzzy cotton of tube socks feels against my penis. I am a tube-sock-masturbator, and I'm not ashamed to leave crusty, jizz-filled socks under my bed for my mom to find," I say in a rush, quickly pulling the microphone away from my mouth.

"WE LOVE YOU, MINIVAN!" Drew screams.

The guests immediately go back to their drinks and conversation, no longer shocked about anything that happens at this point.

Tossing the microphone on top of the table, I wrap my arms around Molly's waist and pull her against my body. "Am I forgiven now?"

She presses her hands against my chest and looks up at me.

"Not yet, but that definitely earned you a few bonus points," she tells me with a smile.

I can finally start breathing normally again and I lean my face down to hers, needing to feel her lips against mine to reassure myself that everything will be okay.

Her hand comes up between us and she presses it against my lips right before they touch hers.

"I really want to kiss you even thought I'm still kind of pissed at you, but I think I'm ready to throw up all the vodka now. Eating that meat was a bad idea," she whispers, moving her hand from my mouth to hold it over her own.

"Oooooh, does Molly have the meat sweats now?" Charlotte laughs as her and Gavin walk up to us with their arms wrapped around each other.

"I think it's the vodka sweats," I tell her as Molly bends forward and puts her hands on her knees while I rub her back.

"Oh, that's nothing. Try having the night sweats because you're becoming a changeling," Jenny announces, walking over with Drew while Claire and Carter and Liz and Jim follow.

"Jesus, Jenny, how many times do I have to tell you it's called *going through the change*, not becoming a fucking changeling?" Claire tells her.

Drew shakes his head sadly and pats her back. "Sweetie, you don't have to make up stories about menopause. It's okay to admit you've been waking up with hot flashes because you're having sex dreams about poop sex. You're amongst family and no one will judge you. I've accepted your fetish, and I promise to take a dump on you the next time I've got one ready."

Molly groans down by my knees and I feel her pain as my stomach rolls with the need to puke right along with her.

"I'm going to pretend I never heard those words come out of your mouth and just say I'm glad you girls finally got your shit together and came clean," Liz says. "Do you have any idea how hard it's been to keep a straight face the last few weeks? Jesus, Claire and I deserve a fucking medal."

Molly's head pops up and she looks quickly between her mother and her aunt. "You knew? This entire time you knew we were lying?"

Liz and Claire share a look and start laughing.

"Duh. Do we look like idiots?" Liz asks.

"Do you think maybe you should have clued me in on this information?" Jim complains.

Liz glares at him. "I was going to until I found out that stain on my living room carpet is actually meerkat jizz and not chip dip, like you swore it was."

Jim groans and Drew starts laughing. "Fucking Tom Brady. That little guy sure did appreciate turtle porn, let me tell you. I've never seen so much spooge come out of such a tiny animal."

Molly immediately turns her head and relieves herself of that pesky vodka, all over my shoes while Charlotte does the same down the front of Gavin's tux.

"But seriously," Liz continues, like the pukefest isn't even happening. "I kind of just wanted to see how far you guys would take it before putting you out of your misery, but then you three girls started getting along like real sisters and that seemed more important than the shit-show you were putting on for us."

I'm not sure who is more shocked right now since Charlotte, Ava, Molly and I all share the same jaw-dropping looks of surprise.

"So, Molly's not pregnant?" Drew asks.

Liz shakes her head. "Nope."

"But she had sex, right? You had sex?" Drew asks, turning to look at Molly, still bent over down by my knees.

"Uh, yes?" Molly replies uncertainly.

"WOOOHOOO, Molly had sex!" Drew cheers, punching his fists in the air.

A painful '*oof*' comes out of him when Jim punches him in the stomach. When Drew recovers, he holds his hands up in front of her to stop Jim from hitting him again.

"I know, I know! She's my niece, and it's disgusting I'm happy, but…it's sex, dude!" Drew explains. "Sex is awesome! But, she's my niece and I should be pissed. But sex is awesome!"

Drew crosses his arms and shakes his head. "I hate being so conflicted."

Liz grabs Charlotte and Ava, pulling them over to Molly as she finally stands back up and takes a deep breath to calm her churning stomach.

"I almost smothered the three of you when you were toddlers and couldn't get along. Then, I tried to sell you on eBay when all three of you had your periods at the same time and almost killed each other," Liz tells them. "Now that you're adults, I'm not ashamed to admit I've done research on turning you into mail-order brides and shipping you off to another country to make you someone else's problem. Can you girls finally admit you love each other and stop acting like assholes?"

The three sisters look at each other quietly for a few minutes before they all smile.

"I'm sorry I ruined your wedding," Molly tells Charlotte.

"I'm sorry I made you lie to everyone and carry my baby," Charlotte replies with a shrug. "I'd hug you, but you still smell like meat."

Molly nods, leaning her head on my shoulder as I shake her puke off my shoes.

Charlotte, Molly and Liz turn their heads towards Ava and wait for her to apologize.

"I'm sorry I've had to put up with you two slutty cock-knobs my entire life."

Liz sighs and Ava rolls her eyes.

"Fine! You know I hate all this touchy-feely shit," she grumbles. "I love you fuckers. I'm sorry I couldn't be less of an asshole than you two and it took *this* shit to bring us together."

Satisfied with the apologies and the love in the room, Liz drops her arms from around Ava and Charlotte, motioning towards the back of the room.

"It's T-Time, assholes. I need a drink."

Everyone cheers and they all follow Liz as she leads them to the bar, leaving Molly and I alone.

I wrap my arms around Molly and hold her tight as we watch Gavin and Charlotte bring up the rear holding hands, staring at each other lovingly despite the crazy train their wedding turned in to.

"I love you and I really like your family, but we're eloping when we get married," I tell Molly.

"Oh, there is no fucking way we're inviting any of these lunatics," she agrees, wrapping her arms around my waist as we make our way across the room to continue celebrating with all the crazies.

Epilogue

One year later...

"GOD DAMMIT, TOM Brady," Uncle Drew mutters, shaking his head at the meerkat he has on a leash. "Your dick is going to fall off if you keep it up."

Mom's face curls up in disgust as she stares at the new stain on her carpet.

"Drew, get that damn animal out of my house. That's the third time today he's jerked-off on my carpet. What the fuck is wrong with him?"

Uncle Drew bends forward in his chair and quickly covers the animal's ears. "Don't yell at Tom Brady! It's not his fault he has a healthy libido."

After the night of the bachelor and bachelorette parties, Uncle Drew got a call from the zookeeper informing him that due to the trauma the meerkat sustained, he was suffering from PTSD and his behavior was scaring the zoo guests. To save the animal from being shipped back to Australia and placed in a home for wayward meerkats, Uncle Drew adopted him. I don't know how that's legal and I don't want to know. It's always best to never ask questions in this family.

"Alright, in honor of this momentous occasion, I think we need a T-Time," mom announces as she goes around the living room handing out shot glasses and filling them with cherry vodka.

I look around the room and smile as my family laughs and jokes with each other while my mom finishes her bartender duties. They're certifiably insane and drive me crazy, but I wouldn't trade them for the world. I spent so long being an outsider that I never felt like I fit in and often wondered if I was adopted. All I needed to do was go a little crazy myself and realize we aren't that different. We might not all be blood, but we're all family and we found each other because of one crazy decision my Aunt Claire made at a frat party all those years ago. We've stuck by each other through crazy situations and continue to love each other because that's what families do, and I wouldn't have it any other way.

"I can't believe you actually want to watch this," Aunt Claire complains when my mom finishes with everyone's shots and sets the empty bottle on the coffee table.

"I feel bad all that footage went to waste. We owe it to Dicky Daren for what he went through," mom explains, taking a seat in between Aunt Claire and dad.

After six months of following our family around and another three months of the production company editing the hundreds of hours they filmed down to two, they were unable to sell it to any network. It's a sad, sad day when even the adult film networks passed because our documentary was just too inappropriate for television.

"I bet it was Tom Brady that put them over the edge," Uncle Drew announces sadly.

"I'm pretty sure it was the audio recording of Molly regurgitating a dick," Ava laughs.

Everyone joins in and my face heats in embarrassment.

"Have I apologized for not remembering to take my mic off that night?" Marco whispers close to my ear.

I turn my face towards him and the tips of our noses touch. "Don't worry, you'll be making it up to me later tonight. I brought home a few new samples from work for us to try."

His eyes light up and he kisses the tip of my nose.

"I hope it's those satin wrist ties. You'll look so hot tied to my bed so I can have my way with you," he tells me with a wink.

Reaching my hand up between us, I pat my palm against his cheek.

"Actually, it's a ball gag and butt plug. You'll look so hot when I violate you on my bed."

His eyes widen in fear and I leave him to his worry when my mom instructs everyone to hold up their glasses.

Uncle Drew puts Tom Brady back on the floor by his feet, wrapping his arm around Aunt Jenny's waste as she sits on his lap and they both raise their shot glasses in the air.

Dad and Uncle Carter, on either end of the couch, hold their arms high while mom and Aunt Claire, squished in between them, tilt their heads together and raise their own glasses.

Gavin stops pacing behind the couch and shifts Molly Marco Ellis, his five-month-old sleeping daughter, to his other shoulder to grab the shot Charlotte hands him. When he takes it, Charlotte softly rubs Molly's back, places a kiss on her daughter's head and holds up her own shot.

"Hey, Marco, I forgot to tell you Ava and I tried out chapter twelve of *Baking and Babies* when we were watching little Molly Marco the other day," Tyler tells him, throwing his arm around Ava's shoulders as they lean against the side of the coffee table on the floor. "Bouncy Seat Brownies and Blowjobs was a hit, man. Well done!"

Tyler points his shot glass in Marco's direction and smiles. He catches Charlotte glaring at him from across the room and shrugs.

"You had sex while you were babysitting our child?" Gavin scolds.

"She was safely strapped into her bouncy seat facing the wall, just like the cookbook instructed," Tyler tells them with a roll of his eyes.

"Remind me again why we let him watch our daughter?" Gavin asks Charlotte.

"Because you wanted to practice chapter nine—Naptime Noodles and Nipples, to make sure we could really do it in thirty minutes or less," Charlotte whispers.

Marco's second cookbook took off bigger and better than the first one and he managed to save enough money to buy his own home. Since I decided it wasn't right to take any of Charlotte and Gavin's wedding money even though I earned it, I stayed with my parents until Marco closed on the house and asked me to move in with him.

By baking me a soufflé, that I'm happy to say he was able to get up, and keep up.

Mom leans forward on the couch and glances around the room with a confused look on her face.

"What's up, slut? I thought we were doing T-Time?" Aunt Claire asks her.

"I just feel like we're missing a few people," mom mutters.

"Well, we did have a shit ton of kids, it's hard to keep track of them all," Dad tells her.

"It's easy to forget what's-their-names since we hardly ever mention them. Wait, isn't one of them our daughter?" Uncle Carter asks.

"Shit, Sophia! That's her name!" Aunt Claire shouts. "I think she's away at college, right?"

Everyone shrugs and mumbles in agreement.

"Don't forget Billy and Veronica, our two precious spawns of Satan," Uncle Drew adds. "I haven't heard from them since they joined the circus. I'm sure they're fine."

We all share a moment of silence for the three people we've mentioned once or twice before but never heard from again. Mom finally raises her glass, waiting for everyone else to do the same.

"Here's to you, here's to me, fuck you, here's to me," she states.

We all toss back our shots and dad grabs the remote from the arm of the couch next to him and aims it at the flat screen TV above the fireplace.

"Alright, you dirty fuckers, let's see what Dicky Daren was nice enough to put together for us," he says, pressing play on the DVD player.

My parents received a package in the mail yesterday with an apology letter from the production company about our documentary not airing on TV and enclosed a DVD that Dicky Daren put together just for us. We all sit back and quiet down as the DVD starts to play, opening up on an interview with mom and Aunt Claire.

"So, yeah, I guess it all started when I got drunk at a frat party one night and gave my virginity to a random guy and then found out I was pregnant," Aunt

Claire says into the camera. *"I became a single mom, found the guy four years later and then Liz and I opened the first Seduction and Snacks. It took off like crazy and here we are now with stores and bakeries all over the country. That's about it."*

The camera pans to mom laughing, sitting next to Aunt Claire.

"Yeah, there's a lot more to the story than that, slut bag. I think you left out a few things."

Mom reaches down next to her chair and pulls five photo albums onto her lap, opening the cover of the first one and sliding a picture out of the page to hold up for the camera. It zooms in to a picture of Mom and Aunt Claire in college with their arms wrapped around each other, holding up red Solo cups. As the camera rolls, she begins going through all the pictures in the albums. There are photos for every event in our lives, quotes that go with every photo and the two of them share the stories for each one. They laugh on camera, they cry on camera, they punch each other several times on camera, and they curse so much it's pretty obvious why no networks wanted to air this thing. Their bleep button would have broken in the first ten seconds.

"Your tits are like Bounty. The quicker dick picker upper."

"Well, fuck me gently with a chainsaw."

"Aaarrrggg, ahoy me matey, thar's a great grand vagina over yonder." Penises talk like pirates when I'm drunk.

"Papa says your friends Johnny, Jack and Jose maded you sick. Friends shouldn't do stuff like that, Mommy. If Luke maded me sick, I'd punch him in the nuts!"

"I wanna eat her Snickers finger but my arm teeth won't feel."

"There is no way you were even remotely as surprised as me. If I woke up tomorrow with my tits sewn to the curtains, I wouldn't be this much in shock."

"In the words of the great Maury Povich, 'You ARE the father'."

"Rule number one: P.O.R.N. is more fun with friends, invite them. Otherwise, you just look pitiful engaging in P.O.R.N. alone. Rule number two: Sharp objects should never be used in P.O.R.N. Poking someone's eye out will ruin the moment. Rule number three: Sneak attacks or 'back door action' must come with advanced warnings or have prior approval. Rule number four: Only two balls allowed in play at all times to avoid ball-confusion, unless approved by the judges. Rule number five: P.O.R.N. is over when the other player(s) say it's over. Otherwise, someone is left holding useless balls."

"Bad boys, bad boys, whatcha gonna do, whatcha gonna do when they cut your wiener."

"Vajingo. As in 'maybe the vajingo ate your penis'."

"Stop by Seduction and Snacks for the grand opening tomorrow and try some of Claire's boobs. They're delicious!"

"You are a gigantic, stinkotic, vaginastic, clitoral, liptistic whore dizzle."

"You're a dick. Go fuck your face."

"FUCK YOU, SAM I AM!"

"No nut shots before lunch."

"These snozzberries taste like SNOZZBERRIES!"

"Wait, maybe it was the nuts. Is Claire allergic to nuts? She might be going into anal flaccid shock."

"I want to teach inappropriate things to our children with you forever. Claire Donna Morgan, will you please, please marry me and love me for the rest of your life?"

"A. SEX. SWING. From the Latin words, 'you are supposed to fuck in it, not rock your kid to sleep'."

"My toilet is your toilet; your spoop is my spoop. I'm on this train, but just so

you know, I don't want to be the caboose."

"It's the fucking zombie virus! Son of a bitch, I told you this day was coming! No one believed me and you all laughed. Well, who the fuck is laughing now?! If I go first, you kill me before I eat ANYONE'S face off, do you hear me?"

"Vagina Skittles are delicious."

"You spidermanned the one you love."

"It's fucking Meerkat Manor in my pants."

"I roofied you because I wanted you naked …. and afraid."

"RUN, VAGINAMAN, RUN!"

"Just say NO to weird sex, Gavin!"

"SON OF A BITCH, TAYLOR SWIFT! I TOLD YOU, NOT UN-TIL THE CHORUS!"

"No, YOU shut your prancing face, Twilight Sparkle, before my parents hear you."

"HONEST MISTAKE?! An honest mistake is speeding, spilling a glass of milk or calling someone by the wrong name. It is NOT sticking your dick in the wrong hole!"

"My tits may be small, but they're deadly"

"Right at that moment, I knew that I would do anything for my best friend. I would hold her hand when she was in pain, scream at my catatonic fiancé when he saw her vagina and sit by her side when she became a mom. There was nothing I wouldn't do for her and I knew that's how it would always be."

The video ends with a picture of my mom and Aunt Claire standing in front of Seduction and Snacks on the day it opened and fades to black with a picture of them standing in front of a map of the United

States filled with red dots indicating every Seduction and Snacks store open today.

Dad stops the DVD and the room is silent aside from a few sniffles every couple of seconds.

"Are you assholes crying? There's no crying in Vagina Skittles!" Uncle Drew shouts. "Dammit, Tom Brady! Get your hand off your dick!"

He quickly grabs the animal from the floor and continues scolding him softly.

"We've been through a lot, haven't we, Slutbag McFuckstick?" Mom whispers to Aunt Claire as she rests her head on her shoulder.

"I wouldn't be where I am today if it wasn't for you, ass face," Aunt Claire whispers back, resting her cheek on Mom's head. "You told me I had nothing to lose by taking a chance and you were right. Everything I have is because of you. Thank you for being my person."

Mom wipes a tear from her cheek and the two best friends, who started us all on this crazy ride, wrap their arms around each other on the couch.

"How about one more toast?" Uncle Carter suggests, grabbing another bottle of cherry vodka from the coffee table and unscrewing the cap.

Everyone quickly passes it around and refills their shot glasses, raising them in the air when the last person's glass is full.

"To Seduction and Snacks—where it all began," Uncle Carter says.

"To Seduction and Snacks!" we cheer, toasting each other and tossing the shots back.

"Alright, enough of this sappy shit or I'm going to grow a vagina," Uncle Drew complains, setting his empty shot glass on the coffee table and pushing himself up from the couch, promptly dumping Aunt Jenny onto the floor. "Who's in the mood for a little Ceiling Fan Baseball?"

Mom jumps up from the couch. "I'll get the dinner rolls!"

"I'll get the frying pans and cutting boards!" Aunt Claire adds, following my mom into the kitchen.

"Can I be up to goal first? Maybe shooting a basket will unstick these Benjamin Balls from my vagina," Aunt Jenny says as she waddles behind everyone else.

Marco stands and holds out his hand to help me up from the couch.

"Does your family ever do anything normal?" he asks as he wraps his arm around me and we head towards the dining room.

"Dammit, Tom Brady! Not in the mashed potatoes!" Uncle Drew shouts from the kitchen.

Marco laughs and I shake my head.

"Normal is overrated. They're bat-shit crazy every day of their lives and that's just the way it should be," I tell him with a smile.

Many, many, many, many, many years later…

CLAIRE AND CARTER ELLIS went on to live a long and happy life together. Just like in a cheesy romantic movie, they died together in their home, peacefully in their sleep on their 75th wedding anniversary, after a celebratory game of Metamucil pong. Well, Carter snored up until the end and Claire gave him one last kick to the shin before she joined him.

LIZ AND JIM GILMORE passed away the weekend after their 78th wedding anniversary, suffering heart attacks at the same time when they decided to test out an entire new shipment of vibrators in one evening. They died quickly and without pain, in the porn room of the flagship Seduction and Snacks store.

JENNY AND DREW PARRITT died in the parking lot of the emergency room, next to their personalized parking space, when Jenny slipped on a sheet of ice trying to dislodge a whisk from her vagina and hit her head, which caused her to swallow the ball from the ball gag Drew's arthritic fingers were unable to remove and she choked to death. Drew passed away shortly after, overexerted himself giving CRP. To her vagina. He choked on the whisk lodged in his favorite place.

CHARLOTTE AND GAVIN ELLIS went on to have two boys after Molly Marco, and Gavin has enjoyed every minute being a father, teaching his children not to give nut punches before lunch and making sure they understand just how dangerous to your life beer pong can be.

AVA AND TYLER BRANSON got married a few years after the birth of their niece, Molly Marco, at BronyCon, in front of all of their friends and family. They bought a horse farm in the country where they went on to host their very own BronyCon every year, spreading the *friendship is magic* message. They too went on to have three children and Tyler is still holding a grudge that Ava wouldn't let him name them Pinky Pie, Shutterfly and Applejack.

MOLLY AND MARCO DESOTO enjoyed a quiet, non-crazy elopement on the island of St. Thomas on Molly's twenty-fourth birthday. Even though they enjoyed the few weeks they spent with Cletus the Fetus, they decided never to have children of their own, fearing that Molly's vagina would one day resemble an Arby's Beef and Cheddar, minus the cheddar. Instead, they adopted two baby boys from broken homes who grew up to be Grand Theft Auto experts, and thanks to their mother, have never, ever collapsed a soufflé.

SOPHIA, BILLY AND VERONICA...uh, yeah. We still have no idea what happened to them, but we assume they had good lives and lived happily ever after, just like the rest of the family.

The End.

Seriously.

Totally not kidding. This is it. Forever.

They're kind of all dead now, so, there's that.

I mean, they could all come back as zombies and I guess that might be kind of funny, but, like, not an entire book funny.

Sorry. This is really the end. Hug it out, bitches.

Acknowledgements

I guess I should probably thank my family first and foremost. It's their fault the majority of the scenes and quotes in this entire series are true. Thank you for being crazy and giving me plenty of material to write about.

A HUGE thanks to Ana's Attic Book Blog for being such a huge supporter of this series and these insane characters. I'm so glad I made you piss yourself all those years ago, which led to the awesomeness that is Wicked Book Weekend, which then led to us making out. Thank you for being a great friend, blogger and all around awesome person (a.k.a. good kisser).

Thank you to EVERY SINGLE reader who took a chance on Seduction and Snacks and continued to follow these characters through all of their stupid decisions. It's because of YOU this series is loved (and disgusted) by so many. Thank you for continuing to tell your friends about it, thank you for refusing to speak to friends who won't read it, and thank you for being so amazing.

For my FTN girls, thank you for always being so supportive and wonderful. I'm honored to call you friends and co-workers and to have people in my life I can happily lose my mind with.

Thank you to Stephanie Johnson and Michelle Kannan for being the best beta readers in the world. I'm sorry for what I put you through with this book, but it was Tom Brady's fault. I love your faces.

As always, saying "thank you" will never be enough for ALL the bloggers out there. You guys work tirelessly to pimp me and support me, and I will be forever grateful for all that you do.

To my Slappers. I love you and I will never forget that you were the first ones to believe in me and support me. Twilight nerds forever!

Lastly, to the entire Twilight fanfiction community, it's because of you I'm able to live my dream and do what I love. Thank you for letting me test my skills with The Vagina Monologues, and thank you to those who have continued to follow me on this crazy train!

25743248R20128

Made in the USA
Middletown, DE
09 November 2015